PROTECTING US

A BLACKTHORNE SECURITY NOVEL

NICOLE VIDAL

COPYRIGHT

Cover design by Designs with Sass

Developmental Edit by Virginia Cantrell of Hot Tree Editing.

Final Edit by Mandy Pederick of Hot Tree Editing

ISBN 978-1-7371689-7-3

TABLE OF CONTENTS

KEEP IN TOUCH WITH NV

Visit me on social media or online to learn about my newest releases:

Facebook (http://fb.me/NicoleVidalAuthor)

Instagram (http://instagram.com/nicolevidal_author)

My website (www.nicolevidal.com)

Goodreads (https://bit.ly/NVGoodreads)

Amazon (https://amzn.to/2XCLSlR)

Pinterest (http://pinterest.com/NicoleVidal_Author)

CHAPTER ONE

JILLIAN

For the first time, I'm chasing something for myself. Flying to another state on Christmas Day is by far the zaniest thing I've ever done to share my feelings with.... I don't even know what to call him. Nothing has ever happened between us, aside from a few near kisses when we were thinking with our hearts instead of our heads.

We first met four years ago at Walter Reed. My brother Jake and his unit mate Connor were injured during a firefight in Afghanistan on their third tour of duty. They've been friends since childhood, and sheer luck had them assigned to the same unit in the military. As such, I think of Connor as my brother too. Recalling my parents sharing about his injury still makes my entire body tense even almost four years later.

Once the guys were situated at the hospital and visitors were allowed, I visited each day after school. I teach severely developmentally delayed students. A few weeks passed before I met my mystery guy. One afternoon about fifteen minutes after I arrived, one of the nurses escorted a gorgeous, though travel worn, man wearing an army uniform into Jake's room.

"I'm sorry to intrude. I'll come back." His voice surrounded me like a cozy blanket on a chilly winter afternoon. The rolling Rs in his words grabbed my attention.

"You aren't intruding. Please take the chair," I said, offering him my seat close to the bed and moving toward the window. My offer made him bristle. Clearly, I shouldn't give up my seat for him.

"Are you his sister?"

"Yes. Jillian. Nice to meet you." I extended my hand to him.

His hand enveloped mine with warmth and softness. The awareness coursing through me was unfamiliar but not unwelcome.

"Cruz. Javier Cruz. I served with Jake and Connor. Your brothers talked about you all the time. I'm sorry it took me a bit to get here."

"Nothing to be sorry for. You're here now." I took him in. The uniform masked nothing. His broad shoulders tapered to a lean waist. He was taller than me, but height wasn't my superpower. His hair was dark, almost black, and his alluring eyes were a deep shade of sable.

The more he spoke, the deeper his voice lured me in as he explained more about the difficulties getting here.

"Cruz?" Jake pushed up to sitting on his bed. His voice groggy from the medication and waking from his nap. Jake strained his shoulder assisting his unit mates before being shot in the arm.

"Hey, Jake."

"You didn't have to come all this way."

Cruz nodded. "Yes, I did."

The palpable tension between them forced me to leave the room. "I'll give you two time to chat. I'm going to visit Connor. It was a pleasure meeting you, Javier."

"You too, Jillian."

I didn't expect to see Javier every single day until the guys were discharged. While Jake and Connor were at physical therapy or group meetings, we would stroll outside or grab a meal, depending on the time of day. A few times before they left the hospital, I thought he would ask me on a date. Unfortunately, Javier took a job with the NYPD, ending our potential relationship before it even started.

We've seen one another at family gatherings, holidays, and military reunions over the years. It wasn't until I realized Connor, Jake, and even Christoph are moving forward in relationships for me to see I need to take control of my love life instead of waiting for the man of my dreams to fall at my feet. No, I need to share my feelings with the man who could be my one and only.

Jake finally admitted his feelings for Norah after two years as friends with benefits. They're due to have a baby in the next few months. Connor and Calliope met and adopted a little girl. They also have twins on the way. Christoph... he's a different story. At one point, I thought he and I could be good together. He's always there when I need assistance around the house, flat tires, and the like. Recently, he fell for Madeleine. He forced me to realize we were never more than friends, quite bluntly, about a week ago. Christoph's advice catapulted me to share my feelings with Javier, terrified as I may be.

"Ladies and gentlemen, please put your tray tables in their upright position and prepare for landing," the flight attendant insists over the loudspeaker, pulling me out of my thoughts.

Once inside the airport, I grab my luggage from the carousel and hail a taxi. The entire cab ride to his apartment, I'm second-guessing my decision.

As I stand at the threshold of his apartment, I give myself a pep talk. *You've come this far already.* I take a deep, calming breath and knock on his door.

A stunning brunette opens the door. She's my antithesis in every way. I'm short; she's tall. Blonde to brunette. Curves to no curves. "Is Javier...."

He steps through my line of sight shirtless with his hair still damp from the shower. "Maris, who is it?"

Holy mother of... he's deliciously cut. I've never seen Javier shirtless until this moment. My imagination has failed me in spectacular fashion. His chest and abs should be on a billboard in Times Square to sell cologne or underwear.

"Would you like to come in?" the brunette offers.

"No, thank you. Traveling here was a mistake. I'm sorry for bothering you this early in the morning."

One foot in front of the other. I repeat the phrase in my head while walking away. I rapidly push the down button for the elevator. When it finally opens, I step inside, drag my rolling luggage, and watch the door close excruciatingly slow, like a snail inching along pavement.

His familiar arm stops the doors from closing. Normally, I don't find an abundance of tattoos attractive, yet his are meaningful. The one on his left arm, which is holding the door open, is the unit crest, and interwoven are the initials of the guys they lost, including Adams, Jones, and Carter.

"Jillian, what're you doing here? Is everyone okay?" He's still shirtless, jeans unbuttoned, and his feet bare. Suddenly my mouth is as arid as the Sahara.

All I can do is drop my head. *Own your crazy decision, Jill!* "I came for you, but…."

This gorgeous specimen exhales sharply. His expressive eyes widen before he demands, "Off the elevator, Jillian."

I'm frozen in place, his eyes locked on mine. There's truly no room for me to ignore him. I certainly can't move him to allow the elevator door to close—although the notion of putting my hands on his sculpted chest makes me want to try. Also, I'm confident the alarm will sound if the door doesn't close soon.

"Jillian, move your fine ass back to my apartment. Marisa is my sister." He's the only person who calls me Jillian. His authoritative tone makes my entire body pay attention. He reaches out his hand to take my luggage while the other continues holding open the door.

Sister? I slide past him and walk back toward his apartment, but not before his crisp, fresh scent assails my senses. I step inside his apartment after he opens the door.

Marisa, the brunette and his *sister*, gathers her purse and bag to leave. "I gotta go to work, Javy. I'll be back tonight or tomorrow to get the rest of my stuff. My place has been cleared."

"Have a good day, Maris. Love you." He kisses her cheeks, and she steps out the door I just walked through.

Javier moves into his kitchen and pulls down two mugs. His apartment is not large, but it's him—well, I think it is from the details I could glean from our conversations at the hospital and the handful of times each year we've talked since. Leather couches with a matching ottoman and a massive television fill the living room. There's a cozy blanket draped over the back of the couch and the matching chair set off to the side. The island has four stools at a granite countertop facing into the galley kitchen.

"You came here on your own?" He hands me a fresh cup of coffee he likely expertly prepared given his knowledge from the hospital. I take a small sip and set the cup on the island.

I wrinkle my brow. "Thank you. Yes. I'm perfectly capable of traveling on my own."

He laughs softly. "I know. Does your family know you're here?"

I shake my head. "No. Last time I checked, I'm an adult. I don't need permission to travel from my parents or my brothers, both blood and found. What's with the questions?"

A thought flashes across his face, but he doesn't share it with me. "Never mind. Why are you here?"

"I want to stop dancing around our potential. Will you go on a date with me?"

In one smooth motion, I'm caged between his muscular form and the island. His hands are flat on the granite that's about the same height as my upper arm. "You live and work a four-hour drive away."

"I know." My words are soft and strained. Maybe this was a mistake, considering how his proximity is messing with my head. The same sexual tension and desire from when we danced at the wedding floods my frame—my heart too, if I'm being honest with myself.

"You're a handful, aren't you?"

I smile and pin my gaze to his. His mouth is a hair's breadth away from mine. I've wanted to taste his lips almost from the moment we met. His bare chest is a mere inch from grazing mine. His nearness has my nipples pebbled in anticipation.

"Will that be a problem?"

"No, ma'am. However, I'm a traditional guy. How long can you stay?"

My belly does a flip-flop. "I can stay until Monday. School reopens on Tuesday."

"Jillian, will you accompany me on a date around my city today and spend time with me until the last possible moment before going home?"

"Yes." *A thousand times, yes.* The longer he's in my space, the more difficult it is for me to ignore the yearning rushing through my veins.

"I need to finish dressing. Make yourself comfortable. I'll be back." He takes his now warm coffee and walks down the hall.

I take a few calming breaths. He didn't touch me, and yet I feel as if I lost something. Is this truly happening? I wasn't sure how receptive he would be when I showed up at his door.

I swallow the rest of my coffee, wash the mug, and set it to dry. When I turn around, Javier slides his arms around me and draws me into a tight hug. Unfortunately, he tugged a thin, gray sweater over his head. Given our height difference, my head is against the hard planes of his chest. He presses a kiss to my hair and slowly releases me.

"Have you ever been here before?"

I shake my head.

The gears in his mind are turning, ideas and plans forming. "Ready to experience the holiday season in the Big Apple?"

"With you, yes." Resisting the urge to rise on my toes and kiss him is increasing in difficulty.

"Do you have a coat and gloves?"

I nod and retrieve both from my luggage.

"Perfect, let's go." He escorts me to the elevator, and we ride in silence to the lobby. He looks over at me but fails to utter a word for a few minutes. Finally, once we're outside, he asks, "Why now, Jillian?"

I turn to face him on the busy street. The hustle and bustle of post-holiday cheer ceases to exist. "We have a connection and chemistry I've never felt before. I need to know if our potential could bloom into...." We spent hours talking about everything and nothing while we waited for our brothers, figuratively and literally, at the hospital, but we haven't spoken really in depth since Jake and Connor returned from their third tour. Well, that's not exactly true. We spoke in depth at the shower for the twins.

"The type of relationship we talked about at the hospital how many ever years ago?" he supplies.

"Yes."

We spent hour after hour talking in depth about so many topics. The qualities we both seek in a romantic partner were shockingly similar. A give and take from both sides, knowing without question that some days you need to give more than you take. Yet on the days you need more, your other half should be willing to pick up and handle whatever is necessary. Sharing those parameters in the abstract didn't make him run away. In fact, we agreed on every aspect, from finances to children to holidays.

He's silent for a few steps. "I always wondered about us myself."

Softly, I murmur, "You never said anything."

"Until very recently, I didn't think I would ever have the opportunity or interest to leave this city. Now it's an option I could choose."

"What are you talking about? You love it here. Your family is here. I wouldn't ask you to leave."

He guides me across the street to a bench right inside Central Park.

CHAPTER TWO

JAVIER

Jillian—who personifies my ideal woman and traveled to visit me on a holiday—is beside me. She's the woman who makes my heart race when she smiles. From the moment we met, I wondered if we could be perfect for one another. A myriad of factors crossed my mind then and now. What about her brothers? The distance between our homes. Is her heart drawn to mine like mine is to hers?

"I know you wouldn't. Nor would I ask you to leave your students," I assure her. "You haven't talked to Jake, Connor, or Christoph about me at all?"

"No, why would I? My brothers, all four of them, if you will, don't know anything about my personal life for my protection and sanity."

I grin at her. She's referring to the fact she's adopted. Jake and Cameron are as well. Connor and even Christoph took on a brotherly role for her when the guys became unit mates and friends.

I chuckle and then push out a harsh breath. I've only shared this information with Christoph when he reiterated an offer for a spot at Blackthorne Security. Not even my mother and sisters know what I'm about to tell her. "A few days before the shower for the twins, I was passed over for captain."

"Oh, Javier, I'm sorry." She sets her hand on my jaw.

The tender caress of her skin on mine sends heat blazing through me. I cover her hand with mine and kiss her palm before lowering our hands into my lap. Only Jillian calls me Javier. My name falling from her plump lips, which I've been yearning to kiss for years, sounds like heaven.

"I've had a little while to grapple with their decision."

"You could've called. I would've listened."

"I almost did actually, but I never had the insane courage you do."

"What do you mean?"

She truly doesn't see what I see. "I pulled up your number numerous times the day I learned I wasn't getting the promotion, and so many days before and since. Not once did I push the green button. There hasn't been a day between the time we met and now when I haven't thought of you at least once a day. Showing up here was one of the most courageous leaps I've ever seen in my life."

A sexy blush creeps into her cheeks. I've catalogued her in my mind over the years. Imagined how her curves would feel in my hands. Whether she would tuck herself beneath my chin or against my shoulder. How her tongue could taste like coffee or apple juice, her drinks of choice at the hospital. Unfortunately, I wasn't lucky enough to kiss her then.

I lift her gaze from our hands to my eyes with a few fingers under her chin. My willpower flew out the window when she appeared at my door. Cupping the side of her face, I drag my thumb across her lower lip.

Her breath hitches, and her eyes flutter closed. Her physical responses to me bolsters my opinion that we may be combustible as a couple. Leaning in, I close the gap between us. It's time to finally kiss this incredible woman for the first time.

"Lieutenant Cruz?"

Jillian jerks away at the interruption and slowly exhales as her attention turns to the woman who called my name.

It takes me a moment to place the woman who derailed what could be my last first kiss—a kiss I desperately want to experience. "Nancy. It's lovely to see you outside the deli."

"You too. Stop in again soon. Billy misses his updates."

"Will do. Have a lovely day." I return my attention to my date. I'm on an actual date with Jillian. "Jillian."

She turns back to face me, her eyes still wide with anticipation.

"I'm sorry."

"Not your fault. Where are you taking me?"

I need to share the Blackthorne offer with her and soon. "I vaguely recall you boasting about your ability to glide along on skates with grace."

A giddy smile materializes on her face, making my heart squeeze. Whether it's because I remembered, her genuine love of skating, or both, I don't care. Her smile lights me up from the inside. I'll find ways to make her smile each day if she'll let me.

"Seriously?"

"Absolutely. Let's go."

We hurry to Rockefeller Center and make our way to the ticket booth. The young girl working the booth asks our sizes and retrieves the skates. We take a seat on one of the benches along the outer wall.

"Can you skate?" she wonders aloud.

I grin at her. "It's been a long time. I'll risk embarrassment and injury to bring a smile to your face."

She looks away from me.

"I meant what I said before, Jillian. Every single day." I guide her gaze to mine and hold it for a few seconds before returning to lacing up my skates.

Jillian reaches for my hand, steady on the thin blades beneath her feet. Me, not so much. I take her hand in mine and wobble.

She tries to suppress the laughter bubbling in her chest but fails. "You weren't kidding."

All I can do is shake my head and grip her hand tighter.

Jillian steps closer and tugs on my arm, bringing my head closer to hers. "Thank you for trusting me with one of your self-perceived shortcomings." She presses a kiss high on my cheek before taking a step closer to the rink.

My intention was to make her smile, her laughter and closeness are an added bonus. Jillian is short, maybe five foot four barefoot. Her curves belie her height. She's perfection in a tiny package. Once she pushes off and my hand is no longer on the wall, I immediately fall on my ass.

Her laughter surrounds me as she helps me up. I'm confident I look ridiculous, but truthfully, I don't care. With one hand linked with hers and the other skimming the wall, I successfully stand.

"That might hurt in the morning." She smirks at me.

"Completely worth it." I draw her closer and press my lips to her forehead.

"Those spikes at the toe will help if you dig them into the ice."

I shake my head. "Now you tell me."

"The girl at the booth mentioned it too."

I lock my eyes with hers. "My attention was focused on you."

Her cheeks flame as other skaters circle around us.

"Should I keep my thoughts and compliments to myself?"

She sighs and drops her head. "Not used to hearing them about me."

I lean down and bring my lips near her ear. "Get used to it. You shattered my self-control the moment you showed up at my door green with jealously over my little sister." Goose bumps erupt along the slope of her neck from my words. Pulling back, I gaze down at her flawless face.

"She's beautiful, Javier. Of course I would be jealous, given she could've been your girlfriend."

"Not as beautiful as you." I haven't had an overnight guest not related to me by blood since we met. The thought of Jillian sleeping in my bed, even without me, makes my pulse increase. I imagine her golden hair spread like a halo on my pillow, embedding her signature scent of vanilla and jasmine on my sheets.

"Thank you."

The tension between us is palpable. Jillian speaks to my soul on a level I've never felt before. She pushes off with her right foot, and we glide along the surface slowly. With precision, she carries us around the rink, my hand branded to her hip and our other hands linked as one. About an hour later, we return our skates.

"Hungry?"

"Starving," she replies.

I thread my fingers into hers and guide her away from the street. I glide my hand along her lower back and interlace my fingers with hers on the other hand. Never before has a woman's hand fit mine as perfectly as hers. A few blocks away, we arrive at the best family-run, hole-in-the-wall pizza shop in this big city.

"Lieutenant Cruz! Come, come," Mrs. Tosetti calls out and waves us toward a table near the rear of the restaurant.

"Hi. Good to see you." I hug her, then pull out Jillian's chair.

"You as well. You're lovely," she tells Jillian.

Her cheeks turn a light shade of pink before she replies, "Thank you."

Mrs. Tosetti leaves menus with us, despite knowing I don't need it. Minutes later, she brings over some garlic knots and a pitcher of Sprite. "I'll be back for your order in a few."

"Any objections to a New York style cheese pizza and wings?"

Her eyes widen. "The hotter the better."

"Bones or boneless?"

"Bones, definitely."

"A woman after my own heart." The words are past my lips before I think to reel them back in.

She's speechless, and her gaze burns through me. Thankfully, Mrs. Tosetti returns to take our order, giving Jillian time to compose her thoughts. After I order, I take her hands in mine.

"What was your plan, *corazón*?

"What does that mean?"

"It loosely means 'sweetheart.'"

"I second-guessed myself a half dozen times since I rushed out of Jake's party last night."

"Why?"

"What if Marisa was your girlfriend? What if you didn't see our potential like I do?"

"Our conversation at the baby shower should have allayed those fears."

"It's been over a month since the shower. You finding a girlfriend in the interim isn't farfetched. You're…. Never mind. It's one thing to talk about us in the abstract but something else to show up heart in hand."

I lift her hand to my lips and kiss it. "Bold and insanely brave, if you ask me. I'm what?"

"You're going to make me say it, aren't you?"

I shrug.

"You're the complete package—smart, charming, career-oriented, and handsome. Clearly, I'm attracted to you, but… you're hotter in person than my imagination conjured up. Do you work out every day?"

Now it's my turn to blush. I feel the heat rising in my cheeks.

"Blushing is sexy as hell on your gorgeous face."

I shake my head. "To answer your question, yes, every morning."

Mrs. Tosetti breaks our conversation by bringing our wings, and we dig in.

"These are amazing!" Jillian exclaims.

Our pizza arrives a short time later, and after a few satisfying bites, I ask, "Tell me something about you I don't already know. I recall the basics."

"What do you remember?"

"Everything. Your favorite color is orange—fall-leaves orange, not like the fruit. You like your coffee light and a tad too sweet. You care about your students as if they were your own children. You're good at disguising your feelings from everyone except me. Today, I learned you prefer when I have my hands on you in some way instead of not at all. I'm willing to bet a kiss placed near the shell of your ear will make you melt against me. What about you?"

She shifts in her seat before answering, telling me I'm spot on with my observation.

"Your favorite color is green. You prefer your coffee darker than me and with not enough sugar. You handle setbacks better than anyone I've ever met. Today, I learned you are affable with everyone not only me and willing to succumb to stares of strangers to make me smile."

Conversation flows freely while we devour our pizza. With our check in hand, we move to the cashier. Light snow has started to fall since we entered the pizzeria. "Where to next?" I ask.

"I'm game for anything with you beside me."

I raise an eyebrow and repeat her words in my head. *Anything? My gorgeous woman, be careful what you wish for. Wait… my?*

We make a quick stop for coffee and reenter Central Park. After securing tickets, we walk to the carriage rides.

"I've wanted to do this since watching it on *Sex and the City*," Jillian admits.

I smile inwardly and help her into the carriage. Frankly, my view of her has inappropriate thoughts for a first date running through my mind. We sit side by side, and she covers our legs while I hold our coffees. I opted for the long ride around the park. The snow adds a romantic atmosphere. About halfway through our ride, my phone starts vibrating in my pocket, but I ignore it.

I twist to look at Jillian fully. "Today has been my favorite day in this city."

"You've lived here your entire life." Disbelief is laced in her voice.

"No other day compares. Second place isn't even close." I slide my hand around her neck and draw her closer.

She sucks in a jagged breath.

My phone vibrates in my pocket again.

"You should answer your phone. It's probably important. Otherwise, they wouldn't have called back again so soon."

Her observation skills shouldn't surprise me given who her brothers are. *Her brothers. How are they going to react to us? Do I care?* "I don't want to answer it. I want to kiss you, repeatedly."

"Answer first, then kisses."

Reluctantly, I answer the call. "Lieutenant Cruz speaking."

"I apologize for interrupting your day off. There has been a development in one of your old cases, which warrants a call," the newly installed captain—the job I applied for and didn't get—informs me.

"I understand. Does it require me to come in or can you share over the phone?"

"I would prefer to discuss this in person," Captain Davidson says.

Resigned that our spectacular date is going to end with me dropping Jillian off at my apartment before heading to the precinct, I reply, "Understood. I can be there in an hour or so."

"I'll see you then, Lieutenant." He ends the call.

"I'm sorry, Jillian. I need to go into the precinct."

Her head drifts side to side slowly. "Nothing to be sorry for. I didn't think you would be free the entire time I'm here. I dropped in unexpectedly."

"Best surprise I've ever had. I'll take you to my apartment and then head in."

"My hotel is fine, Javier."

"You're staying with me." I have no idea what the captain needs to share with me, but I'm confident it isn't good if in person and immediately is necessary.

She starts to object but decides against it.

Our driver pulls along the curb, and I assist Jillian to the ground. Her luscious curves feel tempting in my grasp. Hand in hand, we return to my apartment.

"Make yourself at home. I'll be back as soon as possible. Please know I want to kiss you breathless. However, I won't be able to stop myself if I kiss you right now." With immense restraint, I leave Jillian in my apartment to face an unknown issue with one of my old cases.

CHAPTER THREE

JILLIAN

When I rushed out of Jake's, I had no idea how my impromptu visit would turn out. So far, I'm glad I didn't chicken out any of the numerous times I considered turning back. I roll my bag down the hallway. He has two bedrooms, but the extra one is an office with a daybed for guests. I shrug and lift my bag onto his bed. The master bedroom has heavy, wooden furniture with hunter green linens and blackout curtains. There's a watch box and cologne on the dresser. Otherwise, his bedroom is minimalistic.

I search for some comfy clothes in my luggage and wash up before changing into leggings, a tank, and a slouchy sweatshirt. It takes a few tries to find the right combination of the four remotes to bring the television to life. I settle on *Home Alone* in the background.

I browse the photos along the wall. There are photos of Javier and three women, one of whom is Marisa. I don't recall if he ever shared how many sisters he has. This photo would indicate one more sister and his mom based on the ages of the women. Two photos include my brothers—adopted and found—and a few other unit mates I recognize. I take in the view out his living room window. It overlooks a small courtyard in the center of his apartment building. With the snow cover, it looks serene and beautiful. I was raised in a rural area. The cityscape is stunning covered in white.

A key slides into the lock and the door opens. I barely suppress the smile on my face when I realize it's his sister and another woman, not Javier.

"Hi, again. I'm Marisa, and this is my girlfriend, Ana." Much like Marisa, Ana is stunning as well. She has long, blonde hair and legs for days.

"Hi. I'm Jill. I apologize for being rude this morning. Pleasure to meet you, Ana."

"Likewise," Ana replies before moving down the hall.

Marisa smiles at me. "You weren't rude. Just surprised by my presence."

"Jealous too, if we're sharing honestly, until he told me you're his sister."

"Understandable. I don't meddle in my brother's love life. He's a good man. Please don't hurt him. He can't handle another breakup like Vivienne."

Javier has never mentioned her before. Then again, we haven't discussed our previous relationships yet.

"I won't hurt him." *I'm more afraid he'll crush my heart into a billion infinitesimal pieces, and I'll never be the same.*

"I like you, Jill. No hesitation at all. Where is my brother? He was supposed to be off for a few days."

"He got a call from his captain and had to go to the precinct for a little while."

Ana comes back carrying two bags and sets them near the door.

Marissa continues, "I'm set now. Please thank Javy for me. My place is now freshly fumigated."

"I will."

They leave as quickly as they arrived. If I had to guess, Marisa is about twenty-four and protective of her big brother. As the youngest, I'm accustomed to the exact opposite. I suppose him being the only brother has an impact, whereas I'm the only sister. Not only do Jake and Cameron act crazy protective, but I also have Connor, Christoph, and a few other unit mates who come around every now and then for visits. Javier is their only unit mate who treats me like a woman who happens to be their sister.

Near the end of the movie, my phone lights up on the ottoman.

Javier: I'm on my way.

Me: I'll be here.

I scroll through his Netflix account and start *Die Hard.* It's debatable whether it's a Christmas movie or not. This time when the door opens, Javier steps through it. He doesn't look pleased by the conversation with his boss.

"That bad?"

He tugs off his jacket and hangs it in the closet before dropping his keys and phone into a bowl near the door. "It could be."

"Want to talk about it?"

"Not really."

"Marisa said to thank you for letting her crash here."

"She was here?"

"With Ana."

He slides his hands over the curve of my hips and clasps them at the small of my back. I set my hands on his chest. *Damn.* Seeing him shirtless this morning and touching him now are completely distinct levels of fantastic. I gaze up at him and watch the content of his conversation with his boss dissipate from his eyes. The same heat from our carriage ride takes its place. He slips one hand beneath the hem of my sweater, his fingertips digging into my lower back, as the other winds upward to cup my jaw.

"*Cariña.*" His kiss is soft and tender despite having been thwarted all day. Our tongues delve and explore one another. I fail to suppress a whimper from falling between us. I've never felt this much from a kiss before. I slide my hands upward and hold his face, and the prickle of his stubble tickles my palms. My heart thumps in my chest as I meet the sensual strokes of his tongue with my own. The tenor of our kissing increases, and we dance over to the couch. He takes a seat, and I straddle his hips, my hands gliding back to the sides of his face.

He breaks our kiss and blazes a trail along my collarbone, tugging the neck of my sweatshirt to expose more skin. Slipping my hands beneath the hem of his sweater, I splay my hands on his abs. The muscles jump with each caress over the ridges and planes. How his body feels doesn't compare to the sensations swirling through me from his talented mouth on my skin. *Sweet mercy!* Heat pools between my thighs the longer he marks my shoulder, neck, and mouth with his tongue.

I attempt to add more space between us to lift his sweater over his head. Instead, he tears my sweatshirt and tank over my head and twists, laying me on the couch cushion and hovering over me.

"Good?"

I'm better than good. I wrinkle my nose.

"That's adorable. Do you want me to slow down?"

"No, not even a little bit." I tug his sweater over his head. Pushing myself up onto my elbows, I set my mouth to his chest and explore the expanse of bronze skin before me.

"It's probably a good thing I didn't kiss you earlier today."

I grin against his skin and travel as high as I can go. I attempt to wiggle upward but fail in the sense I haven't moved. Yet the friction of my body against his sends my thoughts plummeting into dangerous territory for tonight. His impressive length is pressed inside my right hip. He rocks back onto his heels and draws me up to sitting.

"May I?"

I nod. He drops his hands behind my back and unclasps my bra before sliding it between us and dropping it onto the area rug. "You're breathtaking."

I feel my cheeks heat from his compliment.

"I'll remind you every day, beautiful." He kisses a path over my chin and lavishes the same attention he offered my lips to my breasts.

I snake my hands down and draw my fingernails upward on his thighs.

He stills when my hands stop at the button of his jeans. "Those stay on, and so do your leggings."

I wrinkle my nose again.

"*Cariña*, we have plenty of time."

There's no inch of my skin from the waist up that hasn't been purposefully nipped, kissed, licked, or sucked on by his talented mouth when he rolls us onto our sides, our bodies tangled from head to toe. I'm quite literally a mushy pile of goo from his capable hands and mouth.

"Do you want to talk yet?" I ask.

He moves his head side to side above my head. I sidle even closer, my breasts pressed against his chest, and draw my hands up and down his sculpted back. I continue gliding my fingertips until he starts to share about his meeting.

"I've been avoiding meeting with Captain Davidson as much as possible since I didn't get the position, especially one-on-one. I'm not angry with him personally, merely how the process played out and I wasn't chosen. I don't flaunt my culture to get ahead in my career or life; however, regarding the promotion, I was confident, along with my service record and closure rate, it would help. Had I earned the promotion, I would've been only the second native Hispanic New Yorker in the position. It didn't.

"One of my first major cases was an art theft ring in Central Park West. I worked closely with Sam Morgan, as his company insured most of the paintings. We determined household staff were working in concert around the city to admit thieves into their employers' homes for a cut of the black-market sales price."

"I assume you were successful in prosecuting most of the staff and thieves," I murmur against his chest.

His fingers dig deeper into my shoulder blades. "For the most part. Since the recovery, the previous owners of one masterpiece dating back decades are claiming it should be returned to them instead of the person who bought the stolen art."

"I see their argument, even if the current owners believed they were purchasing legally, but there must be more to cause Captain Davidson to call you in on your day off."

He pulls back and gazes down at me. "The previous owners are allegedly Irish mob."

"Oh." *Damn!*

"Yeah."

I consider the details he shared. "What does he propose you do with the information?"

He shrugs. "As far as the department is concerned, the cases are closed. Davidson wanted me to be aware of what's going on behind the scenes to increase my awareness."

"You're always vigilant. We sat in the back of the restaurant. You always face the door. You constantly scan the room or street."

He cranes his neck. "I do. Davidson doesn't know me personally. To him, I'm the guy who failed to get his job."

"You don't know how he truly feels about you, do you?"

"No, I don't. Can we drop it for now?"

My heart aches for him. He worked incredibly hard for years before applying for the promotion. I imagine it's going to sting for a bit longer than a month, especially if he has to see Davidson daily. "Of course."

"Tell me about your current group of students."

From the moment we met, Javier has been interested in my students and their progress. "Sure. Do you have anything to snack on?"

"I do, but I don't want to let you go yet."

Oh my. "I'm not going anywhere." I tilt my head and fuse my lips to his. A few breath-stealing kisses later, I tug my tank top on and follow him into the kitchen. While he plates a snack, I share about my current students. "Jesse has ataxic Cerebral Palsy. I work with him to learn through an adapted computer instead of writing. Jesse's ten but functions near a six-year-old. He's a jokester. He's working hard at physical therapy to walk with crutches. Kate has congenital myopathy. She's twelve and a certified genius, but her disease has significantly impacted her ability to speak. Like Jesse, she communicates most effectively through a computer."

In the time I've been sharing about my students, Javier put together a medium-sized charcuterie plate including crackers, cheese, salami, grapes, and a few wrapped chocolates. *How does he remember that?*

"Why do you have my favorite chocolate on hand?"

The corner of his mouth curves up into a sexy smirk. "I may have taken a liking to them after you shared your love of them with me."

I steal a kiss and share about Stevie. "My last student this year is Stevie. He has Asperger's syndrome, along with oppositional defiant disorder. He can compute advanced calculus in his head but doesn't have the social skills to give a napkin to a requesting classmate."

We curl up on the couch and polish off the snack in record time.

"What happened to Kaylin?"

My heart squeezes. *He remembers her too?* "Unfortunately, her condition progressed, and she passed away two years ago."

Javier presses a kiss to my temple. "I'm sorry."

"Thanks. What were your plans for your days off?" He raises an eyebrow, so I explain, "Marisa mentioned you have a few days off when she was here earlier. Was it a secret? As well as forbidding me to hurt you like Vivienne."

"No, not at all. I planned to relax and visit my mom." He shifts before addressing the second part of my response. "I would prefer not to discuss

Vivienne right now, but I'll share with you some other time." The same look crosses his face when he asked if my family knew I was here.

"Don't change your plans for me. I'll be fine by myself."

A confused look graces his face. "Did you truly believe I would turn you away?"

Yes. "It was a strong possibility. Nothing of significance has changed. We still live and work four hours apart."

A devilish grin grows on his face. "I think you're forgetting a few things."

"Such as?"

"We had an amazing date and spectacular kisses."

"True, but our date and kisses were after I showed up here unannounced."

"What if I didn't live four hours away?"

Slowly, I turn my gaze to his. "How?"

CHAPTER FOUR

JAVIER

"I meant it when I said I wouldn't ask you to leave your job for me. You love your profession, and you're a talented investigator, Javier."

I cup the side of her face with my hand. "I know. I wouldn't ask you either, but you're here, despite the obstacles, to make us happen." I take a deep breath and put everything on the line. "Since Jake formed Blackthorne, I've had an open invitation to join the company. Christoph reiterated the opportunity before he left the city with Madeleine about two weeks ago."

Silence hangs in the air between us.

Maybe sharing about the job was a mistake.

She's collecting her thoughts. "That's why you kept asking if they knew I was here. You think they sent me to recruit you."

Honesty is the only way to handle her underlying accusation. "Partially."

"I don't know if I should be flattered or appalled."

Only she would see it both ways. "Neither. I needed to know you came for me."

She exhales sharply, her body relaxing against mine. "I didn't know about the offer. I only came for us, to see if there could be an us."

I draw her close and kiss her hard, feeling possessive and intrigued by the future. "I want there to be an us too."

"What is the deadline for a decision?"

I kiss her again and resettle onto the couch with her tucked against me. "I gave myself a deadline of Sunday night. I've been weighing the offer constantly in my mind."

"What are the drawbacks?" she murmurs against my neck.

"In no particular order: moving away from my family, leaving my colleagues at the department, and forgoing the slim chance another captain vacancy will open in the near future."

"How often do you see your family?"

I shake my head. "Not as much as I should or would like, given we live in the same city. Before you ask, it's unlikely another captain position would open anytime in the next few years."

"Do you want to stick it out and try again?"

Yes. No. "There's no guarantee I would be considered for the position if another were to open."

"What are the positives of the offer?"

She's walking me through this decision with care. "More money, better hours, less stress... you. You were a consideration before you showed up this morning. Each time I saw you—whether it was Connor's wedding, the shower, or other gathering—I always wondered if we could have the type of relationship we're both looking for." *I was right about combustible. Her kisses set my soul on fire.*

"Why didn't you ever say anything? We've seen each other at least three times a year since we met. Clearly, we trust one another enough to share intimate details of our perfect partner."

"For the same reason you didn't until today. We have fulfilling careers in different states. You're a gifted teacher, and your students are lucky to have you. I'm drawn to you and have been since we met. The fact Jake, Connor, and Christoph are your *brothers* doesn't even give me pause. Perhaps it should, but it doesn't. Until now, my career put me in a position that only allowed me to chase one of my desires. Given the job offer on the table, I need to reconcile my willingness to forgo a career aspiration to attain a life aspiration."

"Which is?" Her question comes out tentative, as if she's worried she isn't part of the life aspiration I want.

"Building a partnership and having a family with you."

"You were deciding on your own though."

"Not exactly."

She pushes off my chest and sits back on her heels over my thigh and looks at me expectantly, waiting for an explanation. Ignoring the heat of her core against me is virtually impossible. I want to pin her beneath me and explore the rest of her luscious curves with my mouth and hands, despite it being my choice to slow down earlier.

"I planned to share with you after sharing with my family—more like informing them I planned to accept Christoph's offer."

She leans forward and plants an all-consuming kiss on my lips. Sitting up, I slide her into my lap and return her kisses with equal fervor.

"Seriously?"

"I mean, you did come all this way. You must like me just a little bit."

"No—" She kisses the tip of my nose. "—I—" Kiss to my cheek. "—more—" Kiss to my other cheek. "—than—" Kiss to my lips. "like you."

I can't take any more. Grabbing her hands, I hold them in one of mine behind her back and guide her lips to mine with my free hand.

I whisper, "I more than like you too," against her mouth.

Having her hands restrained doesn't stop Jillian from sharing how affected she is by the passion in our kisses. She rocks over my length in a smooth rhythm. Her pace increases the closer she gets to her release. "We feel better than I imagined over the years."

She isn't wrong. How will it feel when we're actually together? "Yes, we do."

She fights against my hold as her body shudders from the friction between us. "Javier...." Falling forward, her chest presses against mine, and she recaptures her normal breathing. I release her hands, which fall along either side of my torso.

After a few minutes, it hits me. She had no backup plan. "What was your plan for this morning?"

Jillian smiles against my skin. "If you weren't home?"

"Sure, start there."

"I would have checked into my hotel and come back at the end of the day."

"If Marisa were my girlfriend?"

"I would've wallowed in insanely expensive room service dessert. Then I would be a tourist until my flight home."

"I may not have voiced it out loud, but you must know I'm attracted to you, not someone who looks like Marisa. My sister is beautiful, but I've never found thin women attractive."

"It's possible I noticed when we danced at the wedding."

My face heats up. "You looked sexy as sin in your slinky black dress."

"Honestly, I was surprised you danced with me."

"Why?" The aching need in my chest to touch her got the best of me at the reception.

She pushes off my chest to look at my face. "Until then, other than a hug, you never touched me. It even irked me a bit when you kissed Madeleine at the shower."

"I've never kissed Madeleine."

"Yes, you did. You kissed her cheeks when she arrived at the Michelson wedding."

"The only woman I've kissed in the last… is you." I've kissed only two other women with relationship potential since Vivienne destroyed my hope for finding a lifelong partner. Until Jillian.

She shakes her head. "Then your definition of kiss and mine are different. Your lips were definitely on Madeleine's cheeks."

"Your possessiveness is smoking hot. I kiss everyone on the cheeks. My mom, sisters, family, and even acquaintances like Madeleine. I kiss my woman and only my woman on the lips." My woman, I said it. I'm owning it.

Her eyes widen. "Good to know."

My admission hangs between us for a few long moments. Then I ask, "What tourist attractions were you planning on seeing while you were here?"

She taps her index finger on her lips.

Damn! That's hot!

"You unknowingly crossed some off today, including skating and pizza."

"What else? We can check off a few more tomorrow before dinner at my mom's."

"I can stay here if you would prefer."

"What are you worried about, *cariña*?

She shifts and rests her head on my chest, her hair tickling my arm. "It's crazy soon for me to meet your mom. Although, it leads me to wonder about your dad and how many sisters you have. I'm not prepared to answer any questions they may have about us."

I exhale. We didn't share much about our families. Granted, I knew about her brothers when we met, but mostly we talked current movies, music, and couple topics only in the abstract sense, not as if we would become one.

"My father was significantly older than my mom. He passed away when I was fifteen. I helped care for my sisters, Maura and Marisa, until I enlisted in the army."

"How old are they? Better yet, how old are you?"

I chuckle softly. "I'm thirty-two, and my sisters are five and seven years younger than me. Maura owns a salon and spa on Long Island, and Marisa is a barista and goes to school in the evenings for interior design. She's been dating Ana for about six months or so. How old are you?"

"I'm not old." I laugh. "I'm twenty-eight."

"You never shared about your life before. How much do you know about your birth parents?" I tighten my hold on her a little more when I feel her tense a bit. "You don't have to share."

She shakes her head against my chest. "It's fine. Most people don't know to ask about my birth parents. The information I have about them isn't much. When I turned eighteen, I asked Joyce. Joyce is Connor's mom and my adoption caseworker."

"Is that why you think of Connor like a brother?"

"Partially. My parents and Connor's were friends long before the kids came along. Anyway, Joyce shared the information in my file. My mother was a high-end escort in DC. My father was one of her johns. After she recovered from my birth, she had cosmetic surgery to erase as much of me as possible. She died on the table. Joyce was assigned my case."

"That's awful."

She tenses in my arms.

"Do you know who your father is?" I whisper.

"No, my bio-mom didn't list him on my birth certificate. To be honest, I never really thought about him in a parental sense. Ben and Connie are truly the only parents I've ever known. They gave me an amazing childhood and family."

"I'm grateful you were one of the lucky ones."

"Me too, especially after hearing some of Callie's horror stories about the foster system."

Callie was shuttled from foster home to foster home until she ended up in a group home until aging out of the system. At one foster home, she was threatened and harassed by the couple's biological son. Her experience is behind her choice to have both biological and adopted children with Connor.

"You never answered my question, where else did you want to visit while in the big city?" I can feel her heart racing beneath my hands. "Take your time." *I'll hold you as long as you'll have me.* So much time passes, I wonder if she fell asleep in my arms. "Still with me, *cariña*?"

"Yes. I'm reveling in how we feel."

Her lush body pressed against me, despite the topic of conversation, is more than I ever imagined. "Do you want to move to the bedroom?"

"Yes." She pushes up and levels her eyes with mine. After a quick peck, she's on her feet.

With her hand threaded in mine, I lead her to my bedroom. After washing up and removing my contacts, I strip down to my boxer briefs and slide beneath my sheets. Jillian stashes her sweatshirt and bra and exchanges her leggings for short shorts before returning to the same position we were on the couch. The main difference is now more of her creamy, soft skin is exposed to my hands, which itch to glide along the rest of her curves.

"Where do you want to explore tomorrow?"

She presses a kiss to my chest. If she continues marking my skin with her mouth, we won't sleep or plan anything for tomorrow. "I planned to visit MoMa, the Strand, the Ice Cream Museum, and the Color Factory. Oh, and Times Square. Well, those are on the list. All of them may be a lot in a few days."

"Maybe, but we can certainly try."

"Really?"

"I would love to accompany you while you traipse around the city. The only thing I need to do is email my division commander and human resources to resign and inform Christoph."

"I'm crazy excited for you," she murmurs.

"Same. For me and for us."

Jillian snuggles deeper into my arms and drifts off to sleep. Never before has a woman spent the night at my apartment, let alone in my bed.

My alarm startles me awake before six. Carefully, I reach over and press the snooze button to silence it. Neither of us has moved during the night. Jillian is pressed against me, her leg across my thigh and her hand flat on my abs. She's still sleeping peacefully.

I consider foregoing my workout, but I slip out of bed and shut off the alarm. I wash up before tugging on some workout gear and sneakers. Scribbling a note, I leave it near the coffee maker for her. A little over an hour later, with my weight session done for the day, I return to my apartment.

Jillian remains sound asleep in my bed. Waking with her in my arms is perfection, and I want to start every morning with her curled against me. After I finish my water, I brew coffee for both of us.

"Morning, *bonita*." I sit on the edge of the bed with coffee in hand.

"Nothing beautiful about me first thing in the morning," she grumbles.

"You would be wrong."

Reluctantly, she sits up and takes the coffee. "Thank you."

"For the coffee or the compliment?"

"Yes. Both." She smiles at me.

"Get moving so we can start on your list first thing."

"You were serious?"

"Absolutely. I'm sure we'll be apart when I have assignments for Blackthorne. I plan to use this time wisely."

Within an hour, we're both dressed, armed with admission tickets to MoMa, and ready to take on the day together.

CHAPTER FIVE

JILLIAN

The past few days have been spectacular. Unfortunately, it's time for me to leave our little couple bubble and return home. We checked off most of the stops on my list. Dinner with his family was fun, and I didn't feel out of place, even after he shared about his career move.

Javier will be here sooner rather than later. He reached out to the department and resigned. The good news is he's free to work for Blackthorne. The bad news is he has wait until he's no longer on the NYPD payroll to start his new job. Exhausting his vacation and personal time will take about a month.

After a toe-curling kiss at the airport, I settle into my seat and promptly close my eyes to avoid talking about leaving the city with my seat neighbor. Two hours later, I push open the door of my house. My home is decidedly too large for only me. However, it was in shambles and a steal at half the price. Jake was able to help me fix it up. The craftsman has an open floor plan with a gorgeous fireplace in the living room. With Jake's help, I turned the outdated kitchen into a chef's dream kitchen to foster my love of cooking.

Cooking for those I care about is my passion hobby. While I love my chosen profession, there are occasions where the stress gets to me. I started cooking and baking to give me finite and definite results, which is not something I see daily, given all my students are termed severely developmentally disabled. Over the years, I've excelled at cooking to the point where I prepare family dinners and intimate dinners for my family and friends' dates.

Me: I'm home.

Javier: I miss having you near me already.

Me: Me too.

Javier: I'll call you later.

I throw in my laundry and sort through my mail from the last few days. Afterward, I ride into town to browse my sister-in-law's store and pick up some chocolates.

Crescent Bay is a small town within driving distance of our nation's capital. Main Street is exactly as you would picture it. There's a hardware store owned by the same family for generations, a general store, which is also family owned, a florist, and a candy store. Millie runs the candy store and makes the most delicious caramels I've ever tasted. There's a Blackthorne office and Norah's bookstore on Main Street as well. I'm not sure it's a bookstore exactly. The Nook is a store where you can grab a cup of coffee, browse shelves of books, and actually read them. You can purchase books too, but she wanted everyone to be able to enjoy the space, regardless of their ability to pay.

I hurry through Millie's candy store and then wander across the street to the Nook.

"Hi, Jill. Happy New Year."

"Hey, Jessa. Same to you." Jessa is the manager of the Nook. She's statuesque, outgoing, and witty and has colorful hair. I think it's been blue or pink since she started working here.

"Norah is in the office," she informs me.

I nod and wander slowly to the back of the store. Norah has taken great care to make her store comfortable and inviting. I would be here for hours if I had the time. I knock on the door.

"Hey there! How was your 'get my man' excursion to the big city?" Norah takes the bonds of girls' night seriously, despite being married to my brother. Along with Callie and Maia, they called me out on the sparks flying around Javier and me at the wedding and, more recently, the shower. Even attempting to deny my attraction to him is futile. Until our last girls' night, no one knew about our daily chats at the hospital. Hell, I don't even think Jake knows.

I feel my cheeks heat up instantly. Containing my huge smile is—impossible.

"Your grin tells me it went very well."

"For once, my timing was excellent. Did you know Christoph offered Javier a spot on his team?"

"No, Jacob doesn't discuss personnel or security protocol with me." She considers my question. "Wait… Cruz accepted?"

"Yes, he did."

"I'm crazy happy for you. What are you two planning to do about your brothers?"

"We're still working out the details. It isn't as if I chased a guy from a dating app to another city. We have history."

"Who has history?" Jake enters Norah's office and kisses her to the brink of socially unacceptable.

Crap! A twinge of jealousy pings through me. Given our time in the city, Javier is openly affectionate, and I can't wait for him to be here permanently. "Girl talk, nothing to worry about. Thanks for the chat, Norah. I'll consider your advice."

Norah nods, and I make a hasty exit from her office. We may have agreed to date one another, but anything more still requires some discussion. I'm not ready to add my brothers into the mix yet.

I meander over to the thriller aisle and consider a few newer titles, then decide on the newest romance by my favorite author. With a new book in hand, I return home. I curl up near a blazing fire with a cup of coffee and dig into the story.

About an hour later, my phone rings.

"Hi."

"Hey. How was the rest of your afternoon?"

I catch Javier up about my chat with Norah and skirting sharing with Jake.

"What do you want to tell them? You should know Christoph may have an idea about us that I didn't dispel him from," Javier confesses.

"Meaning?"

"When he offered me the job, I hesitated. He asked if there was a woman to consider here. My answer may have led him to believe there was a woman elsewhere. It isn't a big leap for him to know I meant you."

Oh. He wasn't kidding when he said I was a consideration. "I don't want to hide our relationship, but I want to take some more time before fielding their opinions. All they've seen is our recent interactions."

"Agreed."

"How did it go at the precinct today? It couldn't have been easy clearing out your desk."

He pauses a little too long for my liking but answers anyway. "A bunch of the guys were surprised, but overall it went well. I've been working on this decision for a few weeks. The last piece clicked into place over the weekend. You."

"Were you coming to visit to share your new job, or would you have called?"

"I would've come to you. However, the element of surprise would be nonexistent since I don't know your exact address. The only way to get it would be to ask Jake."

"Would've been worth it despite my interest in waiting a bit to share."

"Definitely. When can I visit you to look for a place?"

Now. "Whenever you want. Why don't you stay with me?" *I said it, and it doesn't feel too soon.*

"Do you have enough space for me?"

I laugh. "Yes, definitely."

"Jillian, can I stay with you?"

It takes me a second to realize why he's asking the same question. "You and your traditional norms. Yes, please stay with me."

"The root of most traditions have threads of chivalry, loyalty, and love."

He isn't wrong.

"I think you're forgetting a woman's inability to do things for herself—like open a bank account—at one time. Most of those things have changed."

"True, but those characteristics form the basis for a solid relationship, regardless of changing times and societal norms. I assume your position on marriage and family hasn't changed."

"No, it hasn't changed. My parents are an amazing example of thriving as a couple even with significant challenges, considering they couldn't have children of their own. I want it all. A polite, gentlemanly husband who pulls out my chair, opens my car door, and dotes on our children, but also is willing to wrap my hair around his palm and tug for better access to my neck. Ready to change your mind yet?"

"About us, no. Hell no. I'm making a mental note of the hair thing too."

His confidence in our budding relationship is awe-inspiring. "I expect nothing less." I fail to contain a yawn.

"Get some sleep, *cariña*. I'll call you tomorrow."

"Night, Javier." I smile and end the call. He may not have slept here yet, but I'm not looking forward to sleeping alone even after only a few nights of sharing a bed with him.

The next morning, I oversleep while dreaming of the feel of Javier's arms around me over the weekend and the stolen kisses as we ticked items off my attraction list. Spending time with him has always been smooth, even when we disagree about a topic. Never once have our discussions escalated to disrespect for one another. Thankfully, my bestie is on point for the first day of school in the new year.

"You're my favorite of all time, Deni!" I accept a coffee and a warm donut from her. Denise and I have been besties since the end of high school. She knows there's a guy I've been pining for but not who until I flew to see Javier last week.

"Of course. Are you going to share about your visit to the Big Apple?"

"It was amazing and will get better as soon as he moves here."

She stops near her classroom door. "I'm excited for you. You deserve it! I want all the details."

I lift my coffee in salute and step into my classroom next door. The first day back after a vacation is typically difficult for my students. Kate and Jesse are the first to enter. Their moms assist them putting their lunches in their cubbies and dutifully wave goodbye. Kate's mom, Carol, looks a bit tired from the holiday. She's a single mom. A week straight without a break is a lot to handle. Jesse is being raised by his grandparents. This morning, Grandma Jane dropped him off. The last to arrive is Stevie. He's an only child. His parents are partners and equally share the responsibility of his care, and he looks as if his holiday was special.

Once everyone is settled, I begin with the morning announcements and walk them through our schedule for the day. During lunch, an aide comes into my room. She assists my students while I eat and handle some administrative stuff.

My inbox only contains administrative updates. My phone vibrates in my bag when I reach in for my lunch. A rush of intrigue flies through me. No one texts me, considering my bestie is next door and my family knows I can't answer during the school day.

Javier: Have a wonderful day, beautiful.

I check the time stamp. This message has been sitting here for a few hours. I smile inwardly. I like how we feel. What was I thinking waiting so long?

Me: Thank you. Have a wonderful day too.

I quickly eat my lunch and finish out the day with my students. Today is low drama. Thankfully, the holiday break didn't impact their schedules too much. After they transition to the pickup line, I clean up my classroom.

As I'm almost ready to leave for the day, I'm summoned to the front office. Deni steps out of her classroom with her arms raised in question. I shrug as I walk past her. The main office is near the front of the building to the left. My view is obscured by a throng of married women who have likely never seen a man as gorgeous as Javier, but I know his voice anywhere. It was the first thing I was attracted too. *Liar.* Partially true. I was attracted to his sheepish demeanor, as if he chose how soon he could visit Jake and Connor.

"There she is," Janice, the school secretary, states. Slowly, the sea of ladies parts.

My lord, he's a god among mere mortals. "Hi, what're you doing here? Did I miss something?"

He wraps me in his arms and whispers, "No, *cariña.* I missed you and decided to travel today." After releasing me, he hands me a large mixed bouquet of flowers.

A collective sigh cascades through my coworkers. "Thank you. Consider me adequately surprised and giddy. I never told you where I work."

He leans forward so only I can hear me. "I would be a terrible cop if I didn't notice your badge tucked into your purse."

"Fair enough. Ladies, this is Cruz. Babe, these are my coworkers: Janice, Kylie, and Eve."

"Pleasure to meet you, ladies."

The group of women can't lift their jaws up off the floor. I completely understand, and he's mine.

"I need to grab my bag from my classroom."

"Lead the way." We're barely two steps away before he takes my hand in his. Once we're inside my classroom, he pulls me close and kisses me as if it's been a year instead of a little more than a day. Sensual strokes of his tongue explore my mouth. My knees go weak, and my body heats more than it should from a kiss. He slides one arm higher up to keep me upright. Deni interrupts by busting through the door. She's my only coworker who doesn't knock.

"Oops, sorry, Jill." She starts to leave.

Javier presses a kiss to my forehead and loosens his hold but doesn't release me. Secretly, I love his desire to hold me constantly.

I stop her by introducing them. "Javier, this is my bestie Denise. Deni, Javier Cruz."

Deni extends her hand to him. "You're New York?"

"Yes."

"Hot damn, Jill! How on earth did you wait so long to stake a claim on him?"

I bury my head into Javier's chest and attempt to contain my embarrassment from clearly mentioning him before the recent past. My bestie has no filter, at all.

"I like you. You're straightforward. To answer on her behalf, the timing wasn't right until now."

"It was a pleasure meeting you. I'll let you get going on the correct timing for once."

Javier replies, "Pleasure to meet you as well, Denise."

She leaves my classroom with a backward glance indicating she wants more details later. I nod ever so slightly. There's a fine line between sharing and oversharing. No intimate details will be shared with anyone.

"Ready to go home?" he asks after kissing me again.

"I was going to the grocery store. Here." I hand him my phone. "If you pull up the app, we can order instead of wandering around the store and actually have a worthy meal for dinner."

"You don't have to change your plans on my account."

I pull my lower lip between my teeth. "I want to. You can reorder my last one and add whatever you like to have on hand, including the berry blast Mike and Ike candy."

"How do you remember that?"

I shrug. "Same way you remember my favorite chocolate and happen to love them now yourself." While I gather the rest of my stuff, he places the order, which will be ready for pickup by the time we arrive.

CHAPTER SIX

JAVIER

The travel hiccups were worth it to see her gorgeous smile. From the departure delay with a call from Maura and the insane traffic, I was concerned I wouldn't make it to the school. Then I would have to ruin my surprise. My sister Maura called to reiterate her stance about my decision to leave the city. She feels it's too soon after failing to get the promotion to move on. I appreciate her concern, but my decision was thoroughly obsessed over and rehashed repeatedly over the last few months.

I follow Jillian to the grocery store and, as promised, it's ready for pickup when we arrive. The ride from the store to her home is short. I park in the spot off to the side of her garage so she can leave for school in the morning. If I recall correctly, her house is a little outside Crescent Bay, where Blackthorne is based—a choice I'm confident Jillian made purposefully. The draw of the small town is markedly different from the city. It'll take some getting used to, but I'm ready for this change.

Her home is a gorgeous craftsman. There are likely numerous flowers blooming in her yard in the spring and summer, which is now covered with a dusting of snow. I grab my bags and duck into the garage as the door closes. I add a few bags of groceries in my other hand and follow her inside.

She silences her alarm system. "The kitchen is straight through there." She points to the door directly ahead of me. "Remind me, I'll get you a key."

With all the groceries on the huge granite island, I have a moment to take in her gorgeous kitchen. It shouldn't surprise me, her passion for cooking only rivals her love of teaching.

"Did you design your kitchen?"

A shy smile materializes on her face. "Yeah. I found this house in shambles and convinced Jake to help me rehab it. I created this kitchen from studs."

"It suits you. Why don't you get started on dinner, and I'll fumble around to put the rest of the groceries away?" I suggest.

"Thanks. On one condition."

I raise an eyebrow in her direction. "Which is?"

"I need a kiss or ten first." She steps into my space and plants a kiss on my mouth. I wrap my arm around her waist and hoist her onto the counter near the sink. My hands rest on the tops of her thighs while one of hers clutches my shirt and the other cups the side of my face. Kissing Jillian has levels depending on our location. In her classroom has nothing on my living room and her kitchen. *Coño!* Breathless and more intrigued than I was before, I pull back.

Her lips are red and plump from our kissing, and her breathing is jagged. "We're going to need to add time before everything, aren't we?"

"Definitely." I kiss her softly and guide her to the floor. On one hand, I'm cursing myself for not adding enough space between me and the counter. On the other, her body pressed against mine as she slides to the floor is exquisite torture. "What are you cooking?"

"I probably should've asked. Are you allergic to anything or absolutely hate any type of food?"

I shake my head while replying, "No allergies, and I don't hate any specific food. I'm not a fan of seafood on pizza, but otherwise it's fine."

"I can work with those parameters. I'm making mushroom asiago chicken with rice pilaf on the side."

I continue emptying the bags while stealing glances of her. I've never seen her teaching, but she's mesmerizing while she cooks—focused and beautiful. Jillian is always beautiful, whether she's dressed for a wedding or fresh from sleep. Her dress for Connor and Callie's wedding was perfection. The black dress hugged her curves and dipped exceptionally low in the back. The feel of her skin beneath my fingers while we danced during the reception is branded in my mind. Every touch since then shatters the one before.

"Anything I can do to help?" I ask after I finish putting away the groceries. Her kitchen is similar to mine as far as the layout of the cabinetry and placement of items. I even found the candy stash exactly where mine is.

"Sure, do you want to set the table or make a salad?"

"I'll take the table this time, so you don't have to leave the kitchen."

"Okay."

I step around her but slide my hand along her hip and press a kiss to her cheek on my way to the plates and glasses.

We sit and eat our first dinner together in her home. I suppose it's my home now too.

"How long until you have to tell Christoph and Jake you're here?"

I savor the chicken before answering, "Here in Crescent Bay or here with you?"

She shrugs. "Both, I guess."

"I can start working for Blackthorne in early February. Christoph sent the training manual, procedures, and policies to me right after I accepted. As far as moving in here and being with you, I agree to wait a bit to share with your family. What is the likelihood someone will show up here?"

"Low. My family doesn't show up unless something is awry, and it rarely happens."

"When is the next family get-together?"

She taps her index finger on her lips.

"Do you have any idea how hot that is?"

She freezes and catalogs her movements before smiling slyly and continues tapping her lips. With a wink, she stops and answers my question. "I would think it would be soon after the twins are born. It would give us up to six weeks."

"Six weeks seems like a decent amount of time for them not to freak out on you."

"I'm not worried about me."

"*Cariña*, I can handle the guys if necessary."

"We shouldn't have to handle them. They should be happy for us regardless of their opinions."

"You're right, but you're also a realist. At first, they're going to freak, and we both know it."

She sighs and sets down her fork. I take her hand in mine and lift it to my lips. Her wide ocean-colored eyes meet mine.

"I'm not worried. Are you?"

Her head shakes side to side. "Not even a little."

Of all people, the guys know the damage Vivienne caused as far as her ending our relationship. I will never purposefully hurt Jillian, and I know in the depths of my soul that she won't hurt me.

We clear the table and settle on her couch. She has her back against the arm and her legs draped over my thighs.

"Tell me more about you," she requests.

"Like?"

She smiles. "If you never had to sleep, what would you do with the extra time?"

"Now, I would spend it with you."

"What about before us?" she adds.

"I would've spent more time with my family and friends. I would've fulfilled my promise to Jones, Adams, and Carter."

She links her hands with mine. "What did you promise them?"

"I promised them I would mail their 'what if' letters, which I did. However… I failed to visit their graves when I returned home."

"Why?"

I drop my head and take a deep breath. "Mostly the guilt of not being with them when they were injured."

Jillian leans forward and lifts my eyes to hers with a nudge under my chin. "You didn't have any control over your missions. There's no way for you to know it would go so wrong that given day."

"No, but I was assigned to the mission and then pulled off it early the same morning."

"I'm sure your commanding officer had a valid reason, and you can't internalize his decision. It isn't fair to you, Jones, Carter, or Adams. Do you know where you need to go?"

"Yes." My response comes out as barely a whisper.

"Arlington?" she murmurs.

I nod.

"Maybe you should consider going now."

I shrug. She isn't wrong, especially now considering how much closer I am to them. I've mostly accepted the fact my unit mates died or were injured on that mission. My guilt is more about why I wasn't. Why my commanding officer chose me to stay behind. Why was I spared? Perhaps I should reach out and ask him directly.

"I'm sorry. My question wasn't meant to be heavy."

I draw her into my lap and press a kiss to her cheek. "I will never lie to you, Jillian. My answer was honest. No way for you to know it wouldn't be pleasant."

She turns her head and brushes her lips across mine. "Thank you for telling me."

"I have nothing to hide. We simply haven't had enough time to talk about everything yet."

"Your turn."

"Hmmmm." I take my time thinking about a question to ask Jillian. There isn't anything she could say that would give me pause about us. "What would you do if you had enough money not to have a job?"

"I would open a restaurant with a 'pay what you can afford' type of system."

"That's amazing. You didn't even have to think about your answer."

"Not at all."

"Want to keep going or get some sleep?"

She glances at the clock. "Both." She drops a kiss on my lips and moves to stand.

She's smart and stunning but doesn't see it herself. "What time do you leave for work? Is there a gym around here?"

"I leave no later than 7:30 a.m. As far as the gym, what do you need?"

"Equipment wise?"

She nods, reaches out for my hand, and leads me downstairs while I answer her.

"I prefer to run outside when the weather is good. As far as equipment...."

She flicks on a light. It illuminates a decent-size room with a padded floor, treadmill, elliptical, exercise bike, and one of the new interactive systems on the far wall.

"Do you ever have to leave your house? Do you even want to? Your home is perfect, Jillian."

She smirks at me. "Thank you. It wasn't when I bought it. I only leave for work. You can create a profile for yourself. Jake has a gym at the compound too, if you prefer to work out with other people around."

"Won't you need to work out too?" I don't want to force her to alter her schedule.

"I'm not much of a morning person, as I'm sure you gathered from my visit. Generally, I work out after school and then cook. I usually spend my weekends cooking for family or friends, whether a party or special date. Until you, it was only me."

"No dates or boyfriends?"

She raises an eyebrow at me. "No. In fact, you're the first man in my house who isn't related to me by some familial relationship. The local dating scene is dismal. Most of the guys I would be interested in work for my brothers. I haven't been attracted to any of them enough to initiate anything. If I were to branch out, I'm concerned I might end up meeting my long-lost sibling or even my father somehow."

I draw her against my body, kiss her forehead, and tuck her beneath my chin. She melts against me. Jillian fits in my arms as if she were born for the sole purpose. My heart tightens in my chest. I never considered how her adoption and lack of family history could impact her adult life. The Blackthornes are amazing people and gave her, Jake, and Cam an incredible home. However, not knowing if she has other siblings or even if she were to come face-to-face with her biological father and not know is awful. "I'm sorry."

She shakes her head against my chest. "No way for you to know. I didn't share with you yet."

"I assume at least Jake and Cam know what you just told me."

She lifts her head and looks up at me. "Yes. Both are aware of my fear of stumbling across my biological father or a sibling. I didn't ask, and they never shared about their birth families. It's a deeply personal choice whether or not to dig into your past. It's a near certainty the story isn't pretty."

"Thank you for sharing with me."

She exhales slowly and tightens her arms around me as if there were more space for her to fill. There isn't. There's only one way for her to be physically closer, and tonight isn't the time. "You're welcome. Let's go to bed."

I twist my head in question even though she can't see me do it. My body betrays me though. There's no way she doesn't feel what her proximity is doing to me despite our topic of conversation.

"Sleep tonight, Javier." My name tumbling from her lips sounds like the sweetest song I've ever heard.

"I know what you meant."

She pulls back and slides her fingers through mine. I follow her luscious curves up the stairs to her bedroom. The master bedroom is feminine but not overly so. The furniture is dark, and the linens are white with an arabesque pattern in blue tones. Her windows are covered with matching blackout drapes.

"Do you want to talk more or sleep?" I mumble against the back of her neck. There's no mistaking the goose bumps erupting on her skin.

"I want to talk but need to sleep."

"Night, *cariña*."

"Goodnight, Javier." She burrows deeper into my arms and falls asleep within minutes.

CHAPTER SEVEN

JILLIAN

The bell is ringing as I walk through the front doors of the school building. I have never been late for work. Leaving the warm cocoon of Javier's arms was immensely harder than I anticipated when I invited him to live with me.

"Morning, Jill. I want details," Deni announces from her door.

I wave her off as I open my classroom door with urgency. Thankfully, the parents are waiting for me to arrive. "I apologize for the delay."

Jane speaks first. "We're all entitled to oversleep every now and then. Have a wonderful day, Miss Blackthorne."

"Thank you, Jane. You as well."

The rest of the parents update me on their students' nights and file out the door. During the morning announcements, I set up their lessons for the first block of their school day.

When the announcements end, Kate buzzes through her computer. It's how she raises her hand.

"Yes, Kate."

She types out her question. "What is the boy's name?"

The other students chuckle.

"What boy?"

"Your smile is different today."

Kate isn't wrong. However, I don't plan on sharing too much, if anything, with my students. "Thank you."

"You can share with us. We aren't gossips," Kate quips through her computerized voice.

Her classmates snicker.

I can feel my face heating up. "I appreciate your discretion, but my life outside of school is not up for discussion. Let's get back to work."

A chorus of groans echoes around the room, some through computers and others audible, but my students start their morning tasks. As my butt hits my chair, I see Deni waving me into the hallway. I shake my head and move to the threshold.

"Spill, honey, and fast."

I smile. "There's nothing to spill yet."

"Please tell me you at least saw him naked."

I shake my head.

"What is wrong with you? I only saw a small portion of him kissing you, and it got me hot and bothered. I need to live vicariously through you since I'm single as one can be with no prospects whatsoever. I mean, you flew to another state to catch a good man." Deni's voice sounds incredulous.

I sigh. His kiss is knee-weakening, all-consuming, and possessive. I don't think I'll ever get enough. "We can talk more later, but there truly aren't any details yet."

"I'm still jealous."

"I love you too, Deni. Go back to class. We'll chat more later." As I turn my attention back to my students, all their heads turn back to their work instead of my conversation with Deni. Inwardly, I shake my head and move back to my desk. While rummaging through my bag for my water, I feel my phone vibrate.

Javier: Where can I find a key?

Me: Oops! Sorry. Drawer to the right of the refrigerator.

Javier: Thanks. The alarm code is your birthday reversed?

Me: Close, July 16 my birthyear.

Javier: See you after school.

It appears my class is refocused on their tasks, but I'm not. I'm ecstatic knowing Javier will be at my house after school. I spend my lunch break avoiding telling Deni anything more than I want to. She seems placated until the end of the day when we emerge from the school. Javier is leaning against his truck waiting for me.

"Hi, *corazón.*" He kisses my cheeks and draws me against him possessively. "Nice to see you again, Denise."

"Pleasure is mine."

I'm not sure what to make of his presence at school again. Truthfully, considering the warning from his captain, I'm concerned.

"I'll see you in the morning, Deni."

She gives me the bestie side-eye because she can't continue to drill into me for answers about Javier before she walks to her car.

"Is everything okay?"

"Not sure," he replies. "Captain Davidson called today. There have been some more overt threats toward the department. More specifically, one aimed at the officers, detectives, and their families who worked the case, as well as one directly aimed at Sam Morgan. I know we wanted to wait to inform your brothers, but…."

"Okay. Did you call yet or are we showing up at the office?"

He traps me against his truck and presses a kiss to my head. "I wanted to talk to you first."

"Why don't we take my car to my house, and you can call on the way?"

"No, I don't think you should be by yourself." The sheer worry in his voice gives me pause. I consider objecting, but then I recall who is making the threats—the Irish mob.

Resigned, I reply, "Okay."

He opens the passenger door to his truck and closes it behind me. Once he settles into the driver's seat, he sets his phone in the holder, dials Jake on speaker, and threads his hand with mine.

"Hey, Cruz. Welcome to Blackthorne, bro!"

"Thanks, Jake. I have a security issue that needs to be handled. Where can we meet immediately?"

"I'm at the compound. I can have Christoph and Connor here within the hour. Can you give me an idea of what this is in regards to?" Jake asks.

"It's regarding an art theft chase I worked with Sam Morgan a few years back. Captain Davidson indicated there were threats against the officers and detectives who worked the case, as well as Sam."

"Cruz, Sam is calling on the office line. Come to the compound right away."

"We're on our way." He ends the call and tightens his grip on my hand.

"You realize you said we're, right?" I ask.

He shrugs and continues driving. A few minutes later, he whispers, "I'm sorry, *cariña*."

"For what?"

"Dragging you into whatever this is." Cruz turns onto the driveway for the compound and parks in front of the gate.

Before he hops out, I refuse to release his hand. "Nothing to be sorry for. We're in this together, whatever this is." I lean forward and brush my lips across his. When he returns from the keypad, I realize Jake could've seen me kiss him on the monitor in his office.

"What, sweetheart?" I must look upset.

"Prepare yourself for Jake to freak out when we step into the house."

"Why?"

"He may have seen me kiss you on the security monitor."

Javier kisses me more thoroughly this time. "I'm more worried about Norah than Jake." Norah is Jake's wife. She was an accountant and Jake's friend with benefits for two years before she needed to hire

Blackthorne. She found fraud and other malfeasance while examining the books of one of her largest clients, and they threatened her life.

"Norah knew about my trip to New York, and she didn't share with Jake."

He turns to look at me again before pulling through the gate. "Norah didn't tell Jake." It was a statement, but I answer him anyway.

"No, what's said at girls' night, stays at girls' night."

"I see. Well, Norah and I spoke in depth about us at Connor and Callie's wedding after you and I danced."

"Oh. What did she say?"

"She told me to either walk away or choose to be happy with you." Javier parks near the barn and takes my hands in his. "I was figuring out how to pull it off when I was passed over. When we talked at the shower solidified you would be in this with me, if I asked."

"I would've been years ago, like I am now."

He kisses me again and asks, "Ready to face your brothers?"

"I'm more worried about the threat than my brothers." Javier is a good man. My brothers—all of them—know he is, even if they object to us at first.

Javier rounds his tall truck and opens my door. Jake and Norah are standing at the door as I slide to the ground. Now isn't the time to revel in the feel of his body against me or his fingers digging into my hips.

I reach down and pet Tank and Sabre, their extremely well-behaved dogs.

"How long, Jill?" Jake bellows.

"Hi, Norah. Nice to see you too, Jake." I glance over at Javier only to solidify how far back I'm sharing. "We've been talking since you and Connor were at Walter Reed." If a few years isn't enough time for Jake, nothing will be.

"I see. We have a more pressing matter to discuss." Jake finally allows us inside the house.

"Would you like a drink?" Norah offers.

"A water would be great, Norah," I reply. "How are you feeling?"

"Same for me," Javier states as well.

"Not too bad. I have a few months left." Norah is the cutest pregnant woman I've ever seen. I'm the only female family member not currently with child. Callie is due with twins anytime in the next few weeks. Madeleine is due within a few days of Norah.

Norah hands a water to each of us, and we follow Jake to his office.

Jake takes a seat at his desk and hands Javier a file. "That's the intel from our work with Sam Morgan. When he hired us to protect his now pregnant wife, Savannah, we did a complete review of his life, including the art theft case he worked with the NYPD. What exactly did Captain Davidson share with you?"

Javier reiterates the same information he shared with me from when I was visiting him as well as the more direct threats he learned of earlier today.

"You went to her school before calling me?"

"Yes." Javier's response is unwavering. He told Jake everything he needs to know about our relationship in one small, seemingly insignificant word. He's in as deep as I am despite how new our relationship appears to Jake.

Jake shares, "I've reached out to Blaine. I expect to hear back from him soon."

"Remind me, who is Blaine?" Javier asks.

"He's our investigator, a white hat hacker and purveyor of information. He's exceptional," Connor states from the threshold. "What's up, Cruz? Welcome to the team."

Javier stands and bro hugs Connor. Almost immediately thereafter, Christoph enters the office as well. After a lengthy, practiced handshake, Javier retakes his seat and takes my hand in his. I don't miss the look exchanged among my brothers when they notice. For their benefit, Jake repeats what we know so far.

"Yeah, Blaine," Jake barks into his cellphone. After a few minutes, Jake ends the call and shares what he learned. "Blaine is sending over some intel, including recent movements of the suspected family members of the alleged previous owners of the stolen artwork. There was a blanket written threat of vengeance and death delivered to Captain Davidson earlier today. NYPD is processing it and will share information when it's available. I highly doubt there's any fingerprints or DNA evidence. He indicates there are some photos from your recent trip to New York." Jake pointedly looks at me.

Feeling cornered, I lash out at him and the others. "My personal life is none of your business."

"It is right now, considering you have been identified as someone important in his life by the Irish mob." Jake points at Javier.

"Say what you need to say, Jake. You too." I twist in my chair and glare at Connor and Christoph.

Javier's fingers grip mine even tighter. "*Bastante!* Can we focus on dealing with the threat instead of the ins and outs of my relationship with Jillian, almost all of which are none of your business? Any of you." Javier's is voice louder and sterner than I've ever heard before.

The terms of endearment in Spanish make my chest tighten, but it's something else entirely when his native language and his accent comes through.

Three sets of eyes snap to Javier.

"What about my sisters and mother? Sam and his family? My relationship with the Morgans goes beyond this case. I also worked with Cash and Sam closely when Billie was injured and lost her memory."

After a solid minute of silence, Sabre saunters into the office and lays her head across my feet. Tank takes a spot near the door.

Christoph speaks first. "Who is available from your teams? I have Barrett available for the next two weeks."

"Alex is free for this week, and Drew next week," Connor adds.

"Finn and Maia are free for the next two weeks."

While my brothers talk, Javier leans closer and whispers so only I can hear him. "You're shaking, *cariña*."

I turn my face away so no one can read my lips near the shell of his ear. "I'm pissed at them, but I'll be fine." Despite the situation, I note his physical reaction to my mouth so close to his ear. "I see you, Javier."

"I see you too."

I haven't the slightest clue how long we simply sit there with our faces turned toward one another blocking out the conversation around us.

"You two done?" Jake's voice intrudes on my thoughts.

We pull apart as if we're teenagers who got caught making out on the couch at our parents' house.

I narrow my eyes at Jake.

"How secure is the school, Cruz?"

"There's one secure entrance and numerous exits. However, during school hours, only the front entrance is used for entering and exiting the building unless there's an emergency."

I refrain from looking over at Javier. Instead, I squeeze his hand once. Not only did he come for me first, but he did an analysis of the security of my school too. I feel all warm and tingly despite the threat pushing his need to check the building. My brothers taught me to protect myself in high school, but it's a welcome feeling when it's Javier looking out for me.

"Good. I'll add to the security around her house. You're going to have to move in there. In the event this escalates, we'll find a safehouse for the two of you. You'll need to escort Jill to and from work. If the principal will allow you to be in the building, great. If not, you'll be stationed outside at all times. Currently, there are no direct threats to your mother or sisters. Please reach out to them. I'm going to send Alex to check in on them until the threat is resolved," Jake states, then pointedly turns his gaze to me. "Jill, you will only go to work and nowhere else for the time being. Nowhere else."

I nod. "I need someone to pick up my car at the school if it hasn't been towed yet."

"I'll take care of it. Please give me your keys," Connor interjects.

I fish through my purse, pull out my keys, and set them in his outstretched hand.

"And Sam and his family?" Javier asks.

"Once we're through, I'll call him back again and inform him Maia and Finn are headed his way for the time being. They can stay at Norah's townhouse," Jake responds.

Connor and Christoph have been decidedly quiet during this meeting. Either they don't want to piss me off more, are fine with my relationship with Javier, are willing to let Jake take point, or all of the above. It's probably all the above.

"I'm finished for now. I would like to speak with Cruz alone."

Ugh! Seriously, I'm a grown woman, and he's your friend. I follow Connor and Christoph out of the office with one dog on either side of me.

CHAPTER EIGHT

JAVIER

I don't even give Jake the chance to speak first. My relationship with Jillian is none of his business outside the current threat. "I have no intention of sharing anything else about my relationship with Jillian."

"I'm not blind, Cruz. I would have to be to miss your interactions with one another at the wedding and the baby shower. I would've weighed those interactions more heavily had I known about your history before then. Of all people, you know how important family is to me."

I nod.

"I don't plan to intrude any deeper. I appreciate you putting her first at the risk of angering me. I know you'll protect her like I would. Given your current status, you're in a gray area. Technically, you're still a member of the NYPD for a few weeks. I'll call Jill's school and speak with Principal Platt personally. Ideally, she won't ask too many questions. If she does, Jill may need to take some time off."

"Jillian won't accept being away from her students lightly."

Jake shakes his head. "You're underestimating how much my sister cares about you."

Not even close, but Jake doesn't know the depth of our conversations. The only thing she doesn't know about is Vivienne. "Perhaps."

"I'll call you in the morning and let you know Principal Platt's decision. Jill's security system is equipped with a perimeter alarm she doesn't use and motion sensors in the basement she isn't aware of. I'll text you the admin codes to turn them on. The exterior cameras are looped into the Blackthorne office in town. They cover the backyard, deck, walkout basement door, front porch, and yard. There's a minor blind spot at the rear corner of her garage."

Note to self: nothing overly sexual outside of Jillian's house.

"She doesn't know any of that?"

"No, it was hard enough getting her to allow me to install the system instead of an outside contractor."

My independent woman put her big brother in his place. Still he did more than she wanted. Part of me wants Jake to tell her. "I will blame you when she gets angry later."

"Fine. Do you need anything else?"

"No."

"Good night, Cruz."

"Later, Jake." I turn to leave, but he stops me.

"One more thing, are you armed?"

Always. "Yes."

"You should talk to Jill about where her weapon is stored and the combination to the lock. I don't know the combination to share it with you."

Jillian has a weapon in her home. I'm moderately surprised given where she lives.

"Thanks, Jake."

"We've got your six. Call if anything seems out of place."

"I will." I exit his office and walk toward the sound of soft, feminine voices.

The moment I cross into the living room, all girl talk ceases. "No need to stop talking on my account."

"What if we were talking about you?" Norah asks.

I grin at her. "I have no doubt you were in fact talking about me. Ready, *cariña*?"

"Yes." Jillian hugs Norah before sliding her hand into mine. She pets the dogs with her other hand just before we slip out the front door.

I open the passenger door of my truck and wait for her to climb in. If I touch her, I'm likely to kiss her breathless, and here is not the place. She doesn't speak again until I return to the truck after closing the gate at the bottom of the private driveway.

"What did Jake want?"

"He didn't warn me off or pull the big-brother card. He gave me more information about your security system and a reminder since I'm technically still NYPD."

"You mean the extra features he installed, the ones he believes I don't know about."

All I can do is shake my head. "You never cease to amaze me. Where is your weapon stored?"

"You sound surprised."

I glance over at her. "Partially. I'm sure you can physically defend yourself and confident Jake or even Ben taught you to shoot. I'm surprised you have a weapon in your house."

"Fair enough. It's in a lock box on the shelf on left side of my closet. The code is 986060."

That's my birthday reversed. "When did you pick the code?"

"When I purchased my weapon so... about three years ago."

Timing is everything.

"Can we get food, or should I cook?"

I'm still considering her question when both our phones start chiming at once. Concern slices through me. I can see the preview on my phone from the holder.

Connor: Jill's house compromised. Drive north until we contact again.

"What does yours say?" Her voice is shaky as she turns her phone toward me.

"Same. Please reply to him. As far as food, there's probably some snacks in the glove box."

She types out a reply, rummages through the glove box, and retrieves a protein bar and a granola bar. Jillian unbuckles, lifts the center console, and shimmies beside me. After resecuring her seat belt, she unwraps the protein bar for me.

"Thanks." I don't realize how hungry I am until she sets it in my hand. My first bite is half the bar.

"What does compromised mean to Connor?" she asks.

I set the remainder of the bar in the door and take her hand in mine. "It could mean a lot of things. Perhaps someone was or is in your house. There are signs of forced entry or attempted entry."

"I would've gotten an alert on my phone if someone was in my house."

"Maybe, but I would bet if they're after me, their methods would be sophisticated considering their alleged connections."

She exhales slowly. "What happens now?"

I lift her hand to my lips and kiss the back. "We take a drive until Connor calls back."

She nods and polishes off the granola bar.

"Radio or more questions?"

"Ask me a question." Her reply is shaky and quiet.

She's scared. Understandably so. "Jillian, I will protect you even if it's the last thing I do."

She shakes her head furiously. "No."

"No? Are you crazy? Of course I will."

"We have a life to build. It won't work without you."

She's everything, and she is right in front of me. "I meant—"

"I know what you meant. Either way, without you beside me isn't an acceptable outcome of today or any day far into the future."

I scan the road and continue driving north as Connor requested. What is taking them so long to get back to us? Jillian's home is amazing, and she worked so hard to make it her own. I hope it isn't destroyed. I push those thoughts away and focus on what I can control right now. A question. "What is your favorite day of the year?"

A small smile graces her face. "July 16th." Her reply is definitive and unwavering.

"Why?"

"It's the day I became Jillian Joy Blackthorne."

"*Cariña,* amazing choice." Despite my efforts otherwise, I believe we have a tail. "Jillian…."

She turns to face me. "We have a tail."

"My next statement is going to sound odd, but I love your brothers."

She giggles softly. "I may not work for them, but I can handle myself."

"Yes, you can, and you're correct, we have a tail. As much as I prefer you close to me, move back to the passenger side and call one of them for an update please." The passenger airbag will provide more protection in case of a car chase and accident.

She dials from her phone, puts it on speaker, and retakes my hand.

"Yeah, Jill."

"Hey, Connor. We have a tail. We're on Route 3 near Crofton and the 424."

"Okay. While your house will be fine by morning, you shouldn't come back here tonight. Do you remember where Point B is?"

How much training does she have? Was it purposeful or did she pick it up over the years?

"Yes."

"Christoph is finishing prep right now. He left a new vehicle in the yard. Lock up your current vehicle and go to Point B until we have more information."

"What exactly is wrong with my house?"

"Cut hardline wire to the alarm system and a broken window at the side of the garage. Both will be repaired and fortified as soon as possible."

"Thanks, Connor."

"Cruz, you there?"

"Roger. Once we're there or wherever we end up for some time, I need information to figure out how to close the loop."

"Roger. We'll be standing by to get what you need." Connor ends the call.

I look over at Jillian. She's calm on the outside, but her hand is still shaking in mine. "How much training do you have?"

She smiles. "Not as much as Maia or Alex or even Norah. I can handle a weapon, Dad taught me defensive and evasive driving, and I know Krav Maga too."

"Impressive. Where is Point B and what is he talking about 'the yard'?"

"The yard is a storage unit where Christoph left us a vehicle. We need to go there, store your truck, and go to Point B. Then, we wait."

"The more time we spend together, the more intriguing you become and the more I wish I was stronger sooner."

She leans over and kisses my face. "It wasn't time for us yet."

Deep down, I know she's right. We follow Route 3 for a few more exits before Jillian directs me onto a local road. It's a huge shopping area with multiple plazas and roads of ingress and egress. I pull into a plaza with a few big box stores and drive down one aisle in the lot and immediately exit.

"Our tail slowed to let a couple cross the street," she shares.

I pull into a grocery store and wander through the aisles before idling alongside the building and killing the lights. Our tail passes by on the main road away from us. I move toward the rear corner of the store and ease out the delivery exit onto the local road. It isn't until we're about a mile away from the store when I turn the lights back on.

"Where to?" I ask her.

She directs me to the yard. We exchange my truck for a sleek Q60.

"Whose car is this?"

"Norah's," Jillian replies and inputs the directions to Point B in the GPS.

"Nice ride."

"Yeah, it is. I'm surprised she hasn't turned it in yet."

I pull onto the main road. "Why would she do that?"

"A car seat doesn't belong in a car like this."

"I suppose it wouldn't be practical, but the leather is butter soft, and I can barely feel the engine revving."

"Car guy?" she asks.

"Not really. This is a sweet ride, but I agree it isn't practical for everyday life. Did Norah not want kids?"

She considers if she's spilling girls' night secrets. "At one time, Norah thought she had to choose between being partner and having a family. She had luxury everything—clothes, shoes, and car. After her run-in with the Morettis, she shifted her plans to include having children."

"Is your number still the same?" During one of our many conversations, the topic of children came up in the abstract. Jillian wants at least two children.

"My minimum is still the same. You?"

"Yeah."

Jillian pregnant with my child skates through my mind. Then an image of our child—a dark-haired child with piercing blue eyes like hers. *Slow down, Javier. Medium-sized steps at least.*

I turn onto an unpaved, rocky road as the GPS instructs. "Are you sure this is the right way?"

Jillian chuckles softly. "Yes, I'm sure."

A half mile later, a cute cottage comes into view.

"Who owns this place?"

"My parents. It could be Blackthorne at this point, though. The company has holdings along the eastern seaboard and a few on the west coast. We came here in the summers when we were young. Jake spent a few months here after he was discharged, before he was ready to move forward."

I completely understand how Jake felt. Somedays, I still do. Aside from the circumstances outside these walls, being here with Jillian feels like the start of the rest of our life.

We step inside, and the décor belies the appearances from the outside. The furnishings are modern and comfortable. The kitchen is sufficient—nothing like Jillian's at her home, but it has everything a kitchen should have.

"Can you call one of the guys? I'm going to cook something."

"Sure." I set my weapon and wallet on the counter. As I walk the interior of the cottage, I note two bedrooms and a loft area with more sleeping space. There's a full bath and a small room barely big enough for a desk with a cozy reading nook with numerous colorful pillows and a plush throw blanket. I glance out the window and dial Connor.

"Hey, Cruz. You arrived?"

"Yes."

"Good. We're having a call first thing tomorrow to go over the plans and updates. Figure out what you need to resolve this matter before then."

"Will do. Did Jake call in for Jillian?"

"I believe so, but I'll verify."

"Thanks, Connor."

"We've got your back. Both of you. Talk to you in the a.m." I end the call and stare into the darkness. Having Jillian here is exactly what I didn't want for her. Moving to Blackthorne was intended to make my professional life less complicated, not more. I need to work with Sam to figure out a way to stop the alleged old owners/family members from interfering with my life. Arguably, they've only threatened my family, but as far as I'm concerned, it extends to Jillian. If something happens to her because of one of my cases, I'll never forgive myself. As much as I don't want to, I consider options to separate from her for her safety. However, my thoughts only increase my worry. True, her father and brothers taught her to protect herself, but my heart can't take the chance.

I barely register her footsteps before her arms wrap about my waist from behind. "You okay?"

"Yeah, thinking."

"Forget any thoughts of sending me off with my brothers to be safe at Jake's fortified compound."

She's a spitfire. My spitfire. "You're something else, *corazón*. How is it possible you can read me so well so soon?"

"I would be thinking the same thing if the situation were reversed, despite your skill set."

I turn in her arms and lower my lips to hers. Her wrapped in my arms with my lips fused to hers is the only place I want to be. I kiss her deeply before adding a sliver of space between us. I don't want a day to go by without her, even if she may be safer away from me.

"Come on, food's ready." She takes my hand in hers and leads me to the table.

"You whipped this up in, what, twenty minutes?"

She smiles. "Yes, chicken and french fries is easy and fast with an air fryer. My mom not-so-subtly asked for one for Christmas. She ended up getting three. Now it's here because she didn't have the heart to return any of them."

Before long, our plates are clear. She grabs them and moves to the sink.

I follow her to the kitchen and offer, "I'll do those. You cooked."

She simply continues washing. "I had to wait for the basket to cool. The pans are part of cooking."

"You aren't going to relent, are you?"

"Not likely." She sets the basket on the drying rack and moves on to the first plate.

I trap her against the sink, gather her hair in my fist, and kiss along the nape of her neck. Her hands stop soaping the plate as her head falls forward.

CHAPTER NINE

JILLIAN

He's barely touching me, and the ache between my thighs is building. I set the soapy dish into the sink and shut off the water before sliding my arms down and gripping the outside of his thighs as best I can. He releases his hold on my hair and lifts my blouse overhead. As I turn to face him, his shirt flies to the hardwood floor next, and my hands flatten against his back. His fingers skim up my arm and tease over my laced-covered breasts. My taut nipples reach toward the hard planes of his chest. Containing the shivers his caress causes is impossible.

The storm in his eyes is mesmerizing and makes my heart twist. "What's wrong?"

"This is not how I saw my vacation playing out."

Oh. "What did you want?"

He takes my hand and leads me to the reading area. I burrow into his arms after he leans into the corner of the nook. The touch of his skin against mine almost has me regretting asking the question.

"To answer your question, I wanted time to learn more about you, about us. What 'us' would look like. How we would feel." His lips brush over mine. "The last thing I wanted was to have one of my old cases hanging over me."

"There's no way you could've known."

His body tenses around me. "Maybe I should have."

I slide my hand to cup his jaw, which tics beneath my touch. "How?"

"In my head, I know it doesn't make sense. My heart is a different matter. We may have recently decided to be a couple, but we laid a stable foundation of friendship over the last four years. Given our in-depth conversations, I knew we would be formidable as a couple. Even now, given our current circumstances, I was right. As far as my case, it's the Irish mob. They're notorious for holding grudges and biding time."

"Do you recall who is claiming they own the stolen art?"

He exhales slowly before answering my questions. "I need to review my file, but my educated guess is a member of the Spillane family is claiming it belongs to them. I also need to speak with Sam or, even better, meet with him to discuss how the insurance aspect fits into this scenario."

"He lives in Maine now, right?"

"Yes. Emerson is almost two, and Savannah is pregnant. He won't leave her side this close to her due date."

"I'm sure the guys can get you what you need. What time is your meeting with them?"

"First thing in the morning. How are you so calm about this?" Worry trickles into his sable eyes.

"We're going to be fine. Are you guys overreacting? Probably not, but I know without question or hesitation we'll get through this unscathed."

"How are you so sure?" His voice is barely above a whisper.

My body reacts to the sheer concern in his tone. "You're family to my brothers, and they'll watch your back here like they did while you were serving. Our relationship, albeit new to them, means they will protect me too then worry about us as a couple."

"I wouldn't blame you if you wanted to walk away from me."

"No. Not a chance. I didn't fly to a different state on a national holiday to walk away when being with you gets harder. Do you want me to walk away?"

He drops his forehead against my temple. "I'm terrified something is going to happen to you because of me, but... I can't imagine going back to when you weren't mine either."

His, completely his. "Neither can I."

The storm in his eyes clears only enough for me to see a reflection of my desire staring back at me. I'm flat on my back as he hovers over me. The heat turns molten, and his hard length against me indicates we're absolutely on the same page. I press a tender kiss to his lips. We rush from tender to all-consuming in the matter of seconds. I push him back on his heels and set my mouth on his warm skin. With ease and precision, my bra flutters to the floor. I pop open the button of his jeans and push the denim down to his knees. This time he doesn't stop me. I slither out of my work pants and drop them on the floor under his watchful gaze.

"You're gorgeous." His eyes roam over me in excruciating detail, memorizing each dip and curve.

No other man has ever looked at me the way Javier does. No other man has ever shared his feelings vocally either. I feel cherished and desired for the first time in my life. I'm comfortable with myself. Until him, I never found a man who was as well. There was always something wrong with me—too short, too pudgy, hips too wide. It took some time to realize the issue was them, not me.

He sets his mouth on my collarbone and kisses a path downward before dragging his tongue along the lacy hem of my panties at my inner thigh. My eyes flutter closed. Perhaps it's the anticipation or my lack of attention other than my own hand, but my body is vibrating with need.

"*Cariña, mirame. Dime por favor.*"

As I open my eyes, I'm met with his gorgeous face peering down at me, the warmth of him washing over my entire body. "In no particular order, hearing you speak in Spanish is sexy as hell. No one has ever looked at me like you are right now. I'm terrified of how much I feel for you already."

"*Hablaré español cada día si te hará sonreír.* I'm honored to be the first man to truly see you. I'm scared too, but if we weren't, would it be worth it?"

"No, it wouldn't."

He draws his thumbs over my damp panties and slips them beneath the sides. The slight graze of his fingers sends spikes of pleasure through my body. I nod at his raised eyebrow seeking permission. The window above us shatters. Before I can blink, we're both on the floor and Javier's jeans are pulled up and fastened.

"Get dressed, stay low. I need to get to my weapon and my phone."

I tug on my pants and bra and army crawl toward the kitchen. I throw my blouse back over my head.

"I just pinged the guys. Take this." He thrusts his gun into my hand. "Go into the bedroom and lock the door. Do not come out unless it's me."

"Are you crazy? You're unarmed."

"Jillian. Go."

There's no room for me to negotiate with him. I kiss him hard and do as he asks. I hover against the interior wall away from the window in the bedroom. The curtains are drawn, and the window is locked and has a board in the upper half for the off-season. It's likely why whomever is outside shot out the nook window, which doesn't open.

I hear scuffling and what sounds like a fistfight, including something breaking and a deep grunt.

"What do you want?" I hear Javier through the door.

"Where's your girl?" the unknown voice asks.

His girl. Sounds perfect. Focus, Jillian!

"What do you want?"

"I want what my family deserves. The painting or the insurance money, makes no difference to me."

It takes me a moment to place the sound I hear next—chambering a round.

"I don't have either."

The unknown voice replies, "But you have access to both. You can connect me with the right people. They won't listen to me, but they will if I have you. Let's go."

No! I throw open the bedroom door and hurry toward Javier with my weapon pointed into the living room. My heart jumps into my throat at the sight I see. "Drop it!"

"She's got fire in her. Must be a wildcat in bed."

"Drop it!" I repeat.

"Or what, princess?" The unknown voice belongs to a large, burly man dressed in an expensive-looking, three-piece suit with slicked back hair. His arm is across Javier's chest, and the other holds a weapon to his temple.

I hate being called princess.

"Take the shot," Javier commands.

"I don't want to hit you."

"*Cariña, mirame.*"

I shift my gaze from the gun pointed at his head to his face.

"Focus on my favorite television of all time. What are Rules #9 & #16?"

NCIS. Gibbs' rules. Rule 9 is always have a knife, and 16 is if they think they have the upper hand, break it.

"Now, *cariña*!"

I fire at the burly man. The presumed mob enforcer drops his weapon and grabs his shoulder. The rule says hand, I know, but if I hit his shoulder, I knew he would drop the weapon. As he staggers backward, Javier stabs him in the thigh. He's more concerned with his shoulder than the blood gushing from his thigh. Javier kicks his weapon away and opens the front door.

Quickly, I'm out the front door behind Javier. As we approach Norah's car, we note two tires are slashed.

He takes his weapon and secures it before weaving our hands together. We hurry away from the cottage on foot toward the main road.

We jog between the quaint cottages. When we reach the main road, he tugs me into an alleyway. His mouth is on mine before I can begin to form a question. His kiss is hard, possessive, and something I can't pinpoint.

"You're one of those women who can handle anything life throws at you, aren't you?"

I shrug.

"You are the bravest person I know. You likely saved both of us back there."

"I know you said to stay, but I was worried and figured two versus one were better odds."

"Maybe true, but what's rule #44?"

"Hide women and children first?"

"Exactly. You're clearly capable, but it's my job to protect you."

I shake my head in disagreement. "Maybe we can agree it's my job to protect you too—your body and your heart."

"I'll consider it. Please understand I have a deep-rooted need to protect you. It goes far beyond anything I've ever felt before, even for my family."

Speechless, I'll need to fully process that statement later. "How did they find us so quickly?"

"They probably tracked our phones. Is there another safehouse nearby?"

"Not that close, but what is your objective?"

"Meaning?"

"We could go back toward home or toward New York? Doesn't Sam have a secure home in the city you guys use all the time?"

He kisses me hard again. "You're a genius. I'm going to text Christoph our plan and have Jake get us a flight to New York. Then I need to ditch my phone."

While he reaches out to Christoph and Jake, I scan the street. There's a no-tell motel across the street that may work if we need to wait awhile to get to the airport.

Javier ends his call and destroys his phone. "We need to move. Barrett is on his way to get us to the airport. We're meeting him at the diner in about an hour. It's about half a mile south of here."

"Remind me, which one is Barrett."

"Barrett Beaumont is a member of my Blackthorne team. He's a former marine and Dallas police officer. Like most marines, he would say there is no such thing as former. I have only met him via video chat, and from what I could tell, he's a mammoth of a man who would give even me pause in person."

Given the time of night and the rapidly falling temperatures, we hurry to the diner.

"Good to know."

"Need something other than a coffee?" Javier asks after we take a seat at the counter.

"Only coffee is fine."

The server, whose name tag is stamped Carol, takes our order. As she walks away, the bell over the door chimes. Out of the corner of my eye, I see two well-dressed men enter the diner who clearly don't belong in this lake area, especially in the off-season. I bring my mouth near the shell of his ear. "We have unwanted company at your seven."

He turns his head slightly. "It's insanely hot you know to add location information."

Chills run over my skin. I react to him regardless of the new danger we find ourselves in. Even now his scent surrounds me and settles my fraying nerves. Our server returns with our coffees.

"Is there another way out of here?" I ask her quietly.

"Jake said you two would be arriving. I'm going to come around the counter and distract our new, unsavory customers. Go through the kitchen and to the left. The door exits at the back of the restaurant." Of course Jake knows her. He probably ate here at least three times a week while he was staying at the cottage after his recovery.

"Thank you, Carol." Javier drops a twenty on the counter for the coffees.

Ignoring the pounding in my chest, I use the reflective wall to check on our distraction. Not only did Carol break the touch barrier already, but she's sitting with the heavy-set enforcer and pointing at the menu. Javier takes my hand, and we slip into the kitchen unnoticed. We pause near the rear exit.

I whisper, "How long until Barrett arrives?"

He glances at his watch. It's old and worn. If I had to bet, it belonged to his father. "Fifteen minutes at most."

We hide near the rear exit for a few more minutes before exiting into the cold. As we step outside, a Blackthorne vehicle pulls alongside the building. We slide into the back seat, and Barrett peels out of the parking lot toward the airport.

"Pleasure to see you in person, Cruz. Miss Blackthorne."

"Barrett. Thanks for the assist."

"Pleasure to meet you. Jill is fine."

Javier threads his fingers with mine. "Do you have an update and possibly some supplies?"

"Sorry. There are burner phones and a few small weapons in the bag on the floor. Christoph cleared the cottage and retrieved Jill's purse, phone, and identification."

"How did he get there so quickly?"

"He was retrieving your truck." Barrett continues, "The man you shot was Jimmy Spillane. He was gone when Christoph arrived."

"I didn't shoot him. She did, and likely saved us both."

Shock materializes on Barrett's face, and I can't help but be a tad proud of myself. He doesn't know me personally, and I doubt Jake would share much information about me with a new hire.

Cruz asks, "How did Christoph identify him?"

Barrett responds, "Blaine hacked the tracker on Jill's phone. A plane from Pemberton will be waiting for you at the airport. Jake already spoke with both Sam and Cash Morgan. Miss... Jill has been added to the approved list. Gemma will overnight some clothes for both of you to the penthouse in the morning."

Cash Morgan purchased Pemberton airlines after leaving venture capitalism. Since childhood, he dreamed of being a pilot. When he met and fell for his now wife, Noelle, she gently pushed him to go after his dream. Blackthorne and Pemberton have a long-standing working and personal relationship.

"What about my students?" I ask softly.

"Jake indicated he would speak with Principal Platt personally before your meeting in the morning. He's pushing the start time to ten to allow you both to get some sleep."

"Are you coming with us?" Javier asks.

"Can't. I have a new assignment with Lynn Smith for a last-minute presser in Los Angeles. It's a quick turnaround, just over two days."

I'm not sure how to read into Javier's question. Is he worried he needs backup, or does he prefer it to be only us? Perhaps a little of both. When we arrive at the airport, we part ways. We're ushered onto the plane and greeted by our pilot almost immediately.

"Welcome, Mr. Cruz and Miss Blackthorne. I'm Holden. Please make yourselves comfortable. Our flight time is slightly more than an hour. Ground transportation has been arranged."

"Thank you," I reply.

Exhaustion hits me like a freight train when I settle into the plush seat. The next thing I recall is Javier escorting me into the car after landing in New York.

CHAPTER TEN

JAVIER

I met the Morgans when I was young and reconnected with the family after I retired from the army. I worked on a few cases with Sam and Cash. The most important was their sister Billie's accident. Even though they don't act like it, the Morgans are billionaires. Cash bought this penthouse because of the huge rooftop terrace. I never counted, but I believe there are at least five bedrooms. He graciously allows Blackthorne to use it when things go awry in the Big Apple. As delicately as possible, I slip out of bed. I'm in awe of my gorgeous woman still sleeping soundly in the luxurious bed. I can only imagine the thread count of those sheets.

She blew my mind yesterday. Sharing her skills with me in the abstract is one thing. I'm grateful to Ben and Jake for teaching her to protect herself. Her using her training to protect us both has me falling for her even more. I pad to the kitchen and brew some coffee. Billie was here recently for a design session and sister weekend with Della. Thankfully, she didn't finish the coffee.

The intercom buzzes. "Lieutenant Cruz."

That title still stings. "Good morning, Arthur. How are your wife and family?" I've worked with Arthur on numerous occasions for different cases along with the Morgans.

"My wife is wonderful, and my family is as well. There's a grocery delivery for you."

"Great. Please send it up."

"Have a nice day." A few minutes later, I retrieve the delivery and hurriedly put away the perishable items because it's near time for my call with Jake and Christoph. With a cup of coffee in hand, I boot up Sam's laptop and face toward the master bedroom where Jillian is still sleeping.

"Morning, Cruz."

Jake and Christoph both appear on screen. "Hey, Jake. Did you sleep, Christoph?"

He shakes his head. "Did you?"

"Not much."

"Where's Jill?" Jake asks.

"Still sleeping." I can see the worry on his face. Truthfully, I'm worried myself, but I won't know if it's warranted until she wakes and we can talk more.

"Is she okay?"

I raise my shoulder. "Not sure yet. Her shot was perfect and gave me an opening to get us out of there."

Then Jake asks, "Did you recognize him?"

"Didn't look familiar. Barrett shared he was Jimmy Spillane. Any idea about his current status?"

Christoph answers, "He was gone when I arrived. I noted the signs of a struggle and the broken glass. The window has been boarded and the cottage cleaned."

I nod.

Jake adds, "I tasked Blaine with a deep dive on Jimmy Spillane and where he went."

"Understood." At a minimum, it buys us time to figure out our next move and his.

"I reached out to Captain Davidson," Jake informs me. "He has granted you administrative access to the files you need until this matter is wrapped up. He would appreciate updates at least every few days."

Part of me is grumbling he has the right to request an update, and the rest is still angry. I'm mostly past my anger about the promotion, but the fact I'm the one working to fix this and not him is wearing on me. Working this case falls under his purview as captain. True, he could assign it to me, but I'm technically not an active NYPD officer anymore. "I'll keep him in the loop as necessary."

Jake continues, "Please touch base with Sam today and hash out a plan to settle this matter. He may have additional insights to assist you."

"After I cook something, I'll reach out to Sam."

"You're going to cook?" Jake asks.

"Yes, why wouldn't I cook? I'm hungry."

"Jill is a much better cook than you," Jake admits. He isn't wrong.

I don't know how Jake's relationship works with Norah. Simply because Jillian is a better cook doesn't mean I expect her to cook every meal. It isn't how we work. At least, it isn't how we discussed our relationship would work. "True, but I won't wake her to cook for me."

"Fair enough."

"What about Principal Platt?"

Christoph answers, "I spoke with her and informed her Jill needs a substitute for a least the rest of the week, perhaps even into next week."

"How did that go over?" Jillian is a phenomenal teacher. I'm sure her students won't be easy to deal with for a substitute teacher, and they will worry about her.

"As you would expect. I didn't give her any details when she pressed me though."

"Good. Anything else?"

"Gemma will be shipping both of you some clothes in the next hour."

"Thanks." As I'm about to sign off, Jillian pads to the kitchen and searches for a coffee cup. My tiny woman clad in my shirt reaches up to the second shelf. The libidinous side of me wants to take her against the marble countertop, especially considering how many times we've been interrupted. The rest knows her brothers are still logged into this call and I'm not listening anymore. Her perfect, peach-shaped ass is exposed, and it has captured all my attention. Well, that's not entirely true. She captured all my attention the day we met. Yet the plans swirling in my head are not appropriate for while I'm on this call.

"Cruz! Please tell me you are not ogling my sister right now."

Christoph turns away to contain a chuckle.

Carajo! Part of me would love a mirror to see the expression on my face right now. "I respect you too much to lie to you, Jake."

Jake groans and presses on, "Jill, can you hear me?"

"Yeah, Jake," Jillian answers but doesn't move into the camera frame.

"How are you?"

She huffs as if Jake has no right to be worried. "Good."

"Can you move over so I can see you?"

I can't contain my smirk. There's no chance Jillian will move in front of the camera wearing my threadbare, white V-neck with no bra.

"No. Just pretend you called me on the phone."

Jake huffs, "Truly, how are you?"

"I'm fine, Jake. You and Dad taught me well. My decision to pull the trigger was to protect both of us. I own it, and I'm content with my choice."

"I understand. I'll let Cruz fill in the rest for you. We'll talk again later this afternoon."

"Okay. Bye, Jake," she replies.

I close the laptop and grip my shirt, tugging Jillian into my arms. "We need some ground rules."

Her perfect assets nestle over my now rock-hard length. If she notices, she doesn't indicate as much. My shirt rides up even more, and I would be willing to bet she isn't wearing panties either.

Her nose wrinkles. "Such as?"

"No walking around looking sexy as hell in next to nothing when I have a call."

"Did I distract you?" Her voice sounds sweet and innocent, as if she didn't tease me on purpose.

Perhaps she didn't. All I can do is shake my head and lower my lips to hers. After a deep, sensual kiss, I draw back. "Distract works. My attention was focused on you and how much I want to explore every inch you exposed reaching for the coffee mug."

"Every time we're alone, we get interrupted."

She isn't wrong. The call from Davidson, Deni, then needing to go to the compound after Davidson's call, then Jimmy Spillane showing up at the cottage.

"It does seem that way, doesn't it?"

"What do you need to do today?"

"I need to spend some of my vacation learning how to touch you to feel you shudder beneath me. I want to find every secret spot on your luscious body and hear you sigh with pleasure."

She opens her mouth to respond but pauses. "I would prefer your plans as well, but what should you do?"

There's virtually no limit to how much I would give to hear the thoughts in her head at this moment. If I had to bet, I'm confident it would include marching into one of these bedrooms and spending much of the day naked with her, based on the pink of her cheeks and her lower lip pulled between her teeth.

Resigned her resolve is stronger than mine, I reply, "I need to log onto the server at the precinct and review the files for the case to refresh my memory. Then I need to talk with Sam and check in with Blackthorne again."

"Okay. I assume someone sent food. I'll whip something up."

"You don't have to cook for me."

"I know. I want to. Get started." She leans forward and brushes her lips across mine. Reluctantly, she moves from my lap and steps into the kitchen.

After watching her walk until she disappears behind the island, I focus my attention on the files.

Jimmy Spillane is the nephew of the reputed Irish mob boss, Jackie Spillane. He has two siblings, Caitryn and Kyle. Kyle died in infancy of a rare congenital condition. About thirty years ago, Jackie had beef with a rival faction. Allegedly, Jackie traded the painting in question for refuge from a contract on his head. The truce, if you will, lasted for about eight months.

The head of the rival faction, James Noonan, had Jackie executed anyway and retained the painting. Fast forward about fifteen years, James was arrested for racketeering and fraud. The authorities seized all his assets, including the painting. The government sold his assets at auction. A bona fide third-party, Edward Babylon, purchased the painting. It wasn't insured until Edward bequeathed the painting to his son seven years ago at his death. The son, Stephen Babylon, insured it with Morgan Insurance. The painting was stolen from his home four years ago. Morgan Insurance paid the claim to Mr. Babylon. A year later, the painting was recovered by my team when we outed a theft ring and located their warehouse of stolen goods.

I consider the facts. At this point, Jimmy is unaccounted for, but there must be someone else looking to retrieve the valuable painting. It seems unlikely he would tackle retrieval alone especially given his failed attempt to abduct me. As far as I can tell, the Spillanes didn't insure the painting. I also question how the Spillane family came into possession of the painting in the first place. The painting is currently locked up in an FBI warehouse under round-the-clock surveillance. Arguably, Morgan Insurance is the rightful owner as it paid out on the policy and it has since been recovered.

According to this report, Special Agent Alex Bishop has been assigned the case. If I recall correctly, he assisted Jake with his case against the Morettis. As I consider all the angles, Jillian alerts me the food is ready. She set the plates on the dining table.

I rise from the couch and move into the dining room until she returns with two coffees. I pull out her chair and then take a seat. "Thank you. This looks amazing." Each plate has a western omelet, toast, and some fruit.

"You're welcome. Can you share what you learned?"

"I suppose it can't hurt. You could read most of it if you google the case." Between bites, I share with Jillian the details of the case.

I see the wheels in her mind turning. "What if Stephen wants the painting back?" she asks.

"I want to verify with Sam, but it's my understanding, if he has the funds to reimburse Morgan Insurance for the payout, he gets the painting back. I'm sure Sam has an attorney who handles these types of matters for him."

"Sam doesn't abide by Gibbs' rules? Rule #13: never, ever involve lawyers."

I laugh heartily. "You truly know all the Gibbs rules?"

"Yes. I started watching *NCIS* the day after you told me it's your favorite of all time. I made notes of the rules, even the unnumbered ones."

"Then you know Rule #51: Sometimes you're wrong, which would lend itself to say sometimes lawyers are necessary."

"Yes, Gibbs wrote it on the back of a card with Rule #13 on it. Why are the Spillanes coming after you?"

I exhale. "Jimmy believed the authorities and lawyers would listen to me if he had me as his hostage. I figure his plan was use me as ransom for the painting or the insurance money."

"What happens now? We wait?"

"Yes and no. Yes, we wait until someone contacts either Davidson, Agent Bishop, or Sam. No, because Sam and I will figure out a plan to make a deal with the Spillane family and the Babylon Family. I'm sure there will be attorneys involved on both sides—well, at least the Babylon side."

Her head falls.

"*Dime, cariña.*"

"Are we safe here?"

I turn my chair, then hers, and pull her legs between mine before taking her hands in mine. "I meant it when I said I would protect you."

"I know, and I did too. My question is more about if I can let my guard down here."

"Yes, completely. There's a limited list of people who have access to this place. Not one person listed is a threat to you or me."

"Okay. What time is your call with Sam?"

"One. Do you need something?"

She raises an eyebrow. "Are there any books here?"

Ignoring the undertone of the look on her face increases in difficulty the longer we're alone. "We can look after I wash these."

"If not, I'm sure I can order something and have it here fairly quickly, right?"

"As long as it's here in the city, yeah."

The moment we clear the dishes, the burner rings on the ottoman.

"I've got this," she states.

I hurry over and answer the call. The number of people who have this number is miniscule. "This is Cruz."

"Davidson here. I have a quick update for you."

"Of course."

"Attorney Shannon Jameson has contacted my office on behalf of Caitryn Spillane. Rumor has it she's the brains behind the family now."

Interesting. Caitryn was a wallflower from my earlier research during the case.

Davidson continues, "They're requesting a meeting to discuss options. What is the status so far?"

"Thank you for your call, sir. I reviewed the files earlier this morning. I'm scheduled to speak with Sam Morgan of Morgan Insurance early this afternoon. Did Attorney Jameson indicate what Miss Spillane is seeking?"

"Either the painting or the value of the painting with interest from the time it was allegedly stolen."

"Can Miss Spillane prove the painting was stolen from her family all those years ago?"

"Excellent question, Lieutenant. I doubt it, or she would've by now one would think."

"Exactly. Part of my discussion with Mr. Morgan will include if money or returning the painting to Miss Spillane are even an option. Have you spoken with Special Agent Bishop of the FBI?"

"No. I haven't."

Bishop is a key player in this matter. This case has levels of implications and, therefore, has a representative in each of the branches of law enforcement, both local and federal. Davidson should be in contact with him as much as me, if not more. I set my concern aside for now.

"I'll keep you in the loop, Captain. Have a good afternoon."

"Thank you, Lieutenant."

I cringe at the title as I end the call. The pit in my stomach from the conversation isn't helping. My gut rarely fails me. Just like I know Jillian is the one for me, something feels hinky about Davidson not being in contact with Bishop. I pause my thoughts and search for Jillian.

CHAPTER ELEVEN

JILLIAN

After finishing the dishes, I explore the entirety of Morgan's penthouse. The furnishings are more modern than I would select but comfortable. Each room is set up as a guest room, except the master with limited personal touches. The first room past the office appears to be decorated for a child.

I only know the Morgans by name and reputation. I've never met any of them. Blackthorne takes its duty of privacy seriously as they would expect the same for themselves.

The phone Barrett provided is ringing. "Hello."

"Hey, Jill."

"Hi, Norah. Is everything okay?"

She laughs softly. "I'm calling to check on you. I've been where you are. Well, at least trapped with your man and unresolved issues. The only difference is Cruz needs to work out the puzzle, not you."

"Thanks, Nor. I'm hanging in there."

"How did the call go this morning?"

Now it's my turn to laugh. "Jake scolded Javier for looking at me suggestively."

"He'll get over it. Cruz is a good man. Jake knows that."

"Honestly, Jake's opinion doesn't truly matter to me. His approval would be appreciated, but it isn't necessary for me to choose Javier."

"Good for you, Jill."

"Thanks."

"Do you need anything other than the clothes Gemma sent?"

I shake my head. "If it isn't against some rule, could you get a message to Deni?"

"Sure."

"I'm sure she's messaged a million times. She's likely freaking out because I haven't answered and I wasn't at school today."

"I'll check with Jake, but I don't think it's an issue."

"Thanks, Norah."

"Of course. If you think of anything else, call. I'll see what I can do."

"I appreciate you softening my brother's rough edges, Norah."

I can almost hear the smile in her voice. "You're welcome. Hopefully, we'll see you sooner rather than later. Bye, Jill."

"Bye." I end the call and start to peruse the small collection of books in the office. I pull one down and realize it's a first edition of *The Great Gatsby*. I browse the titles and decide I'm not in the mood for a classic. Truthfully, I wasn't expecting a shelf of thrillers or contemporary romances. Hoping is more like it. I'll find a movie or something to watch instead while Javier finishes his work.

"Hey, there you are." He pulls me into his arms at the threshold of the office which isn't the best plan given today's schedule.

I haven't changed, and neither has he. He's still wearing his casual shirt and jeans with the top button open.

I smile at him. "This place is huge."

"It is."

"Who was on the phone?"

"Davidson."

His favorite person in the whole wide world. "You look unsettled."

"I am. According to Jake, Davidson has been working this case for a few months, yet he hasn't spoken to Special Agent Bishop with the FBI at all. It doesn't make sense."

"You know what to do. Why are you hesitating?"

"I know this *adventure* is disrupting your life, but I'm grateful you're here." His arms tighten around me. Attempting to ignore the heat of him pressed against me clad only in his shirt is messing with my head.

"Nowhere I would rather be than with you." I kiss him lightly. "Why the hesitation?"

"It'll look petty to dig into Davidson."

"Doesn't matter, if you feel it's necessary."

"I know you're right, but the optics aren't pretty. It's just my—"

"Your gut is telling you something is off about Davidson, and it could somehow fall back on you personally, professionally, or both." *Gibbs' rules #36 and 40. If you feel like you're being played, you probably are, and if someone seems out to get you, they are.*

"Exactly."

"Have Blaine dig. If he comes up empty, no harm done. If your gut is right, which I assume it usually is, Blackthorne can figure out the best way to handle the dissemination of the damaging information."

He kisses me hard. "You're amazing. I need to call Sam. Did you find something to read?"

"There are a bunch of classics. I'm going to look for a movie in the bedroom while you work. Then we can figure out dinner."

He rushes away with newfound gusto. Unfortunately, Javier is likely correct about Davidson. The bigger question is his motive. After locating the remote, I curl up on the huge, comfy bed and scroll through available movies. I select *Harry Potter and the Deathly Hallows.*

"*Cariña.*" Javier's voice floats through my mind.

My eyes flutter open.

"How was the movie?" He grins at me.

"I've seen it before. I guess I was tired." I glance over at the clock. It's near six. "How were your calls? I'm sorry I fell asleep."

"Don't worry. Clearly you needed it. I checked on you between calls."

"What happens now?"

"We leave this room and eat dinner."

I smile. *He cooked for me.* Everyone from my family to my friends, except Deni, expect me to do it because I can cook well. "Thank you. No one has ever cooked for me before."

"You're welcome."

"I meant from your calls though."

He presses a kiss to my temple. "I know. We can talk while we eat." A groan surrounds me as I scoot to the edge of the bed.

"What?"

Fire flashes in his eyes. His shirt is bunched at my waist, and my lace panties are in plain sight.

"You saw these yesterday."

"Doesn't diminish my desire to lower them down your toned thighs and fulfill my promise to learn you."

I'm speechless. No man has even been as clear, definitive, and open about his feelings with me.

He continues, "We should eat first. I plan to take my time with you, despite the pounding in my chest and the rush to my brain when we're alone. We won't leave this room until morning."

A myriad of responses flood my mind, but none are anywhere near an appropriate response. I rise from the bed, thread my fingers with his, and follow him to the dining table. He pulls out my chair, then hustles to the kitchen.

He comes back carrying two plates heaping with delicious-looking food. I could dissect it but prefer to ask what he made. "What did you cook?"

"*Fricassee pollo y arroz con gondules.* Fricassee chicken and rice with pigeon peas." His eyes are pinned to me.

I lift the fork to my lips and pause. "Why are you staring at me?"

He smirks. "Staring at you is rapidly becoming one of my favorite things to do. Plus, I want to see your reaction."

"I'm sure it's fine, Javier."

"I'm nowhere near as good a cook as you are."

"You don't have to be. We're a team." I slip the fork between my lips. The mixture of flavors, both sweet and spicy, is perfection. "It's delicious, Javier. You can breathe now."

He pushes out a breath slowly.

"In fact, can you teach me how to make this and any other traditional dish you like?"

Surprise crosses his face. "Sure."

"Why the surprise?"

"Long story. It would require me to share about Vivienne, which I will, just not right now."

"Okay."

His shift in demeanor, which he's desperately trying to mask, indicates Vivienne hurt him deeply. We eat about half of our meals before turning back to the content of his calls.

"Can you share about your calls?"

He finishes the forkful in his mouth. "The short version is Sam agrees with my take. If Babylon can reimburse Morgan Insurance, he's the rightful owner unless the Spillane family can prove it was legally theirs before Noonan was arrested."

"Can they?"

"I doubt it, but Caitryn Spillane will spend copious amounts of money to fight for a settlement either way."

I consider his opinion. "Who is Caitryn?"

"She's Jimmy's sister and, according to Davidson, the brains of the family now."

"What is Bishop's opinion?"

Javier's head lifts in my direction. "You're truly unlike any woman I've ever met. You see all the moving pieces like Jake. Bishop was at a scene. I expect to hear from him tomorrow."

"Did Blackthorne have an update from Blaine?"

"Not yet. For now, we wait to hear back from Blaine, Agent Bishop, and the attorneys who are now involved."

"Can we talk about something else?"

"Sure." He sets his fork down and takes a drink.

As a host of questions float through my mind, I'm momentarily distracted by the movement of his throat. Who knew that was a thing? "What is the one thing you are absolutely determined to accomplish?"

"I want to be a dad. More accurately, I want to have a family. I only had my father for a short time. My sisters had even less time with him. Choosing Blackthorne gives me more financial security, less potential danger, and more time to achieve my goal."

"No hesitation. I appreciate your steadfastness."

"My turn. Who inspires you to be better each day?"

"You could probably answer this one yourself. My students push me each day. Each of them has some quantifiable obstacle. Assisting them to overcome, or at least manage, their inabilities is the best part of my day. I gather the same feeling would extend to my children one day."

He presses a kiss to the back of my hand and carries our plates to the kitchen.

I follow with our glasses and move to the sink. "I'll wash."

"I can't promise to keep my hands to myself."

We seem to have a penchant for starting things in the kitchen. "You have a thing for kitchens?"

A smile breaks at the curve of his mouth. *Damn, that's sexy!* "No, you do, and I have a you thing."

I sigh inwardly and start washing the plates. He's merely standing behind me, and I can feel need rolling off him. It's vibrating through me in equal measure. Javier skims his hands up the back of my thighs, over the curve of my ass, and inches slowly up my back.

His hands brush around my rib cage and palm my breasts. "Did you even put a bra on today?" he whispers near the shell of my ear. Ignoring his arousal pressing against me is impossible.

"I...." I push out a ragged breath. The sensations cascading through me from his fingers rolling and pinching my nipples has stolen my ability to multitask. I close the faucet, reach back, and lower the zipper of his jeans.

"You done trying to wash those for now?"

A breathless "Yes" falls from my lips.

Javier lifts my arms into the air before grabbing the hem of his shirt that I'm wearing and lifts the garment over my head. I lower my arms and grip the sides of his jeans. He dots warm, tender kisses along my skin as he trails a path down toward my waist and over the curve of my hip, shifting our bodies as he moves.

He lowers himself to his knees, but he pauses, lost in his head. His breath whispers over my skin, sending ripples of anticipation through me. Wetness pools between my thighs at the mere thought of his tongue dipping between my folds.

My fingertips graze the tops of his shoulders. "Javier."

His eyes lift to mine in time for me to observe a flood of emotions zip through them. He presses an open-mouth kiss below my navel, rocks back onto his heels and then comes to his feet. Silently, he retrieves the shirt on the floor and weaves his fingers with mine.

He leads me into the bedroom, near the edge of the bed. I take the shirt and let it float to the floor before reaching for his jeans and pushing them to the dark hardwood. After stepping out, he returns to the same position as the kitchen. Only this time, he doesn't stop at one kiss on my belly. His thumbs hook my panties and draw them off my legs. Lifting each foot, he slides them away and drags his tongue up my leg to my knee before switching to the other side. I steady myself with one hand on the top of the mattress and the other laced into his soft, almost jet-black hair.

The flutters of anticipation grip my chest. I exhale slowly as he drags his finger from my nub to my puckered hole and back. My stance widens almost involuntarily, inviting him to continue. While moving his finger, he alternates nipping my inner thighs. He has me on the verge of splintering faster than I anticipate. Replacing his finger with his tongue sends ripples of pleasure deep into my already pulsing core. The instant his tongue delves into my heated center, I careen over the edge. My legs give out, and he guides me onto the bed without breaking contact.

Waves of tantalizing bliss wash over me. He doesn't slow or stop the deliberate and demanding strokes of his tongue. A second decadent climax spirals tighter in my belly. As the trembling in my legs increases, Javier's intoxicating lashes increase in frequency.

"Javier... never...." My entire body shudders, and I bow off the bed. Slowly the cascade of pleasure decreases to a bereft feeling as if I lost something. It's been a while, but being with Javier is more than I imagined, and we haven't.... I was falling before. Sharing these moments of ecstasy will shove me over the edge.

He travels up my hip, removing his boxer briefs before climbing onto the bed, nipping and biting a path along my torso until he reaches my mouth.

"*Corazón.*" The flare of emotion on his face causes me to believe he very well might hear my innermost thoughts. "Are you sure about this? We can't go back from sharing ourselves completely with one another."

"I couldn't even if we don't." We may not have acted on our feelings over the last few years, but we were wholly honest about our needs and expectations, even though our conversations weren't meant to apply to us. Our conversations aren't hypothetical anymore. Adding in the physical aspect of a relationship will only add strength, not detract from it.

He lowers his mouth to mine as I drag my fingernails along his flank to cup his face. As I spread my legs, he settles between my thighs, and the tip of his length grazes my hot, wet core.

"Are you on some form of birth control?" he murmurs against my lips.

"Yes," I whisper.

He exhales slowly and slides forward inch by enticing inch. Javier seals his lips over mine as he withdraws completely before burying himself to the root in my throbbing inner walls.

"We feel—"

I cut off his words by pulling his lower lip between my teeth. "I need you to move."

Javier's rhythm is demanding and on the cusp of hard. He lifts one of my legs to his shoulder.

"That feels… don't stop…."

Pleasure radiates from my core as goose bumps skitter over my skin. My body tenses as my climax thunders from my low belly. Clawing at his back, I hold on to savor the rapture of us as he empties into me in hot bursts.

He hovers over me as our breathing regulates, our gazes locked on one another. I feel untethered but grounded in him at the same time. My body is languid and pliant in his skilled hands. Lowering himself, he turns us to our sides.

"*No tengo palabras.* I have no words."

"Same," I reply in kind simply because it's absolutely too soon to share I've fallen hard and fast for Javier Cruz. The fast part is debatable, but, either way, I can't go back to a time without him in every single day. I sidle closer, my head nestled against his shoulder, our limbs tangled, rendering it difficult to separate us.

CHAPTER TWELVE

JAVIER

The safety of the Morgans' penthouse is preferable to the chaos outside. I never wanted my life to impact her negatively. Yet I can't return to a time where she isn't the first and last thing I see each morning and each night. Near midnight, she woke me with her tongue gliding down my body. With precision and perfect form, she took me to the back of her throat and milked me dry with her mouth.

I've been alternating my view between the sprinkle of freckles on her nose and the snow falling outside the large window.

"I can feel your gaze on me." Her voice is raspy and sultry.

"*Eres hermosa a la luz de la mañana. No, eres hermosa siempre.*"

She melts deeper into my arms. "Thank you."

"Do you even know what I said?"

"No, but you won't say anything to hurt me, and hearing you speak in Spanish is sexy as hell."

My face falls, and I fail to school my features before she notices.

"What just happened? Did I say something wrong?"

"No, not at all. First, I said, 'You are beautiful first thing in the morning.' Then I said, 'No, you're beautiful always.'"

She closes her eyes in acknowledgement. I'm confident Jillian has never been treated well by a man in her life before me. Even without her sharing the details, I know in my heart no man ever appreciated her. Then she looks up at me, expecting an explanation. I would prefer to never have to share my relationship history with Jillian. However, I'm confident she won't judge me or run away.

"My reaction has to do with Vivienne. I'll start from the beginning. She and I met in high school through acquaintances. We ran in the same circles, if you will. Vivienne was the epitome of wealth. Her parents sent her to public school to mingle with regular kids her age. We were only friends at the beginning. She stood beside me at my father's funeral, even though we weren't a couple. Despite the obstacles of dating because I was caring for my sisters, I asked her on a date about six months after my father died. For the next few years, we were inseparable. She would come over and hang out at our apartment without complaint when I needed to care for my sisters."

I press a kiss to Jillian's head and hear her sigh softly. Her breath on my skin is pulling me in opposite directions: continue sharing or pin her beneath me and make love to her again.

"We discussed our future in detail. She planned to go to NYU and stay in the city. Initially, I planned to go to college."

"What were you going to study?"

"I wanted to… I've never shared this with anyone." Vivienne didn't know my deepest thoughts and feelings, a notion that isn't lost on me. Jillian did before we were dating. "I was going to be a math teacher."

She sets her hands on my chest and skims her lips across mine.

"When I realized we couldn't afford it, I enlisted. Vivienne was furious at first. Eventually, she saw my position, and we continued dating, including all the trappings of your first relationship from homecoming to prom to senior skip day. My intention was to complete my first contract and then go to college. Fast forward to the end of basic training, Vivienne and I are still together, but she's living the life in her own apartment her parents provided for housing during college."

I pause to settle my nerves. This isn't even the most difficult thing I'm going to need to share with Jillian. "She came to my basic training graduation, but she was distant and more interested in hurrying back to school. Our calls became less frequent and short, especially when I learned I would be stationed in Texas while she was in New York."

Jillian's hand slides along my chest and cups my face, her thumb dragging along my lower lip. "You don't have to share if it's too painful."

"I appreciate that, but it'll make our conversations at Walter Reed and after readily understandable."

"Okay."

"We continued long distance for another six months. Vivienne and I talked about our future broadly, but nothing like how I set out what I was looking for when I talked with you. She knew I wanted a white picket fence, two point five kids, and a dog. When my deployment order came through, we had a frank discussion about our future as a couple and agreed to stay together. Our letters and emails were strained from the moment I left the United States. She couldn't handle the long stretches of no contact or the nights alone. Her *Dear John* letter came when I was two weeks from redeploying home from my first tour."

"That's awful."

"Unfortunately, it gets worse." I pause to compose myself. "Her letter not only ended our relationship, but she included her decision to terminate her pregnancy after my graduation from basic training."

"Oh, Javier. She didn't tell you at all. Despicable. You had a right to know. It may not have changed her decision, but…. Please don't ever let me cross her path. I won't be able to control my mouth."

I grin before kissing her head. "Thank you."

"You're welcome. Does anyone else know all the details?"

"My sisters know the details. The guys probably put the details together, although I didn't specifically tell them."

I nod.

He continues, "After her betrayal, I went wild and crazy in my personal life. Nameless hookups and excessive partying if I wasn't on duty. Reporting on time and fully sober was definitely not a given for a while. I didn't decide to pull myself together until the orders for my second tour came through."

"I hadn't met you yet, but even now, I'm proud of you."

Utter shock floods my veins. "What?"

"Your reaction is completely normal, one would think. No one is perfect, Javier."

"*Eres perfecto para mí. Me estoy enamorado de ti,*" I draw her lips to mine and kiss her breathless.

We spend most of the snowy morning tangling up the sheets in the bedroom instead of facing our current dilemma.

After a steamy shared shower, I scan my email and learn I have an invitation to a call with Agent Bishop in thirty minutes.

The intercom buzzes. "Good morning, Lieutenant Cruz. Miss Blackthorne."

"Morning, Arthur," we reply in unison.

"I have a delivery for you from a Gemma Watson."

"Perfect. Please send it up. Thank you," I reply.

"Of course. Have a wonderful day."

Jillian is almost giddy at the prospect of having more clothes. Me, not so much. Perhaps it's less about the clothes and more about *clean* clothes.

"I'm going to change quickly before my call."

She attempts to follow me, and I shake my head. "If we go into the bedroom together, I won't make this call."

She raises her hands in mock surrender and says, "I'll make some coffee and then brunch for after you talk to Bishop."

I steal a kiss and hurry down the hall with the large box in my arms. I change and settle onto the couch with barely enough time to log on.

"Lieutenant Cruz, pleased to make your acquaintance officially."

"Agent Bishop. Just Cruz is fine. What do you mean officially?"

"Bishop works for me as well. Not a fan of titles in general. I've read your case file for Spillane, Noonan, and Babylon, as well as the Morgan accident case."

"I understand. What are the options here? Has Davidson made any headway with the attorneys?"

"I haven't spoken with Davidson since this case erupted again. Each time I reach out, he's unavailable. It wasn't until last week his office directed me to you."

I grumble inwardly. "I see."

"I'll get down to it. The painting is secure in our warehouse and under guard 24/7. It's my understanding Caitryn Spillane is seeking the painting itself."

I nod, and he continues, "Legally speaking, the painting currently belongs to Morgan Insurance. I spoke with Sam earlier today. He indicated the company would be willing to be reimbursed by Babylon in exchange for the artwork."

"Has Mr. Babylon made any indications of his preference?"

"No, he hasn't responded to any of our requests."

"As morbid as this sounds, has anyone heard from him in the last two weeks?" I ask.

"No, now that you mention it. Can you do a welfare check since you're in the city?'

"Technically, I'm on terminal vacation from the NYPD until I exhaust my benefits."

"I thought you were working for Blackthorne."

"Yeah, after I'm off the NYPD payroll."

Bishop taps a few keys on his keyboard. "I see. Give me a few hours, and I'll get you covered either by FBI or NYPD again."

What about Jillian? "Got it." I end the call and pad to the kitchen.

"That didn't sound good."

"Which part?" *The part where I likely must leave you here alone while I go investigate in my city where the Irish mob has put a target on my back?*

"All of it. Is it safe for you to leave here?" She wrings her hands in front of her.

I draw her into my arms and hold her against me. "I don't know." I do know. It isn't, but I won't share with Jillian.

"Don't hide information to protect me," she accuses.

She's perceptive. I shouldn't be surprised. "It's unclear if the threat is still viable. If my hunch is correct and Babylon is no longer in the picture, the Spillanes have more leverage."

"Why?"

"Babylon is an unmarried man with no children. Unless he's a philanthropist and left his art to a museum, the fight would likely end there. The Spillanes could agree to reimburse Morgan Insurance and get the painting, despite their suspect claim of ownership."

"I see. Then the bad guys win again?"

I slide my hands up and down her sides and note the absence of panties at her hip. Containing the groan isn't possible. "The bad guys might win again, yes."

"Is there anyone at the NYPD you trust?"

"Maybe, why?"

"I'm not a fan of you going anywhere alone. I realize how ridiculous I sound. Either way, backup is never a bad plan. I'm certain you won't take me, and I won't ask, but no one from Blackthorne is authorized, nor can they get here in time."

"It's not ridiculous, *cariña*. I wouldn't want you to be in the same position either. The only difference is, it's my job."

"It was your job. Plus, there are more underpinnings and concerns you have about Davidson now than before. Speaking of which, did you get any information from Blaine yet?"

True. "No, I haven't heard from Blackthorne yet today." My phone vibrates on the island. "I have to take this. It's Bishop."

Her shoulders drop as she turns away. Clearly she wasn't done with our conversation. I'm not sure how to read her right now. She understands the risks of my job. My *old* job. She's basically dating a retired cop. Yet I'm going to need to go back into the field to close this case for good.

"Yeah, Bishop."

"Getting you back into the field took some maneuvering. I had to agree to come down to the city. I'll land in thirty and pick you up in forty-five. I'll have credentials for you."

"I'll be ready." Ending the call, I take a fortifying breath and search for Jillian.

She's curled up in a chair watching the snow falling over the cityscape below. "I—"

I kneel on the floor near her feet. "Jillian—"

"Go ahead."

"No, you."

She sighs. "I'm sorry. I should've kept my concerns to myself. I wasn't thinking with my head. It happens frequently where you're involved."

"I'm sorry too. How you feel is important to me, whether it's your head or your heart, especially when it's your heart. I agree with you. The last place I want to go is out in this city. Too many unknowns. I don't have a choice."

"You don't?"

"No, my past is looking for you, to hurt you. I need to tie it up to move forward with you."

"Can't someone else go with Bishop?"

She's terrified something is going to happen to me. "Maybe, but I need to handle it myself. Then I'll know the case was closed properly this time. Knowing there's an active threat to you puts me on edge. I need to render your world safe."

"At what expense though?"

"Ideally, none. I know this isn't what you signed up for, but it's on me to protect you."

Her head drops and sways left to right slowly. "I signed up to be with you. I thought I was prepared to be a cop's wife. It's harder than I expected."

Wife. Our future plans are the same. "I'll take every precaution necessary to get back here to you. You need to promise me you'll stay here. I need to know here—" I point to my head. "—and here—" I point to my heart. "—you're safe. No one comes in and no deliveries either. I can't handle if something happens to you because of me."

"I promise."

I haul her forward to the edge of the chair and surround her in my arms. Jillian is fraught with tension, even in the place I know she feels safest. Going into the field has never caused so much turmoil within me. There's only one explanation. *Her.* My phone vibrates in my pocket. Drawing back, I cup her face and kiss her softly. "I'll be back as soon as I can."

Before I second-guess myself, I walk out of the bedroom and check the phone. Bishop's ETA is ten minutes. I grab my weapon and coat and ride to the foyer.

"Good afternoon, Lieutenant."

"Hi, Arthur. Please do not let Miss Blackthorne leave the building."

"I'll do my best."

With a little reassurance, I step into the elevator and ride to the parking garage below the building. As the doors open, a sleek, unmarked SUV glides to a stop, the window lowering.

"Bishop." I open the door and slide in.

"Cruz. Here are your credentials, a vest, and an FBI-issued weapon. Please lock your personal weapon in the safe beside you before we exit the vehicle."

I nod and stow my personal weapon as requested.

Stephen Babylon lives only a few miles from the Morgans' penthouse. With traffic, it takes nearly twenty minutes to arrive. As we approach the concierge, Bishop takes point.

"Good afternoon. Special Agent Bishop and Lieutenant Cruz to see Mr. Babylon. Is he in?"

"Good afternoon. As far as I can tell, Mr. Babylon returned home four days ago and hasn't left," the lanky concierge named Tyson informs us.

"Have you or your colleagues spoken with him?"

Tyson shakes his head.

"Is this entrance the only way he can leave the building?"

"Unless he chartered a helicopter and left from the roof, yes. To answer your next question, no landings were authorized by the staff in the last week."

Bishop nods.

"Has he retrieved his mail, accepted any deliveries, or had any visitors," I ask.

"No, he hasn't picked up his mail, nor had any deliveries. However, one of his girlfriends stopped by for a few hours two days ago."

"One of his girlfriends?" Bishop inquires.

Tyson nods curtly. "I use the term 'girlfriend' very loosely. There are about three or four who rotate. He has company at least twice a week. The woman who arrived a few days ago was new, never seen her before."

Mr. Babylon utilizes a high-priced escort service.

"What did she look like?"

"She was average height, even with stilettos, thin, with other assets surgically enhanced. Aside from those descriptors, her hair was purple."

Whoever she was, the hair was likely a wig. "Which unit?" I ask.

"Penthouse two, sir."

We enter the elevator, and Bishop waits for the door to close. "How many high-end madams work the Upper West Side?"

"Two, maybe three," I reply.

The door opens into an anteroom, not directly into Babylon's home. Luckily, or unfortunately for him, the front door is ajar.

Bishop knocks and announces himself. "Special Agent Bishop of the FBI. Mr. Babylon, are you home?"

Through the open door, it's clear there was a struggle. The foyer and living area are trashed—lamps askew, pillows litter the floor.

"Stephen Babylon, FBI. We're coming in," Bishop repeats and takes the lead clearing the penthouse.

Room by room, we check the home and come up empty. Most of the spaces are untouched until we reach the master bedroom. It would appear Mr. Babylon had a raucous party with his purple-haired lady friend before disappearing.

"I assume the property has camera footage of the lobby?" Bishop asks as we complete the sweep.

"Not sure. We can ask when we speak with Tyson again."

"Let's go. Nothing else can be done here," Bishop announces.

Tyson is sorting through a few deliveries when we reach the lobby. "Is Mr. Babylon okay?"

"His condition is unclear. Are there cameras in the lobby?"

"No, Agent Bishop. The owner's association decided against one."

"I see. Thank you for your cooperation, Tyson." He hands him a business card. "When Mr. Babylon returns, please have him reach out to me."

"Of course."

We exit the building and ride back to the Morgans'. My trip into the field today was smooth. Yet my gut is screaming. Coming to the city may have been a mistake. I resolve to talk to Jake and, at a minimum, get Jillian away from here.

CHAPTER THIRTEEN

JILLIAN

The snow continues to fall on the city. It's beautiful but different than snowfall at home. It seems less peaceful. Perhaps it's me. Worrying about Javier, knowing he had to go. The part making me uneasy is… he went for me, for us.

I need to talk to someone. I pad to the kitchen and dial Norah.

"Hey, Jill. Freaking out a bit?"

I nod furiously, even though she can't see me. "Yes."

"It's a little different for you. I called Jake. You got caught up with Cruz and his old case, but the toll is the same. You're worried sick and you feel caged."

"That's disturbingly accurate, Norah."

"I recall those feelings well. Does Cruz know how you feel about him?"

Yes. "I think so. We haven't said those all-mighty words, but…."

"Trust me. I get it. Everything else screams commitment, love, and attachment, but the words haven't been spoken." Norah is referring to her and my brother. They had a two-year friend-with-benefits arrangement before my brother pulled himself together and shared his feelings with Norah.

"Exactly. Our history will now seem short by some meddling brothers' standards."

"The guys will get over it. Cruz is a good man, and they know it. Securing you first before even calling Jake was pretty much the clincher for him. Mum's the word though."

"I won't divulge my sources."

Norah chuckles. "How long has he been gone?"

I sigh and glance at the clock. "A little over an hour. I know, I'm losing it."

"No, you're not. You're terrified and rightfully so, in my opinion. I would be too."

"Let's chat about something else. How are you feeling?"

"I feel great. Our little person is too active at night if you ask me, but who needs sleep anyway? I can only imagine how Callie feels with two babies due any day now."

I laugh. An image of me pregnant crashes through my mind. Javier will be an amazing dad. Vivienne's actions are unforgivable. "Two is a lot of baby at once. How is she feeling?"

"I saw her this morning. She's ready to be a mom of three. Amara started sleeping through the night. Callie's ready to start the process over again with twins. I give her credit. I'm concerned about one baby, let alone three."

"Jake will…."

The elevator door opens, and Javier steps into the penthouse.

"Nor, Javier's back. Thank you for talking me off the ledge."

"Anytime. Talk soon."

His posture visibly relaxes as his eyes sweep from my toes to my face. He closes the space between us in a few large steps. One hand grips my hip while the other cups my face. "*Gracias, cariña.*"

"I never break my promises, Javier."

His mouth captures mine. The relief I stayed mixed with his emotions is a potent combination I never want to lose. Breathless and thoroughly kissed, he adds a sliver of space between us. "Neither do I."

Our gazes catch and hold for longer than necessary. I could stare into his chocolate eyes for the rest of my life. Not could, I want to. I consider heeding Norah's veiled advice but decide against it for now.

"Can you share any details or…."

Javier shucks his jacket, vest, and sets two weapons, along with his knife, on the island. "He wasn't home, and there appears to be signs of a struggle. Bishop is going to request footage from the street cameras while I work the high-end escort angle."

I raise an eyebrow.

Javier laughs. "According to the concierge, Mr. Babylon has a rotating stable of female visitors at least twice a week. My connections in this city are deeper than Bishop's."

"Okay."

He leads me to the couch and draws me against his body.

Mine.

"His status as missing has good ramifications too," Javier shares.

"How so?"

"It means we don't have to stay here. We can go home, and you can teach with me as your shadow."

I shake my head. "My students are going to have a field day. Jesse called me out about my smile the day you showed up."

"Good, old-fashion ribbing from your students, huh?"

"I told them my personal life wasn't up for discussion."

"I'll be on my best behavior." He winks at me.

"Going home sounds wonderful, but I'm confused. Isn't there still an active threat?"

"Yes, but if Babylon is out of the picture, whether missing or dead, nothing can happen with the painting. Nothing definitive anyway. I'm sure the Spillanes will create some procedural aspect to keep the painting in play. Babylon won't be able to appear in court or make any requests regarding its disposition."

"Which means the threat stays active, but the Spillanes play the long game because they still need you alive." That realization tears my heart out.

Javier hangs his head. "That's one way to look at it. I'll close the case permanently this time. I assure you."

I have no reason to doubt him, but a small voice reminds me he thought it was closed before. "Okay."

"I need to ask Blaine to pull some footage and talk to Jake. When do you want to go home?"

My eyes widen, and I pull my lower lip between my teeth. "Never. Our little bubble is mostly fantastic."

He grins and tightens his arms around me. "It is, but it isn't reality."

"I know. Whatever you need to get security in place at school on Monday is fine with me."

"You amaze me, *cariña*. I have completely disrupted your life, and you're handling it better than me."

"I want you. I want us. Our current situation is temporary. I'm confident you and the guys will finish the case and we can move forward together."

"Me too. I'll make these calls as short as possible. Are you opposed to ordering dinner?"

"No, why?"

"I would like to share another family restaurant with you before we leave."

"Perfect. Make your calls. I'll be fine." I push up and sit on my heels. A sultry kiss with promises of more later, and he's gone. Armed with a plush blanket from the back of the couch, I slip outside onto the terrace. Snow is still falling lightly, but a portion of the roof extends over a double chaise. There's a heater as well. Being a billionaire certainly has its perks, or staying at the home of a billionaire does anyway.

I curl up beneath the blanket and listen to the city. Even up here, and despite the snow falling, the traffic noise travels. With my eyes closed, I can separate the sounds and focus on the crinkle when the snow hits the surfaces around me.

Cold drops hit my face. I open my eyes slowly and find Javier sprinkling snow over my head. Fire flashes through me. "Javier!" I swipe down, hoping to grab some snow to retaliate but fail.

"*Si, corazón mio.*"

I should've never shared how his Spanish affects me. "You chose your words on purpose to soften my response, didn't you?"

"*Sin duda.*" He leans down and presses a kiss to the tip of my nose and then my lips.

I hold the sides of his face and deepen our kiss.

He breaks our connection to seek absolution. "It was either the sprinkles of snow or a full snowball. Forgive me?"

"Forgiven, this time."

He slips beneath the blanket beside me and hauls me against his warm, hard body. "Much better." He kisses my temple.

"All set with work for now?"

"Yeah. Jake is going to work on a flight home and possibly some backup as well."

Fear bubbles in my belly, replacing the butterflies Javier causes whenever he's nearby. Not true, I feel swoony and mushy whenever I think about him. "Did something else go wrong?"

"No. He's being overly cautious considering we're in the city. I believe his plan is to have Maia and Barrett fly here."

I burrow deeper into his embrace. Even late afternoon, his cologne is still present—fresh and crisp. Gemma is truly gifted at anticipating people's needs. Not only did she send casual clothes, but she sent workout attire and loungewear for both of us, along with all our toiletries and Javier's glasses. Jake needs to give her a raise.

As his fingertips draw circles on my lower back, sparks of awareness sprint the length of my body. I lift his shirt and set my mouth to his rib cage. A hollow groan echoes around us. Straddling his thighs, I kiss his chest with the blanket falling over my shoulders. Javier's hands imprint the curve of my hips, his grip leaving no room for me to question him or his interest in me. *Holy hell! The possession feels right.*

Our pace increases exponentially, despite the moderate insanity of losing our clothes outdoors in winter in New York City. He tears my sweatshirt and tank overhead and resecures the blanket over my bare shoulders to keep me warm. A devilish glint materializes in his eye.

"No bra?" He kisses a circular path around my nipples before nipping both.

"First, not my fault you didn't notice earlier. Second, the tank is fitted. I don't need one."

"No, you don't. Panties?"

Ignoring his question, I shimmy his athletic pants and boxer briefs off his ankles and then remove my leggings as well. He changed while making his calls. As I hover over him, his shaft jumps between my thighs.

"What am I going to do with you? Do you skip underwear regularly?"

I lift my shoulder teasingly. "You'll have to stick around and find out."

"Yes, ma'am. You weren't lying when you agreed you were a handful."

"Not at all." I lean forward and kiss him tenderly but thoroughly. Reaching back, I surround him with my hand. His shaft lengthens and hardens with each stroke. Javier squirming beneath me gives me a heady feeling.

"*Cariña, te necesito.*" His words emerge strangled with desire.

I need him too. Breaking our kiss, I move downward and impale myself on him and push up to sitting. Fuller, I feel inexplicably fuller in this position. Our gazes lock as I lift and push down, meeting his thrusts one after the other. A spiral of pleasure tightens in my abdomen as I increase my pace to frantic.

The moment his thumb grazes my swollen nub, my inner walls convulse around him. "Oh… we feel…."

His fingers mark my skin as he chases his release beneath me. "Let go again with me."

I slide my hand down and flick my clit in time with our movements. Prickles of ecstasy rush through my veins and collect at the base of my spine more potently than ever before. Tightness takes over, and I career over the edge again with Javier exploding in short bursts at the same time. Once the waves subside, I lower myself against his heated skin.

A contented sigh falls from his lips.

"Please share with me."

He kisses the top of my head. "I truly didn't think our conversations at the hospital would lead us to one another. I'm grateful I was wrong."

"Me too," I murmur against his chest.

"Are you cold?"

I chuckle softly. "Not even a little. I'm not ready to move yet either."

"Same."

I can feel his heart beating against my cheek, strong and steady.

A little bit later, his stomach screams for nourishment. "We should at least place our order for dinner."

"Fine. What's our plan though? We have two options, I guess. A mad, naked dash inside or we dress out here first."

"I'll follow you naked anywhere."

My cheeks burn with embarrassment. "The things you say."

"I mean every single one. There's one more option."

I raise an eyebrow.

"We can stay wrapped in the blanket and walk inside together."

"Your plan is better. Let's move. I'm getting hungry too."

We clumsily stand up and twirl into the bedroom. After cleaning up and donning fresh clothes, I retrieve our clothes from outside while Javier orders dinner.

I hear a notification from my phone but don't recall where I left it. I locate it and find a text from Norah.

Norah: Feeling better?

Me: Yes. Thanks again.

I wait for Javier to finish ordering.

"Food should be here in less than an hour. I have messages from Jake and Bishop to return."

"Go ahead. Then we can go to bed after dinner." I wink at him as he rushes into the office with his phone.

While I wait, I gather our dirty clothes and start a load of laundry. At least we'll have options to travel home in. Then I set the table with plates and silverware. When I return to the kitchen for glassware, the intercom sounds.

"Good evening. I have a delivery for you."

"Good evening, Arthur. Please send it up."

"Right away."

"Thank you."

Within minutes, I accept our food from Arthur and set it on the dining table. I pad to the office to get Javier.

As I reach the doorway, I overhear Javier's call. "No, Jake. There's no reason for her not to go back to work. I'll go with her as long as necessary. Her students are of the utmost importance to her. A week is long enough." He turns to face me when I set my hand on his forearm.

Not more important than him, but a close second. "Thank you," I mouth.

He nods. "Jake, she'll be fine at school with me or someone else from Blackthorne if it can't be me."

I shudder at the thought of it being someone else, but I'll handle it for him.

Javier continues, "Blaine found nothing notable between Davidson and Caitryn Spillane until our run in with Jimmy at the cottage. Maybe my gut is off because I'm angry or it involves Jillian. Either way, the connection is professional, not personal."

He listens more and ends the call.

"How adamant is Jake about us staying here?"

Javier kisses me and guides me out of the office. "He's fine with you going home to the farm but not to school."

"No, if I go home, I'm going to my home, not his. You told him yourself the security at school is adequate unless there's an emergency. What's his problem?"

"I didn't get a solid answer out of him. Perhaps he's growing stricter because of the baby's pending arrival."

We take a seat and dig into the meal he ordered from Romano's.

"This manicotti is melt-in-my-mouth delicious. I dare say the best I've ever tasted."

"Mama and Papa Romano craft the best Italian in the city in my opinion."

"You're right. Should I not go back to work?" Asking nearly rips my heart out.

"I understand Jake's position. I'll protect you here—at home, at school, everywhere until the threat is over."

"This isn't really about me though. It's about you."

"Arguably true, but the Spillanes won't think twice about using you to get to me."

"What can you do for them at this point?"

He shrugs. "I don't know what they think I can do. Perhaps they think I have access to Davidson simply because he's my captain. I doubt their information sources would fail so spectacularly. The only other avenue is my personal relationship with Sam. Frankly, the connection there is tenuous as far as Caitryn's claim the painting belongs to her. Morgan Insurance doesn't figure into it at all unless they broker a deal if Babylon is out of the picture."

"What do you need me to do?" *Whatever you need, it's yours.*

His fork clangs onto the plate, and he takes my hands in his. "I don't want any of this for you. I want you to live your life with me as your partner, not live a watered-down version because my job—my old job— threatens your safety. The fact you would even consider not returning to teaching until I resolve the case speaks volumes to me." *Yo tambien te amo, Jillian.*

"If it's what you need, I won't teach."

"*Cariña.* I won't ask you to stay at the farm or take more time away from teaching if it can be rendered safe."

"Jake won't relent. It'll be an uphill battle with him. He kept Norah at the farm for over a month, regardless of her self-defense skills."

"I'll certainly do my best to persuade him."

We polish off our meals and snuggle in bed to watch a movie. Within thirty minutes, Javier is out cold with his head on my chest.

CHAPTER FOURTEEN

JAVIER

My internal alarm wakes me bright and early in the morning. Shifting slightly to get a better view, I catalog Jillian's features and sear them deeper into my brain. I consider working out but decide to remain snuggled next to my other half.

I know the timing wasn't right before, and despite the current security issues, our time is now, and I refuse to let her go.

"You're staring again." Her periwinkle eyes fly open and meet mine.

"I will unabashedly stare as long as you'll allow me to."

"I have no plans to decrease your staring privileges anytime in the future."

I close the minimal space between us and brush a kiss across her lips. "Good, because I don't want to give up my staring privileges either."

"What time is your call with Jake? Why isn't Christoph handling this considering you're on his team?"

I laugh heartily. "You could answer your question yourself, sweetheart."

"Jake pulled the brother card. Of course he did." Her head falls.

"It's fine. Both are protective of you, but not in the same way I am. To answer your first question, Jake is set to call at eight."

"Is it a video call?"

I raise an eyebrow to her. "No, but you should be dressed in case his plan to leave is complete."

She frowns at me, then pins me to the mattress. "Fine, I call dibs on the shower."

"Seriously, woman. The shower is large enough for four people, and I don't plan on wasting the opportunity to share it with you."

"Fine, I'll share." She kisses me lightly and heads into the elegant bathroom.

The marble walls are barely steamy before I join her, despite taking in the water flowing over her full breasts, down her toned thighs, to her pink toenails. A sexy shared shower is the perfect way to start every single day. Truthfully, every day with Jillian is perfection. We dress in plenty of time for me to take Jake's call.

With coffee in hand, I answer the call on speaker. "Morning, Jake."

"Cruz. Maia will arrive at the penthouse by ten this morning. Barrett should arrive by noon. I added him and the rest of the new team members to the approved list with Arthur. Your flight is at three."

I take the last gulp before answering, "Fine. What are my transportation options to the airport?"

I feel her approach before she touches me. Jillian slides her arms around me, clasping her fingers.

"Vehicles have been arranged for travelling to the airport. Maia will don a blonde wig as a precaution."

I scrub my hand down my face. "You realize I'm the target, right?"

"Yes. It's the sole reason she's staying here and you won't be accompanying her if I let her go to work on Monday."

"Like hell she's going anywhere without me. If you let her? Do you even hear yourself, Jake?"

"I can hear you, and if you're going to discuss me, I should have a say," Jillian interjects. "Jake, I won't stay at the farm. My home is adequately secure."

"No, the Spillanes know where you live."

"And?"

"J—"

She cuts Jake off. "Could someone still be watching my house? Sure. I'm confident the Spillanes and their henchmen know we're here as well. If Javier believes I can go to work safely, I'm going. If I need him and someone else with me, fine. Good luck with Platt though. If you two want to continue your measuring contest, find something else to argue about."

A resigned, frustrated sigh floats through the speaker. "Cruz?"

"Yeah, Jake."

"Please get yourself and my sister to the farm safely. Then we can discuss the next steps in person."

"See you tonight. Bye, Jake." I end the call and pull Jillian around me.

She's vibrating with concern and possibly fear, even though she's cocooned in my arms where she feels safest. Her body is molded to mine, exactly where she belongs.

"What if there is another option, a compromise of sorts?"

My heart sinks. She's willing to sacrifice her students for me. I would for her as well. However, she shouldn't have to. "Please elaborate."

"As much as I don't want to give Jake the satisfaction of winning this argument between the two of you, am I risking my students by going to work?"

"*Cariña*, you amaze me more each day. Arguably, yes, especially if I'm there with you."

I watch the wheels turn in her beautiful mind. "What if I could set up distance teaching for the time being? If Suzie can be in the room, I can teach via video conference. I don't want to stay at the farm though. I want to be home."

"Who is Suzie?"

"She's one of the aides at school. Suzie gives me breaks throughout the day for admin stuff, lunch, or meetings with parents."

"Are you sure? You were pretty adamant with Jake."

She buries her head into my chest. "I'm not a fan of being told what to do, especially by my brothers. The flip side is Jake's talented in his profession. If he's nervous and you are as well, perhaps my opinion is flawed and the two of you are right. If you tell Jake I said that, I'll deny it until my last breath. I expect you to be honest with me about the risk, Javier." Her reply is muffled until she lifts her eyes to mine.

I smile inwardly, noting she didn't list me. "I never said there was no risk. Your students are important to you. I can and will keep you safe at work."

"At the risk of yourself?"

I dip my head to her shoulder.

"No. What happened to wholly honest, Javier? It's one of the parameters we discussed as paramount to a stable relationship."

"I didn't lie to you, *corazón*. I will never lie to you. Sacrificing your career for me isn't acceptable."

"But potentially sacrificing yourself is? No. Absolutely not!"

I will sacrifice myself for her without hesitation or reservation. "*Te amo desde lo más profundo de mi alma.* I will do everything in my power to love and protect you as long as you'll have me."

"I love you, Javier. Sometimes a love like ours requires difficult choices. You chose before; now it's my turn."

"Choosing my career instead of you was one of, if not the hardest, decisions I've ever made."

She skims her lips across mine. "Then you understand you need to let me choose for both of us now."

"I understand, but I don't have to like it."

"The give and take is on both sides, Javier. Giving falls on me this time. If Jake can work it out with Platt, I'll teach from home until the threat is resolved. If Platt refuses, then perhaps a leave of absence is necessary. We'll figure it out. I want to maintain as much of our little bubble as possible. Staying at the farm would destroy any hope of privacy. Our relationship doesn't need to flourish under my brothers' noses. I would prefer to be home with you or someone else from Blackthorne instead of work or the farm."

I shake my head. "You're coming to the meeting with Jake and how many ever more of your brothers are present."

"Okay. We should pack before Maia and Barrett arrive."

With precision and speed I didn't know she possessed, Jillian packs her clothes and toiletries in one bag and sets it near the bedroom door.

"Are you sure you weren't in the military?"

Her soft laugh surrounds me, warming me from the inside out. "Not only was my father in the military, but he was a cop too. Add in my brothers, it kind of rubs off."

Before I fully process the information, Maia arrives. After some chatting and a delicious late breakfast prepared by Jillian, Barrett arrives as well. We review the plan again, which includes Jillian going with Barrett. I'm not a fan of Jake's hidden curveball at all. We leave the building in separate cars from the underground garage.

"She's fine with Barrett," Maia whispers fifteen minutes into our ride to the airport, clearly noting my uneasy posture.

"I would prefer to protect her—"

Our phones light up at the same time.

Barrett: We're being followed. Will evade and meet you at airport when safe.

"Fuck!" As I scan the road, time screeches to a halt. The thoughts in my head have questionable value. Fear grips me. She's in danger because she loves me. She chooses me. I understand the stalwart desire to protect one's queen at all costs. Jillian is my person. My everything. I need to end the chaos as soon as possible. Finding Babylon is likely my only chance of shortening the timeframe to actual safety and freedom.

"Cruz."

I hear my name again.

"Cruz, I only know you as a friend and former unit mate of the bosses. Now you're a teammate. The guys don't mess around when it comes to protecting family. If Jake willingly allowed me, Nolan, and Christoph to protect Norah, then he trusts the training Blackthorne provides. I'm sure you know Barrett was a marine and former cop. Jake wouldn't trust his sister with someone who lacks the requisite skills."

I nod and note we're ten minutes out from the airport. Then I spot a potential tail. "Maia, we may have a tail as well."

"I think that's Barrett, not a tail. I'll confirm."

Maia: Is tag #69817 you?

Barrett: Yup. We're at your six.

Maia: Well done.

Barrett: Thanks.

Maia shows me the text thread. "It's Barrett, not a tail."

I relax slightly and increase speed to the safety of the private hangar. Within twenty minutes, we're wheels up with Holden at the controls again. Once he shuts off the seat belt sign, I escort Jillian to the onboard living room away from Maia and Barrett.

Once the door clicks closed, I run my hands over her body. Only a thorough and tactile inspection will suffice.

She cups my face and ends my examination. "Javier, I'm fine."

"I needed to verify myself." I lean down and kiss her softly.

"It was scary but not as bad as the cottage. It only took a few sharp turns and a serendipitous red light."

"Any idea who was following you?"

"No. It was a dark SUV with tinted windows, but I texted the plate to Jake."

That's somewhat comforting. "I shouldn't be surprised, should I?"

She grins at me. "Not at all."

"I can't guarantee my reactions will change until I know this case is finished."

"I understand. I'm sure you feel the same way I did when you went out with Bishop."

Damn! I've never been on the waiting side before. "I'm—"

She stops me with her index finger against my lips. "No apologies necessary."

Over the intercom, we hear, "This is your captain speaking. Please take your seats. We'll experience some turbulence for the remainder of our flight."

Our landing can't come soon enough if you ask me. Turbulent is putting the rest of our flight mildly. Barrett and Maia escort us to the farm and hastily scurry away. I don't blame them. I wouldn't stay if the situation were reversed. My truck is parked in a spot near the barn.

"Jake is in his office," Norah informs us when we step into the house. I don't miss her noting our threaded fingers and close body proximity. With her blanket permission, holding Jillian in some way is an extension of me.

"Thanks, Norah."

We walk down the hall toward the office. Jake is seated at his desk with Tank and Sabre curled up on the leather couch. We stand side by side at the corner.

"You were right—" Jake begins.

Jillian cuts him off. "In an effort to diffuse the brewing tension between you and Javier, I have a few ideas." She shares her suggestions that she told me before leaving the penthouse.

Surprisingly, Jake listens intently to the options before finishing his sentence when we first arrived. "You were right, Jill. We shouldn't have discussed your security without your input. For a regular client, it would make sense. For you, not so much. Your suggestion about remote teaching has promise as a potential compromise. I'll reach out to Platt when we're done. Ideally, I can get it approved for Monday. What, if anything, do you need to pull it off?"

"Only for Blaine to reinstall the VPN he put on my system for remote learning last year."

"You should probably add the VPN anyway. If Platt says no?"

"I would appeal as far up as the superintendent and then take a leave of absence."

Shock passes through me. She's not like Vivienne at all. *You already knew that. This just confirms it.*

"Understood. As far as where you sleep, I agree with you. Your home has adequate security with all the features enabled and Cruz. Once you're home, you stay home. When you order takeout, groceries, or whatever you need, either shop as a guest or use the office account."

I feel her bristle at the notion she wasn't able to take care of herself before we became a couple—a fact she's proven handily in my opinion at the cottage.

Jake addresses both of us. "Blaine was able to track Jimmy to the cottage. After your *discussion,* he called a burner phone. Two others arrived and drove him to a private residence owned by Dr. Mitchell Svenson. A few hours later, the EZ pass for their vehicle pinged near the New Jersey state line."

"Okay. Is Blaine still tracking Jimmy or do I need to share with Bishop?"

Jake gives me a sideways glance. "Both."

"Understood."

Jake continues, "Blaine should have the footage for you soon. I forwarded his findings from Babylon's phone records to your Blackthorne email. You should be able to make progress narrowing down the escort companies with the information. Please keep me in the loop with Bishop as necessary."

"No problem."

The tension in the office is high, though the reason is unclear. Sure, there's still a threat out for me, but Jillian's compromise will allay most of Jake's concerns.

"I'll let you know what Platt decides. Have a good night."

"Night, Jake." At the threshold, I turn back. "Where are the keys to my truck?"

He slides open his top drawer and tosses my keys toward me. I catch them and lead Jillian outside. We wave to Norah who is on the phone in the living room as we pass. I open the passenger door and wait for Jillian to take her seat. Then we're on our way to her house after I relock the gate at the base of the driveway.

"Dinner?"

"I'm sure we can find something at my house."

I pull into her driveway, input the pin to her garage door, and pull inside. After a quick and simple chicken dish, we fall into bed until late morning on Saturday.

CHAPTER FIFTEEN

JILLIAN

Whether for her sanity or mine, Platt agreed to allow me to teach from home temporarily. With a little assistance from Suzie, I'm up and running on Monday morning as my students enter the classroom.

"Morning, Kate and Jesse."

"Hi, Miss Blackthorne," Kate's mom, Carol, replies. "Is everything all right?"

"Yes. We are taking a few precautions with one of my brother's clients." The parents were made aware of my connection to Blackthorne as a preemptive measure to allay any fears. I never considered his business would impact me personally when the school board politely requested I share the information. I greet Stevie, and the class settles in for the morning announcements.

The first remote teaching day is moving along fine until lunch. Deni barges into my classroom as the students leave.

"Oh my god. I was so scared when I couldn't reach you."

"Hi, Deni. Didn't Norah call you?"

"Yes. She placated me. I understand why though."

Javier steps into my office while tugging his shirt on. "*Cariña*, oops sorry. Hi, Deni."

"Cruz. Nice to *see* you."

"You as well. Jillian, lunch is ready."

"Thanks. I'll be right out."

"Ohmigod, girl!" Deni exclaims the moment he's out the door. "I'm not feeling sorry for you holed up with that gorgeous specimen of manliness! He has abs for days and even the coveted V. His abs have abs."

I can feel my cheeks heat from her on point but still inappropriate words. "Stop!"

"No way! You of all people know the dating scene here is dismal. Not only did you find a good man but eye candy to boot. Can you get him to come back into your office and create a replay for me?"

"No. What am I going to do with you?"

"Find me a man who looks like Cruz, and I'll be out of your business in a jiffy. I'll have my own to handle."

I laugh out loud. "I need to eat before lunch period is over. Hopefully, remote teaching will be a short-term thing. I miss hanging with you."

"I wouldn't miss me with him warming my bed and making me meals."

I shake my head. She isn't wrong. "Bye, Deni."

"Byeeeee!"

I end the session and pad to the kitchen. "Sorry about her."

"Don't be. You two are exactly like my sisters and their friends, more so Maura than Marisa. Although, I wasn't the eye candy they were referring too."

I take a bite of the sandwich. "Thank you. This is tasty. What's in it?"

"Family secret. Stick around and I'll share all of them."

"Deal." I savor my food a bit more before asking, "Any updates?"

"Nothing major. I cross-referenced the phone logs and narrowed Babylon's madam down to one. However, the number has been disconnected since his disappearance. Caitryn Spillane has filed a request through her lawyers to have the painting authenticated and appraised."

"Progress and a roadblock. How would Sam pull off her request?"

"The painting is currently in FBI custody. Sam would simply need to give permission for it to be viewed or moved to complete her request, assuming it's approved by the court."

"Any reason it wouldn't be approved?"

"Not likely. The only downside for Caitryn is the value could have increased significantly given the press coverage and Babylon's mysterious disappearance."

I glance at the clock. "Shoot. Thank you for lunch." I gobble down the rest of my sandwich, kiss him quickly, and hustle back into my office. The afternoon proceeds smoothly. Suzie handles the students with care, and I appreciate her for it. After a short chat with Suzie about the day and things to improve or add, I sign off. Javier is typing away on his laptop in the living room.

I pull out some beef for dinner, change my clothes, and hustle downstairs before I lose my urge to work out. Halfway through a high-intensity, interval workout, Javier hops on the treadmill and is running at a decent pace expeditiously. I finish my final set and sip water while he runs inexplicably faster. When I finish the bottle, he slows to jogging. Soon thereafter, he slows to a moderate walk and stops.

"Everything okay?" I lean against the wall and wait for an answer.

He shrugs and steps off the treadmill. "Yes, as far as your safety, but no considering I'm not making any progress finding Babylon so you can get back to your life."

I don't miss the *before I disrupted it* that he didn't say.

"Yes, because being in our comfy home indefinitely is simply *awful*. I mean, all the alone time without interruptions is simply unacceptable."

He hauls me into his sweaty arms and squeezes me against his chest.

"Ewww, gross!"

He laughs heartily and releases me. "You're sweaty too!" His genuine laughs gets me every time.

"True, but not as much as you."

He raises an eyebrow in my direction. "Help me understand how this is different from getting sweaty together?"

I don't have a conclusive answer to his question. "I...."

"Let's hear it, *corazón*. Give me one good reason how post-workout sweaty is different from hot, naked, sexy sweaty."

"Because we get hot and sweaty together." My response is soft and low.

"Fair point."

"And… hot, naked, sexy sweaty feels exponentially better than a workout."

"Better point."

We both laugh and clean up for dinner. After a delicious meal prepared by yours truly, we spend our evening hanging out.

Our routine has been pretty much the same for the last three weeks, working from home and spending time together—whether watching a movie, talking, reading, or simply being together. You would think we'd be at one another's throats, but we aren't. Perhaps our years of getting to know each other before dating and living together helped ease the shift to being a couple.

Tonight, Javier has taken over the kitchen. I negotiated my way into the room, but I'm not allowed to assist or ask any questions about dinner. To keep my promise, I ask a random question to learn more about him for fun.

"Which celebrity has the perfect body in your mind?"

Many answers come to mind—Megan Fox, Scarlett Johansson, and Kate Upton being at the top. I'm floored by his answer.

"I would choose Marilyn Monroe or Sofia Loren from old Hollywood. Modern Hollywood… hands down Salma Hayek."

Holy hell! I'm not a mega star, nor is my skin as flawless as Salma Hayek's, but physically speaking, she's a close comparison to me. Even with every option available, he would choose normal.

He adds a dash of this and that into the pot and ponders his question for me. "If you were forced to relive one ten-minute block of your life again and again each morning, what ten minutes of your life would you choose?"

"Digging deep, huh?"

"Worth it."

I consider his question for a few moments. "I can narrow it down to two. First, I choose the two minutes before Joyce handed me to my parents and the eight minutes following. I would give almost anything to experience those emotions as an adult. Second, I would choose to start those ten minutes the moment you stepped into Jake's hospital room. I felt deep in my bones when you took my hand in yours that my life was never going to be the same."

He sets the spoon on the stove and rounds the island. Within a second, his mouth covers mine. Seemingly pent-up emotions pour from his lips to mine. He marks my mouth, jaw, and neck with possessive and passion-laden kisses as he draws me to my feet and I melt against him.

In the recesses of my mushy, desire-addled brain, I hear the lid of the pot bouncing. "Javier, the pot," I mumble between the sighs he's eliciting from me.

A deep groan bubbles between us. He kisses the tip of my nose and reluctantly returns to cooking. "You never shared that with me before now. Why?"

"We were wholly honest in our discussions from our career aspirations to marriage and children. I knew building a career as a police officer was your next step, not building a relationship with me. It wasn't time for me then either. I was barely into my first year as a teacher when we met. You were a bright spot in my days when I saw you."

"Does right now work for you, Jillian, considering my current work drama?"

"Right now is perfect, Javier." I didn't intend for my answer to bring about a discussion about our relationship. He doesn't press for more though.

He plates chicken, rice, and plantains and sets one in front of me and the other beside me. I'm confident when he shares the actual name for the dish it will sound sexy and decadent from his lips.

"Water, juice, iced tea?"

"Water, please."

He kisses my cheek and sets my water in front of me. After he joins me, I ask about the food. "What are we eating?"

"Chicken."

I laugh and playfully push him. "Seriously."

"You want me to speak Spanish again, don't you?"

My eyes are wide with anticipation. "Maybe."

"Fine. *Pollo guisado y arroz con habichuelas y tostones.* I made flán for dessert too."

"When did you have time to make dessert?"

"While you were teaching. Taste it so I can stop being nervous and you can tell me about the kids."

The chicken literally peels off perfectly and melts in my mouth. I can taste the adobo, sazon, and a bit of garlic. He covered the white rice with stewed beans and the plantains on the side. "This dish is delicious too. No more cooking without me. I want to learn."

"Agreed. We can cook the next one together."

"Good. The kids, as you call them, have adjusted well to the shift to remote teaching. Would I prefer to be there? Sure, but I know it's safer for me and them for me to be here." We continue chatting and eating. I share more about Deni's quest for love. She's failing miserably. I understand her plight completely. Her dating pool needs to expand outside a twenty-mile radius of her condo if she plans to find a decent guy.

Javier's phone vibrates on the island beside me. The caller ID indicates it's Christoph.

"Go ahead. He wouldn't call unless it was important."

Unfortunately, Javier's right. "Hey, Christoph. I'm going to put you on speaker," I answer.

"Hey, C-Top. What's going on?" Javier greets Christoph.

"I have some fantastic news and some not-so-fantastic news. Which do you want first?"

"Not so fantastic," I request.

"I'm going to need Cruz to take an assignment in a few days."

He threads his fingers through mine before speaking. "What is your plan for Jillian?"

"Someone will stay with her—either Jake, me, or Ben. Mostly likely Ben."

I take a deep breath and exhale slowly. "The fantastic news?"

"Callie and Connor are the proud parents of Myers Connor and Sutton Mara Michelson as of about an hour ago."

"Congrats to them. I'll visit when they get home." Other than the time travelling, I'm safe at the farm as well.

"Can you send me the file for the assignment, C-Top?"

"Sure, it's a press event before a cast premiere and dinner the following evening for Lynn Smith. Her next movie, directed by Ellis Barnett, is releasing in two months. The job was assigned to Callen, but Miss Forrester's filming schedule was extended."

"It's no problem. We knew it would be a possibility. How is Madeleine feeling?"

"Thanks, Cruz. She's tired but refuses to slow down. At least I got her to forgo her sky-high heels for work."

"Happy to hear it. Let me know when you have my departure details set."

"All details are in the file."

"Thanks. Later, Christoph."

I end the call and push my food around my plate.

"*Cariña*, I'll be fine."

"I'm reserving judgement until I know where you're going." I drop my head.

"I'm sure Christoph wouldn't send me back to the city."

"You're probably right, but I need to see it in black and white."

"Can we consider this from my perspective for a minute?"

I lift my gaze from our hands to his drawn face.

"It's my fault you need security in the first place. Now we're impacting your family due to your need for security and my obligation to do my job. Not to mention your inability to attend school in person."

"Javier, I will never lie to you either. I'll handle whatever is necessary to get us to safety. The blame doesn't fall on you. It falls on the Spillanes. I'll be fine with Dad for a few days."

"Thank you. I don't want security for you. I want you to be as free as you were before your unexpected, serendipitous, and amazing visit to my apartment."

I lift our hands to my lips. "We'll be safe and free as soon as we can. Did Christoph send the file yet?"

"Anxious?"

"Enough for both of us, yeah."

He grabs his phone and checks his email. It takes him a few minutes to find the information I desperately want to know. "The assignment is in Chicago."

I exhale a breath I didn't know I was holding. "Why don't you read the file while I finish today's grading?"

He nods.

About an hour later, we fall into bed until morning.

CHAPTER SIXTEEN

JAVIER

I take a seat on the edge of her bed—our bed—and watch her sleep peacefully for the last time in the next few days. I'm not angry about the assignment. Part of me is looking forward to it, but the other part is worried about Jillian. She's demonstrated her ability to protect herself and me, but I'm uneasy about leaving. Having Ben stay with her is a huge comfort, but I don't want her life to be upended for mine.

"Is it time already?" she grumbles.

"Unfortunately."

Her eyes flutter open and meet mine. "Please call me when you can."

"Of course. I know you understand, but please heed your dad." I press a kiss to her forehead.

"I will. I love you."

I kiss her softy and reply, "I'll be back soon. I love you." Hurrying out of the room is my only play. I refuse to turn back. If I do, I won't leave. Moving to Blackthorne was the right move. Soon it will be less muddy in my mind.

As promised, Ben Blackthorne arrives at five thirty in the morning to stay with Jillian. Ben is a former marine and cop. "Good morning, Mr. Blackthorne."

"Cruz. Nice to see you again. I would prefer different circumstances," Ben states after crossing the threshold.

"As would I, sir."

"Jillian is on my concise list of strong women. She would be fine even without me here."

"She would, but I think you fail to give yourself and Connie credit for her strength."

"I appreciate the sentiment, but she was fiery and fierce from the day we were entrusted with her care."

I can almost imagine Jillian as a child. "I would love to hear about her childhood someday."

"You'll be around long enough to ask every question you could think of."

Damn! He saw our feelings on display too. "As long as she will have me."

"Go. She's got this despite my presence."

"Thank you, sir."

"You're welcome. Perhaps we could shift to Ben for the time being?"

I extend my hand to him. "Thank you, Ben." I heft my bag onto my shoulder and walk out the door.

Before bed last night, I reviewed my assignment profile again. Lynn Smith, acclaimed actress, working on a film with Ellis Barnett. If I recall correctly, Cash Morgan's wife, Noelle, is Ellis's sister. His full name is Nicholas Ellis Barnett. He uses Ellis as he screen name. Mrs. Smith will be accompanied by her husband, Gerald. There's a press event this evening and a dinner tomorrow.

I arrive at the airport, park, and move expeditiously to the private terminal Christoph indicated in the file. Within ten minutes, I'm buckled in my seat after greeting Holden again. After a failed attempt to sleep, I review the file again despite having studied the details thoroughly since Christoph sent it.

I suppose doubt should be filtering through me as this is my first job for Blackthorne. The procedures Blackthorne follows are similar to the police department, except Blackthorne doesn't require a firearm. While I do have one on me, I won't while I'm with Mrs. Smith.

I thank Holden before deplaning and arrive at the hotel thirty minutes later. My phone has been vibrating in my pocket the entire ride. I check into my room and plan to handle the myriad of messages.

Me: Have a great day. Love you.

Jillian: Thank you. You too. Love you.

I check my voice mail and note one from Bishop and Davidson. Davidson, first.

"Good morning, NYPD. Captain Davidson's office."

"Morning. Javier Cruz returning his call."

"One moment please."

"Cruz. Thank you for returning my call so quickly."

"Of course, sir." That still stings, but I'm nothing if not appropriate when addressing my commanding officers.

"There were two reasons for my call. First, it's my understanding Miss Spillane has requested an appraisal and authentication of the artwork."

"Yes. The parties are working out logistics and security as far as I know."

"Wonderful. Please keep me in the loop when you learn the plan."

"I will keep you informed as necessary." I'm skeptical about this call. Davidson should be in the loop about this transfer through the attorneys and perhaps the court or even from Morgan Insurance directly.

"Second, you have officially exhausted your vacation and personal time as of midnight last night. I'll leave your administrative access to the servers and file open until the Spillane case is complete. Otherwise, all access to NYPD resources will be terminated effective at noon today. As per my agreement with Agent Bishop, you'll shift to an FBI consultant for this case."

"Thank you, sir. I hope to wrap up the Spillane matter as soon as possible."

"I expect nothing less. It has been a pleasure working with you, Mr. Cruz."

"Good day, sir." I end the call and barely refrain from chucking my phone against the posh hotel room wall. Unsettled about Davidson but elated I'm mostly done with the NYPD, I tug on my suit jacket and make my way to Mrs. Smith's room. Her event is scheduled for 4:00 p.m. local time.

I knock on the door and introduce myself when it's opened. "Good afternoon. I'm here from Blackthorne."

"You must be Cruz. I'm Lynn Smith. That's my husband, Gerry, and my personal assistant, Jamie."

"It's a pleasure to meet you, Mrs. Smith."

"You as well. I need a few more minutes, and I'll be ready." She's dressed, but it appears I interrupted the final touchups on her hair and makeup.

I'm not sure what I was expecting, but she's refreshing and down-to-earth. "No problem."

Jamie offers me a water, which I accept and hover on the perimeter for the room. Without hesitation, I answer the knock at the door.

"Good afternoon. I'm here to see Lynn."

"Good afternoon, Mr. Barnett. Please come in."

"Thank you." Ellis steps into the room and greets Lynn with a kiss on both cheeks. Then he shakes Gerry's hand before turning back to me. "Cruz, right?"

"Yes, pleased to meet you in person, Mr. Barnett."

"Please call me Ellis."

I nod and wait for my cue to escort Lynn to her event. With Lynn and Gerry slightly behind me, we make our way to the press event. Flashbulbs illuminate the moment she and Ellis step into the room. They take their seats side by side and answer questions from the throng of reporters present. Slightly over two hours later, I escort Mrs. Smith back to her suite for the evening.

"Good night. I'll be back tomorrow evening for your dinner with the studio executives."

"Thank you, Cruz. See you then."

I exhale and push the down button to my room. As far as security goes, I understand her desire to have someone present. This assignment hasn't been difficult, and I'm grateful. I scan my messages and respond to Jillian first.

Jillian: How did your event go?

Me: The client is nice. It went well. How are you?

Jillian: I'm fine.

Me: I'll call you in a bit.

I consider running but opt for a quick shower before calling Bishop and Jillian.

"Cruz. Thanks for returning my call."

"You're welcome."

"I'll get right to it. The parties have agreed to allow the painting to be appraised and authenticated in an undisclosed location chosen by Morgan Insurance by an appraiser selected by the same. The circle will be small, including Sam, myself, and you."

Interesting, not Davidson.

He continues, "Sam has selected to have the painting appraised by Antonia Caffey. Once the process is completed, the painting will be stored in the vault at the FBI field office in New York city until the parties come to an agreement regarding its disposition. I understand Sam has secured armored transportation for the transfer in the next few days."

"Not Davidson?"

"No. As a colleague, you'll understand when I say I'm wary of him."

"I understand more than you know to the point of having him checked out by Blackthorne. Even though I came up empty, I'm not fully sold on his motivations." I'm comforted Bishop's gut is roiling regarding Davidson as well.

"Agreed. It merely means there's an avenue neither of us have considered."

"Do you have an update on Babylon?"

"His last whereabouts was his penthouse. No flight plan was required if he took a chopper off the roof. I have no access to cameras in the area. Judge Mapleton feels the connection between our case and Babylon's disappearance is too tenuous to allow unfettered access—her words."

"Okay. I'll dig into Babylon more, especially considering the escort angle disintegrated within hours of our visit to his penthouse."

"You're no longer an active member of the NYPD, correct?"

"Yes, you're correct."

"I'll reach out to Jake or Christoph to let them know I need to extend your FBI consultant access to cover you. Acceptable to you?"

Davidson shared that information earlier. It's hinky, if you ask me. There are too many disconnects between Davidson and other law enforcement agencies. "Yes, thank you. I would like to complete this case quickly though. Splitting my focus between the case and my Blackthorne assignments isn't ideal." Sharing the impact on Jillian isn't necessary as far as I know. It impacts me all the same.

"Understood. I would prefer to close this case again myself."

"Thanks, Bishop. I'll let you know if I learn anything."

I take a few minutes to order a meal and then call Jillian.

"Hey, sweetheart. How was school today?"

"Hi. Jesse had a rough day, but the others were great. I appreciate they heeded Suzie when she had to leave them alone with only me on the screen."

"Was Suzie able to handle it?"

"Yes, but Platt wasn't happy Kate and Stevie were essentially alone for almost fifteen minutes."

"As much as I don't want to agree with her, I see her point."

Jillian grumbles, "I do too. How was the press event?"

There's a knock at the door. "Hold on, Jillian. I need to get my dinner." I hurry to the door, admit the server, and sign for my food. I switch to speakerphone. "Thanks. I'm back. To answer your question, the press event went smoothly with no issues. Mrs. Smith is nice. I also met Ellis Barnett. He's quite down-to-earth as well." I take a few bites of my burger. Jillian hasn't made me a burger yet, but I know without a doubt, hers would be exponentially better.

"Is he as dreamy in person as he appears to be on screen?"

"Seriously, woman?" I pop a few sweet potato fries in my mouth.

I hear a soft chuckle. "Sort of serious. I mean, even you can admit he's good-looking."

"I'm not sure how I feel about you ogling Ellis Barnett or any guy."

"Really?"

"Nah. I'm kidding. Yes, I suppose he's good-looking. The actress who plays Lynn's daughter in the film, Angelica Swisher, she's stunning." She is, but I'm seeing how far Jillian plans to take this discussion.

"Hold on. Let me google her."

I hear movement, a thud, and them some tapping.

"*Corazón*, what are you doing?"

"I moved into the office." She pauses for almost a minute. "Wow, you're right. She's gorgeous. A bit too young for you, but...."

I wait her out. She bursts into laughter mere moments later. "I only want you, but I'm not blind."

"Same for me. The wanting you and the blind part. Truthfully, how are you doing?" she asks.

"I would prefer to be with you, but I know it isn't realistic. I'm sure Ben has you under control."

"Excuse you."

Now it's my turn to burst into laughter. "Your facial expression must be priceless right now."

"Since when do you call my father Ben?"

"He corrected me this morning."

"I see."

"Don't worry. I'll win them over as your other half instead of your brother's unit mate."

"Not worried, just surprised. We haven't shared our relationship with anyone other than Jake, Christoph, and Connor. I know they wouldn't out us to my parents."

"We weren't exactly hiding anything at the wedding or shower, even though it wasn't official then," I offer as I polish off my dinner.

"True. Norah said my feelings are unmistakable, especially when you're in the room. My father's investigative skills are finely honed. He pegged Jake's feelings for Norah long before he admitted them to her and himself."

"I was kidding myself as well, thinking I could mask mine from everyone other than you."

"We didn't have to hide them then, nor do we now. It's exciting."

"I agree."

She fails to stifle a yawn.

"Go to sleep, sweetheart. I'll call you tomorrow. I love you."

"Okay, but only because it'll hurry this up. I love you."

I end the call, set the plate in the hallway, and turn in for the night a little early.

CHAPTER SEVENTEEN

JILLIAN

My once inviting huge bed no longer calls to me when I'm alone. I finish brewing the coffee and check on my dad in the guest room. He's still sound asleep. I know he's here on Jill duty, but there's no reason to wake him. I won't leave.

After a quick quiche for breakfast, I login to my class and start my day. All are accounted for, and Suzie is finishing setup for their modified art project. I worked with the IT department to create a simple program that will allow Jesse and Kate to create the same project as Stevie.

Jesse and Kate will input the desired colors into the program while Stevie paints. In the end, all three will have expertly decorated winter scenes for hanging on their wall of fame at home. Soon after they get started, my dad peeks his head into my office.

"I'm sorry I overslept, sprite." It's nice to hear my childhood nickname again.

"No worries. You clearly needed the rest. I won't leave, Dad. It's important for Javier's sanity for me to stay here."

"Mine too, sprite."

I hug him before answering, "I know."

"Need a refill?"

"No, thanks. I'm fine for now."

I continue monitoring my class as they work on their art and scan my administrative emails as well. There's nothing of note, other than a potential issue with spring parent-teacher meetings. Hopefully, I'll be able to attend in person with security or schedule video conferences with the parents.

While Suzie is printing the artwork for Jesse and Kate, I open the floor to them.

Kate buzzes first. "When are you coming back?"

I sigh. "I don't know yet. I would prefer to be there too."

Stevie adds, "Suzie is nice, but you're… funner."

A laugh bubbles up from my belly. "Thank you, Stevie."

"What about you, Jesse?"

"Is it because of the boy?" Jesse asks.

"He means the man who changed your smile," Kate's computerized voice adds.

Indirectly. "No, it has nothing to do with him."

"So there is a man?" Kate asks.

Damn it! "You guys set up me!" I shake my head. "Yes, there is a man in my life now. However, you'll get no more details out of me."

Groans surround me as Suzie returns. I sign off and craft a simple sandwich for myself and Dad for lunch.

"When would you like to talk about your relationship with Cruz?" Dad asks.

"We can talk over dinner. There probably isn't enough time for you to get your interrogation done before I need to log back in with my students."

"Fair enough."

I stew in my thoughts while I finish my lunch and anxiously wait to get back to my students. I'm not worried about sharing my relationship, but how we got to now isn't anyone's business but ours. I'm distracted for the remainder of the day, wondering exactly how my father plans to handle his line of questioning. As if he knew I needed support, I get a message from Javier.

> *Javier: I hope your school day was amazing. I'll call you later. It may*
> *be late.*
>
> *Me: Almost done. Call no matter what time it is here please. Update?*
>
> *Javier: I will. Nothing positive. Love you.*
>
> *Me: Love you.*

I say my goodbyes to my students and clear out my email for the afternoon. Dad is watching an old movie in the living room.

He pauses the movie. "School done for today?"

"Yeah."

The doorbell rings, and he points into the kitchen. I hesitate only long enough to realize I didn't order anything. A trickle of fear climbs into my chest. While the Spillanes likely know where I live, they must know I'm not stupid enough to accept an unwanted or unordered package.

"Can I help you?" I overhear Dad say to the delivery person.

"I have a delivery for Jonas Appleton."

Relief washes over me. My father's heart is probably racing too fast for his age.

"Next door," I state for my father to hear.

"You have the wrong house. Jonas lives next door."

"I apologize for the error, sir. Have a nice day."

"You too, young man." Dad closes the door and enters the kitchen.

"Better safe than sorry, sprite."

I nod. "Thanks. I know. What are you thinking for dinner? Spicy chicken and rice or meatloaf with greens and potatoes?"

"I'll never say no to your delicious meatloaf. Working out first?"

"Yeah."

"I'm going to call your mom."

"Tell her I love her for me."

He smiles. "Will do."

I change and head downstairs before I pick up a book instead. After a strength training workout, I hurry through the shower before cooking. Having Dad here is likely unnecessary but comforting to the guys, all of them from Cruz to Jake to my dad himself. He's been here since Javier left but not underfoot. I appreciate his respect of me and my home despite being my father.

I twist my hair up into a topknot, pull out the ingredients for dinner, and get to work.

Dad joins me about halfway through peeling the potatoes. "Want some help?"

"Sure. Do you want to finish peeling or snip the green beans?"

"Green beans." I'm sure he's simply formulating his series of questions in his mind.

"Ask what you need to ask, Dad. Please don't grill me like a suspect though." Sometimes, as a former cop, he can't help himself when he's digging for information.

"I'll do my best. The first time I noticed a hint of anything between you and Cruz was at the holiday party two years ago. It wasn't overt, but I considered there might be something between you then. Is that when you started dating?"

"No, and the truth is more complicated. Javier and I have been talking since Jake and Connor were at Walter Reed. From the day he arrived until the day the guys were released, we talked about anything and everything, including specifics we wanted out of life. We left no stone unturned, from expectations in a marriage, finances, and even children."

Surprise crosses his face, but he doesn't interrupt.

I continue preparing dinner and sharing. "There were a few times all those years ago, I thought he would ask me out. Deep down, I knew he was determined to follow his dream of being a big-city police officer. I wasn't going to stand in his way. I also knew my career was starting here. Giving it up so soon wasn't an option for me. We saw one another a few times a year since then. We had an in-depth discussion about us at the shower for Sutton and Myers about five months ago."

"How did you get to him living with you so quickly?" His question skims the surface of judgmental.

I pour the potatoes into the strainer and check the meatloaf. "On Christmas day, I flew to New York and knocked on his door. The rest is the two of us deciding to be together. One factor I wasn't aware of is the guys offered him a spot at Blackthorne from day one. He never shared with me because he was set on the NYPD. Recent events in his life, in conjunction with our conversation, pushed him to take Jake up on his offer to work at Blackthorne. As far as him living here, he was going to look for a place, and then the Spillane case put a wrench in the plans." That's only partially true, but Dad doesn't need every detail.

"Thank you for sharing. Cruz is a good man. Your relationship seems less rushed knowing you have been building a foundation for the last four years."

"He is. Thank you for trusting my judgment."

"It's much better than your brother Jake's. Hell, he kept Norah at arm's length for over two years."

I laugh softly. "True. Jake wasn't ready until Norah was in actual danger and she threatened to walk away when she was safe from the Morettis."

Dad laughs heartily. "I thought it was my heart-to-heart with him at the Michelson's that made him see the light."

I smirk. "It absolutely was." I pull the meatloaf from the oven and let it rest while I mash the potatoes.

"When you can move freely, please bring Cruz to Sunday dinner. Your mom and I would like to get to know him better as your other half instead of a buddy of your brothers."

"I will." We take a seat at the island after I plate dinner. "Now the bigger question is what to do about Cam."

Dad laughs and digs into his food.

"Cam is a goofball with a good career ahead of him. I don't remember the last time he went on a date."

"To be fair, you didn't know about Javier and me either," I offer.

"Accurate. However, I doubt Cam is as discreet as you."

"Point taken." We finish our dinner and clean the kitchen. "I have some work to do on my students' individualized plans."

"I'll watch a movie or read."

I nod.

"Good night, sprite."

I hug him close. "Good night, Dad. Thank you for being here for us instead of Jake or Christoph."

"Anytime. Love you."

"Love you too." I retreat into my office and plow through the plans for my students. For Jesse and Stevie, their current plans simply need to be renewed. Kate needs some additional support at home. More succinctly, her mom needs more help. Kate hasn't been sleeping well, which means neither is her mother. The trick is going to be how to assist her without it looking like charity. Hours later, with painstaking word choices, I fall into my bed.

Near eleven, my ringtone pulls me out of a deep sleep. "Hi, *cariña.*"

"Hi. How was the dinner?"

"Long but security hiccup free. The client is tucked away in her suite, and I'm snuggled in this huge bed by myself."

"I miss you too." Silence stretches between us. Not because we don't have anything to say, but we would prefer to be together when we talk about anything important.

"Go to sleep. I'll be home around lunch. I love you."

"I love you." I end the call, sigh, and burrow deeper into the soft covers of my bed. The only good news I can muster right now is Javier will be cuddled next to me tomorrow.

My alarm blares, startling me awake. I make my way to the kitchen for some coffee and find my dad sound asleep on the couch instead of in the guest room. I tiptoe around making my coffee and close myself into my office.

Stevie is the first to arrive this morning.

"Hi, Stevie. How was your night?"

"Good." He takes his seat and waits for his classmates.

While I would prefer to be physically present, they seem to understand it isn't possible right now. I'm grateful for their resilience. Kate takes her spot at the same time I receive a note concerning Jesse.

He was rushed to the hospital last evening after a fall while practicing on his crutches. His prognosis isn't good.

I force my emotions down and focus on greeting Kate. "Morning, Kate."

"Hi, Miss Blackthorne. Are you okay?"

"Yes, I'm fine. How are you?"

"Good." Her answer through the computer sounds drawn out today. Logically, it isn't possible, but given this news, it would be fitting.

Once the students are content with morning announcements, I text Jake.

Me: What's the likelihood you can get me to the children's hospital safely?

Jake: Right now, low. I have no free staff.

Me: Perhaps this afternoon?

Jake: One of your students?

Me: Yeah.

I watch Kate and Stevie for a moment. Losing Jesse will crush them. Me too if I'm being honest.

Jake: Let me see what I can do.

Me: Thank you.

I push through the rest of the morning with a brave face for my class. It's harder than I expect. I've lost students before, but the sheer fact I can't simply go to Jesse is tearing my heart out. The deeper issue is I wouldn't ever put the blame on Javier either.

I log off for lunch and join Dad in the kitchen.

"How was your morning?" he asks.

"Not great. One of my students fell last night. He's hospitalized, and his prognosis isn't good. I asked Jake to see if I can see him. He's working on a plan."

"If he can, he will."

"I know. I wouldn't ask if it wasn't important."

"He knows," Dad assures me.

I'm busy making a sandwich when I hear the front door open. Part of me wants to rush over and leap into Javier's arms, but I won't with my father here. Javier steps into the kitchen.

Dad saves me from deciding. "Cruz, glad you're back."

"Thanks, Ben. All quiet here?"

"For the most part. Small little scare yesterday but was merely a mistake by the delivery kid."

"Glad to hear it." His shoulders drop despite the fact there was no actual threat to me; he's still upset he wasn't here.

I'm anxious for a kiss, but I'm still dutifully waiting while they talk. Javier's gaze shifts from me to my father and back a few times.

"I'll pack up unless you want me to stay in case Jake needs me." His words are aimed at me.

Javier's eyebrow raises.

"I'll pack up and wait to hear back from Jake. Does that work?"

"Yes. Thanks, Dad."

The moment he's out of the room, Javier sweeps me into his arms. All my pent-up concern drains from my body. I trust Dad implicitly, but I prefer he not be anywhere near my security detail, if you will. The concern etched on his face will hopefully dissipate some when he leaves me in Javier's capable hands. Not only as my bodyguard but otherwise.

The sheer relief cascading off Javier is thick. His lips cover mine, and I melt into him. Our kiss is possessive, passionate, and all too short.

"As much as I want to march you into our bedroom, I need to get back to class. Jesse fell last night. He's in the hospital. I reached out to Jake to see if I can visit. Please talk to him for me."

"I will. I missed having you beside me, Jillian."

"Me too. I'm not going anywhere, Javier, except to class." I kiss him quickly and scamper back to my office for the rest of the afternoon. I'm anxious to see if Jake can pull off a visit or if he'll even allow me to visit. Part of me also regrets asking. I don't want Javier to blame himself when Jake says no. My gut tells me the best I'm going to get is a video call with his parents from the hospital.

I log off and steel myself for bad news when I step out of my office. Dad and Javier are chatting in the kitchen. The solemn looks in my direction would indicate Jake turned my request down handily.

"I'm going home, sprite. Give your mom a call when you have a few minutes." Dad pulls me in for a hug. "Love you."

"Thanks. Love you too." I can tell from his hasty exit and the strength of his hug that I'm not going to like the news Javier has for me.

Javier doesn't speak until the front door closes completely. "I'm sorry, *corazón*, you can't go to the hospital."

I slide my hands over his flank and dip them beneath the hem of his shirt. Oh how I missed the warmth of him beneath my fingers and his muscles jumping from the caress of my skin on his. "Jake made you the messenger, huh?"

"I volunteered to tell you. It's my—"

"No, do not take any additional, unnecessary blame on yourself. There was no way for you to anticipate these circumstances, none of them."

He adds enough space between us to slide his hand to my face. "You're truly the most understanding and unflappable woman I've ever met." His thumb drags across my lower lip.

"No, not even close. You see more cracks than anyone else. You're the only person who truly knows me."

"I could say the same for you about myself."

I pull my lower lip between my teeth. "Do you have anything you need to do immediately?"

"Yes."

My heart falls. "Oh, okay." I attempt to pull away.

His arms close tighter around me. "I need to be with you."

His words. I rise onto my toes and seize his lips with mine. With each step toward the bedroom, another article of clothing litters our path. My shirt on the island lifted off so he can savor the curve of my breasts with his tongue. His shirt and jeans halfway up the staircase, giving me an expanse of skin to explore with my mouth as we climb to the bedroom. We fall onto my bed clad in only our underwear.

Javier admits, "Slow will be impossible for me right now."

"Yes, please."

He grins at me and tears my panties down my legs while I unhook my bra. He turns me onto my belly before rejoining me on the bed.

Gripping my hips, he pulls me up to my knees and positions himself behind me. The round tip of his length teases my core. "You good?"

First time for everything. "Uh-huh." My response comes out low and uneasy.

"*Cariña,* talk to me."

The level to which he is attuned to me is terrifying and comforting at the same time. "I'm fine." *Nervous but fine.* "Never tried this position before."

A harsh exhale flows from him. I glance over my shoulder. His eyes are clamped closed.

"Javier, open your eyes." A mere moment later, he pins his gaze to mine. An emotion I can't pinpoint is staring back at me. It's a combination of love, anticipation, and perhaps a tiny smidge of fear. "I trust you completely. We can talk more later."

He nods curtly, exhales again, and draws his hands over the curve of my hips. Slowly, he pushes forward inch by glorious inch.

Ohmigod! The fullness in this position is considerably more than the others I've tried.

"Jillian…." His voice is strained with concern.

"I need you to move, Javier."

At my request, he withdraws and pushes fully forward, filling me again. With a moderate pace, he continues to find his rhythm. My inner muscles throb around him. The knot of pleasure at the base of my spine tightens faster and more deeply than ever before. Holy hell! He feels so good!

His demanding thrusts increase as he nears his climax. My core pulses around him as I shudder and career over the edge of ecstasy. His fingers bruise my hips when he follows me over. When his breathing slows, he withdraws and gathers me into his embrace.

He presses a kiss to the nape of my neck before speaking. "We should talk more in depth about our history."

"Not necessarily. I'm sure it was hard enough to share what you've already shared. I'm fine. No, I'm more than fine. Are they all different?"

I feel him grin against my skin. "Yes and no. The angles and depth vary, which increases or decreases the feeling of fullness."

"How many are there?"

He laughs. "More than enough to keep us busy for a very long time."

"I'm game. You?"

"Without question. I need a promise you'll tell me in the future."

"I promise."

We stumble into the bathroom, clean up, then scrounge for leftovers for dinner. After dishes, we curl into bed until morning.

CHAPTER EIGHTEEN

JAVIER

We oversleep the next morning after a few more rounds of twisted sheet time during the night.

When I realize how much, I hurry Jillian into dressing and send her straight to her office. "Sweetheart, go. I'll bring you coffee and something to eat."

"With a shirt on this time," she demands.

"Are you sure?"

She shakes her head and turns at the threshold. "For me, no shirt necessary... ever. For my coworkers and students, it's a must."

I wink at her and get moving in the kitchen. Within fifteen minutes, I prepare her coffee and some avocado toast. I attempt to sneak into her office, but one of her students catches a glimpse of me. I round the desk and hang my head.

"Who's he? He's handsome," a computerized voice echoes around me.

Jillian shakes her head. "Don't you worry, Kate. Focus on your work."

"Is he Smile Guy?" Stevie asks.

A fierce blush takes over her cheeks. "If I answer your question, will you refocus on your work?"

Kate and Stevie answer in stereo, "Yes."

"Yes, he's Smile Guy. Now back to work."

I scribble a note asking for details, blow her a kiss, then exit her office. Before handling my email and work for the day, I hustle to the basement and tackle a long, demanding workout. Jillian makes me want to skip them each morning. Almost two hours and a soothing shower later, I spread my files on the dining room table.

The only case-related email is Bishop requesting an immediate call.

"This is Bishop."

"Morning. You could've called if it was urgent."

"Yeah, well, I know your assignment ended yesterday. Wanted to let you get some sleep."

I smile inwardly. *Sleep, not after waking up without Jillian for a few days, highly unlikely.* "What happened?"

"The painting arrived as required and was dutifully appraised by Antonia Caffey."

Her reputation is stellar. I'm not surprised Sam selected her. "But?"

"The painting was stolen en route to the FBI warehouse in the city. A crew of ten held up the armored truck caravan. The drivers were tased, hogtied, and left in the middle of the street about eight hours ago. I requested assistance from Blackthorne to locate necessary footage. I realize I'm skirting the line of good and evil, legal and illegal, but Caitryn Spillane has gone too far this time."

"First, who else knew about the transfer?"

"The armored car company and the evidence clerk, aside from the core four."

"We need to investigate both. The core four is airtight."

"Already started."

"Why do you believe Caitryn is behind this?"

"There's still no sign of Babylon. None of his money has moved, no credit card usage, nothing. He's likely dead or living off cash not in his name. Also, he gains nothing from stealing the painting. Arguably, he's a bystander in this. If Morgan Insurance wished to be reimbursed, Babylon would be able to get the painting back."

"Does he have the funds?" It's the only reason a deal with Sam hasn't yet occurred. Babylon doesn't want the painting, or he lacks the funds to reimburse Sam.

"I hadn't considered checking. He hasn't indicated either way whether he's interested in the actual painting or not. I'll look into it. Any concerns with Jillian's security while you were gone?"

"Nothing of note." *Only the aching need to protect her myself.*

"Good. I'll continue to investigate those outside the core and keep you in the loop."

"Thanks. I'll reach out to Sam to see if there's other avenues we can take to locate the painting off the radar."

"Understood."

I end the call and finish scrolling my email. I shift to a different seat so I can see Jillian leave her office. I want to plan a surprise date for her at home for this weekend. It'll be our first Valentine's Day as an actual couple. We were together on the holiday when Jake and Connor were at Walter Reed, but we merely acknowledged the holiday and continued learning about each other.

I order the last item necessary for my date as Jillian leaves her office for lunch. Closing my laptop, I join her in the kitchen. I kiss her lightly and ask, "Smile Guy?"

She laughs. "Smile Guy is my students' nickname for you because I refuse to share your actual name. I'm sure my students will hound me to meet you in person soon enough."

"I would love to meet them. They're a huge part of your life, Jillian."

Surprise crosses her gorgeous face. "Seriously? You would be willing to subject yourself to the feisty scrutiny of my students?"

"Absolutely. I'll do anything for you." I haul her against me and kiss her slowly and deeply. Our kiss explodes to groping and clawing feverishly until the alarm on her phone rings to get back to class.

"I'll be done in a few hours," she murmurs between attempting to pull away from my kisses. "Javier, I need…."

"I know what you need. I'll give it to you… later, over and over until you're hoarse from screaming my name."

"Damn!"

"Too much?"

"No, perfection. I wish we could start now."

I press a kiss to her head and shoo her into her office without eating lunch. The heavy petting was worth it. Pushing my lustful desires away for now, I reach out to Sam.

"Hey, Cruz."

"Hi, Sam. How are you? Has Savannah had the baby yet?"

He exhales sharply. "No, and she is ready any minute now."

Someday I will be in his shoes. I'm looking forward to it. "I'm sure she is. I won't keep you on the call too long. I spoke with Bishop. We're working with Blaine to get footage of the heist."

"He shared as much with me. I was skeptical about moving the painting. My gut told me to decline her request."

"I understand completely given the outcome. Rarely is my gut wrong, seems yours is as well."

"Hasn't failed me in business or my personal life yet, at least with the relationships I can control."

"How is Margaux these days?"

He chuckles. "I haven't spoken to my mother in a while, and I intend to keep it that way. She made her choices, and they don't include me or my family."

"Your father?"

"Dad is doing great. He and Eloise are engaged and moving to Maine in the next few months. We've made great strides in our relationship since his divorce from Margaux. What about you?"

"Glad to hear it. Mama and my sisters are doing well. Marisa is crushing school, and Maura's spa is turning a healthy profit after only a year in business. For the first time in a long time, I'm happy in my personal life, and I will be in work when this case is closed—again."

"Good for you. What's her name?"

"Jillian."

"Jake's sister?"

"Yeah."

"You took a huge risk there. How did Jake take the news?"

I laugh. "I did. He was surprisingly chill about it. Clearly Jillian and I haven't been as discreet as we thought over the last few years."

"You been dating for years?"

"No, but we've been friends with potential for the last four years. Only recently did Jake notice our friendship looked like more."

"You deserve to be happy in love considering your history." Sam knows broad strokes about Vivienne but not her decision to terminate her pregnancy.

"Thanks, Sam. What is your plan for recovery?"

"I may reach out to a retrieval expert. Bishop asked me to hold off a bit. If it isn't recovered in the next few weeks, I'll enlist her services to locate and return it to me. Then I'll lock it up and throw away the key."

I laugh. "I wouldn't blame you."

"Honestly, I would prefer it out of my possession. I don't care who gets it. Reimburse the company and do what you wish with the art."

"I agree completely. Let me know when you involve her."

"Will do."

"Good luck to you and Savannah. Emerson will be a great big sister."

"Thanks. Same for you and Jillian."

I end the call and then answer a few texts.

Marisa: Hey there! I miss you.

Me: Hey! Miss you too, Maris. How's Ana?

Marisa: She's good. She landed the modeling gig in Paris.

Me: Good for her. How's school?

Marisa: Stressful but awesome. Love you, Javy.

Me: Love you too, Maris.

I answer Marisa then move on to Maura.

Maura: Are you alive?

Me: Of course. Miss me already?

Maura: Only because I can't pick on you when you're so far away.

Me: You can. My responses will take longer to arrive though.

Maura: Ha ha ha. Honestly, how are you?

I hesitate only because I don't want to alarm my family any more than they already are.

Me: I'm happy for the first time in too long.

Maura: You're different with Jill.

Me: It's her. She smooths me out.

Maura: I'm happy for you, Javy.

Me: Thanks. Love you, Maur.

Maura: Love you too.

I glance at the clock and make the final call of the trifecta today. All three women in my family in one hour. It's a record for me. Usually one at most is enough for me.

"*Hola, Mama.*"

"*Hola, mijo. Cómo estás?*"

"I'm well and you?"

"Good. Don't worry about me. I'm fine."

"I know you're fine, Mama, but I still worry, especially now."

"At first I was concerned about you leaving for a woman. Jillian is different than the other one. *Ella es la única.*"

Jillian is *nothing* like Vivienne. Mama doesn't know every detail. It crushed me. I can only imagine the fallout if she knew the whole story. "No, she isn't. Jillian is *the one.*"

"*Mijo,* I need to go. It's time for my bingo night with the *vecinos.*"

"Mama, it's barely after three."

"*Sí,* early bird dinner first."

I grin. "Have fun, Mama. Love you."

"Love you too."

I end the call and consider the facts. My mother and sisters are doing fine without me. I took on caring for them as the man of the house after my dad passed away. Not only am I grateful to them but sad too. My sisters are grown women who can take care of themselves—a fact they dutifully remind me of every chance they get. Mama is one of the strongest women I know, a notion which made me pause in making decisions for myself until very recently. I don't regret the extra time I stayed in the city, except to the extent I could've been with Jillian sooner.

Jillian leaves her office and heads straight to her impressive wine rack. If I recall correctly, Jake has exceptional taste in wine. It clearly rubbed off on his sister. She pulls a bottle of Mayacamas 2014 and two glasses out. Then she turns back for the corkscrew.

I surround her in my embrace and murmur, "What happened, *cariña*?"

Tears fall before she even utters a word. I lower one arm and take the corkscrew from her hand and draw her fully against me. Her entire body is wrought with tension as the sobs increase.

Between heaves, she mumbles something I can't make out. If it's within my power, I'll fix whatever is upsetting her. I'll plow through anyone and anything to never have her cry again. Her sobs lessen, and the heaving decreases. She lifts her bloodshot and puffy eyes to mine. Even now she's stunning.

"Jesse… isn't going to… make it."

My heart breaks for her. I resolve to get her to Jesse's service in whatever form it looks like. As much as I love our bubble, truly I do, she needs some girl time too. If I've learned anything having two sisters, girls' night can soften almost any blow a woman can suffer.

I lead her to the bedroom and curl up with her in bed until she falls asleep. I leave her only long enough to set into motion a few things she needs and soon. Calling Jake is the first step.

"Hey, Cruz. Everything good?"

"No."

"Is Jill all right?"

"She's physically fine." I share the news about Jesse and my plan to get Deni and the ladies together tomorrow night.

Jake pauses too long for my liking. "You're truly in this with Jill, aren't you?"

"I love your sister with everything I am, Jake. I'll do anything to make this easier for her." The sole reason she needs assistance in getting what she needs is me. "Persuading her to refrain from visiting Jesse at the hospital is one thing. His funeral service is something else."

"It's less risky to get Jill to the farm. It protects Deni if the Spillanes are still watching her house. Between you, me, and Christoph, we'll bring her here. Can you reach out to Deni?"

"Sure. Can Norah and Callie handle the food, or do you want me to order it?"

"Norah and Callie will be happy to handle it. We can determine the service details when we know when and where."

"Thanks, Jake."

"We're family in more than one way now. We've got your back."

I end the call and search for Jillian's phone. I locate it on her desk. I opt to call from there simply because I doubt Deni will pick up a number she doesn't recognize.

"Hey, Jill. How are you?"

"Deni, it's Javier Cruz."

"Is she okay?"

"Not really. I assume you heard about Jesse."

"Such a tragedy. He was making progress with his independent walking and then this happens."

"Are you free tomorrow night? Jillian needs some girl time."

"Yes."

"Perfect. Have you been to her brother's house?"

"Yes."

"Does six thirty work?"

"Yes. See you then." She starts to say something else but pauses twice. "Thank you for taking care of her. She deserves the world, and I'm glad she found you."

"She does, and I'll give it to her if she'll allow me to."

"Do you have a brother?"

I laugh. "No, sisters only, sorry. Good night, Deni."

I plug in her phone and slip back into bed with Jillian. Closing my cold case is my top priority. It'll eliminate her need for security and get her back to school with her students where she belongs. I won't quit until she's safe, until we're safe.

CHAPTER NINETEEN

JILLIAN

"Everything is going to be all right," Javier whispers as I snuggle deeper into his hold. "I've got you."

If I could burrow under his skin, I would consider it. Even half asleep his words make me melt into a mushy pile of goo, especially considering his sentiment does nothing for him. Unfortunately, I know it's near time for me to get up for school.

A few tears slip past my eyelids. "Thank you."

"Always." He presses a kiss to the nape of my neck.

Goose bumps slither down my spine despite the circumstance that led us to this moment. There will never be a time where I don't react to Javier's touch.

"Go take a shower. I'll make you breakfast."

"Okay." I'm immediately cold when I remove myself from the cocoon of Javier's warm, sculpted body. Shuffling into the bathroom, I turn on the water and brush my teeth before showering. A personal day would be spectacular right about now. *Sigh.* I can't shirk my responsibilities to Kate and Stevie. Plus, it wouldn't be wise for me to push my luck with Principal Platt either. I'll get through this day for Kate and Stevie, for me, and for Jesse.

When I pad into the kitchen, Javier sets a plate of food before me. It's gorgeous—an egg scramble with red peppers, green onions, and cheese paired with a slice of toast, a cup of fruit, and coffee. I savor my first bite.

"You've been holding out on me."

A sexy smirk appears on his gorgeous face. "No, I haven't. The other times I cooked for you was dinner. The avocado toast the other day doesn't count as a meal. I knew you needed something easy to eat while teaching. Today requires actual nourishment since we skipped dinner."

"Where's yours?"

He grins at me. "Can't run on a full stomach."

I polish off the food in near record time. With a quick kiss, I hurry into the office with a fresh cup of coffee. I fortify myself and login. Stevie joins me first and then Kate. The school counselor informed them about Jesse's fall as the cause of his absences. I haven't been informed whether they shared his prognosis with them yet.

The morning drags, but the class seems to be handling the cause of Jesse's absence well.

Suzie gives me a brief update during the midmorning snack. "Academically, the students are working well. Even with the video conferencing, they're on target with their lessons."

"You deserve the credit."

"No, you're plans are stellar. I simply assist when something goes wrong with their computers or walk them to the restroom."

"I appreciate you, Suzie."

"Thanks. Any news on J-man?"

Kate and Stevie are working on a music lesson with headphones; nonetheless, I'm grateful for her discretion.

"Nothing since last night. As far as I know, he hasn't regained consciousness and his brain activity is limited."

"How awful."

"I'm worried about Kate and Stevie. Honestly, myself too. It'll be difficult to handle if he doesn't pull through."

"The entire school community will be affected. He's vibrant and loved by everyone."

I note she used present tense. I appreciate her choice immensely, even though it could be false at this very moment. "I agree. I'll be back after a quick lunch." I sign off and take a few deep breaths.

I feel him before he touches me. Javier's arms slide around me from behind, and his head rests on my shoulder. "Hi, *corazón*."

"Hi."

"Any news?"

I shake my head. "I didn't ask you for an update last night. I'm sorry."

"Nothing for you to be sorry for. Jesse is more important than my case right now."

"Not really, but I love you for saying so."

He presses a sultry kiss to the slope of my neck and leads me to the kitchen. "Eat and I'll update you." While she eats, I share the information from the last few days.

"I assume Sam's recovery specialist is like Blaine?" Blaine is Blackthorne's independent white hat hacker. When the firm needs information, he's their guy. He's elusive. As far as I know, only Jake and his friend and former client Peter Harpin know what he looks like and where he is based.

"She bends the rules without blatantly breaking them."

"Sorry, I need to get back. Thank you doesn't begin to cover how grateful I am for you."

"I could say the same for you."

"I haven't done anything."

I cup her face in my hands. "You have sacrificed the most for us at this point. You've given up your ability to move freely, teach in person, visit your critically ill student, and socialize with your friends. I should be thanking you. I love you, Jillian. Go show Kate and Stevie how to rock a Friday preholiday afternoon."

I force a small smile. "Okay. I love you."

The afternoon zips by, especially with the Valentine swap and special snack for my class. I ordered heart-shaped cookies and sent handwritten cards to Kate and Stevie earlier this week. It's bittersweet when Suzie shows me their cards for me via video. I bid them farewell and slump into my cozy chair in the corner of my office. A workout is not in the cards for me today.

"All set with school for today?"

I nod.

"Perfect. Time to get dressed, something causal with sneakers, a coat, and gloves please."

"What's going on?"

"We're leaving the house."

"Really?" How could he possibly know? I never said aloud my need to leave these four walls. Our couple bubble is fantastic, but I need to leave for a little while.

"Yes. First, we're going for a long walk to the point at Jake's, and then I have a surprise for you."

I literally leap into his arms and pepper his face with kisses. "Thank you. Thank you. Thank you."

"While I'll gladly accept your grateful kisses, why didn't you say something, *cariña*?"

She shakes her head. "I didn't want to add to the stress for you or my brothers."

"What happened to full disclosure?"

"I refuse to force you to choose between your jobs and me. It's important to you and your piece of mind for me to stayed tucked away here in virtually complete safety. I won't take the small amount of comfort away from you."

"Promise me you'll share going forward." He presses a kiss to my forehead, his chest sinking with his deep exhale.

"I promise. How much time do I have?"

After a quick glance at his watch, he replies, "About thirty minutes."

After a peck on the lips, and I scamper upstairs to change. I hear male voices as I tug on jeans and a hoodie. It takes more time to find my gloves than anything else. As I descend the stairs, I'm able to discern the voices—my brothers, including Cam.

"Hey, guys. Thanks for coming." I hug each of them, then move beside Javier, and thread my fingers into his. Jake and Cam shake their heads while Christoph and Connor don't react.

"Let's go," Jake orders.

Javier leads me to Jake's truck, which is conveniently parked in my garage. My car is nowhere to be found, and a Blackthorne vehicle is inside as well. However they want to do this, I'm game and excited to go out.

"Follow the longer route through the nature preserve," Christoph reminds Cam who is sitting in the driver's seat of my car, which the guys moved outside.

"Will do," Cam replies and pulls away.

Javier opens the door for me and rounds Jake's truck. "I'll take route B."

"Meet you there in about twenty." Connor and Jake pile into the Blackthorne SUV and ease into traffic. Christoph drives Javier's truck and turns left at the end of the driveway away from me.

"I appreciate all this effort, but I didn't want to cause any unnecessary work for them."

He lifts my hand to his lips. "I'll do anything to make you happy. If it includes imploring your brothers for a little help, I'll do it. They're family. There was no question they would help, knowing you needed to leave the house."

"How did you know?"

"Nothing specific you did or said. I know being trapped inside isn't fun."

I raise an eyebrow. "Do you want to qualify your statement a bit?"

He laughs. "Being trapped inside with you is fun and sexy, especially with dirty, naked time sprinkled in, and it would be fine indefinitely if it were by choice."

"Better."

Javier hops out to input the code into the gate. Jake and Connor pull in behind us. As he rounds the truck, Jake and Javier exchange a few words. He leaves as Javier pulls through the gate and waits for it to close behind us.

"What happened?" I inquire.

"Nothing to worry about. Christoph witnessed an accident and rendered assistance. It'll be a bit before he gets back. The guys are going to assist."

"Okay."

Javier parks near the barn and opens my door. Hand in hand we walk around the building toward the far point of Jake's property. There's an overlook set up with tables, chairs, and, the newest addition, a designated bonfire circle. We walk for about ten minutes before I ask, "Cam?"

"I'm sure he's fine. Why are you so worried? Jake would never risk your safety or mine regardless of how we shared about our relationship."

"I know in the general sense. Either way, they're my brothers. While it's true there haven't been any more issues here, I'm still on edge. I don't like them taking risks for me, even though I'm ecstatic to be out of my house but can only go to Jake's. You are... never mind."

"*Cuentame, cariña.*" He presses a kiss to my temple as we continue to walk.

"That's dirty, Javier." I'm fairly certain those words themselves aren't dirty. However, the effect of him speaking Spanish is filthy. My heart rate increases, and the heat pools between my thighs. I instantly need a fresh pair of panties. Every. Single. Time.

He shrugs. "*Tal vez un poco.*"

"I know this is temporary, but my fear is deeper for you."

He stops walking and pulls me against him, his eyes boring into mine. "We aren't temporary." His tone is emphatic and unwavering.

His words. They aren't always eloquent, but he gets his point across each time. "No, we aren't. I meant the situation."

"Admittedly, it has taken longer than I anticipated. With Sam's help, I'll find the painting so the Spillanes will back off. I understand why Jimmy thought kidnapping me was necessary to gain access to the information. Caitryn seems savvier. More of a paper enforcer rather than a physical enforcer. Perhaps it's why there haven't been any more incidents, but I'm not willing to ease up on your security yet."

"I wouldn't ask you to with Jimmy's whereabouts only loosely known. It protects you as well. Can we not talk about the Spillanes, the painting, security, or anything other than normal stuff for the rest of the weekend?"

"We can try like hell."

He takes a seat in one of the Adirondack chairs and hauls me into his lap.

I laugh and skim my lips across his. "How willing would you be to get naked out here with me?"

"If I didn't know Jake has cameras monitoring the far corners of his property, I would be completely on board even in the dead of winter."

"Noted. I'll tuck the information away for a later time and a different outdoor location."

"As you should."

I attempt to snuggle closer, but truthfully, there isn't any space between us, literally and figuratively. "Thank you for getting me out of the house."

"You're welcome. Our little hike is only the beginning."

"You did say there was a surprise involved. When are you going to share with me?"

He checks his watch. "Soon."

"Was the watch your father's?"

He nods and kisses me. "It was the only item he left for me. I wear it as a reminder of the advice he left with me."

"What advice?"

He takes a deep, cleansing breath. "My father gave me lots of advice in the short time I had with him. Given my age, some of it didn't make sense. Most of it was about becoming a man I could be proud of. Two pieces of advice stand out actually. He said, 'Whatever our souls are made of, hers and mine are the same.' I now know, it's a paraphrase of Emily Bronte. I believe he meant there's a soul mate for everyone; we simply have to find him or her. The second was something like 'a good marriage is where both partners secretly believe they got the better deal.'"

"Both are beautiful."

"He lived by the last two. Most people were against my parents marrying. Reasons such as their age gap being too significant and nothing in common to build on. They had almost twenty years together. Mama always says it was enough for her lifetime."

"Has she dated since he passed?"

"No. She's adamant no other man would ever compare."

"She's even more impressive than I originally thought."

He brushes a kiss across my lips. "You blew her away."

Shock materializes on my face. "How? We were only there for one meal."

"Truthfully, it was more about me."

"Meaning?"

"She called you the one. *Ella es la única.* Her observation was more about how you balance me out like my father did for her."

"Is she correct?"

"More than you know. I've shared this before, and I'll share again. I never thought our conversations at the hospital would ever turn into an us."

"Me either. I'm grateful and ecstatic it has though."

"Me too, *corazón.*"

I snuggle deeper and revel in our conversation and shared words. When his case is closed, we'll be able to be a normal couple.

He glances at the watch again. "Ready for your surprise now?"

"Thank you. The hike would've been enough."

"You're welcome. Maybe for you. There's no length I won't chase to make you happy."

My head shakes furiously. "No. I meant I'm handling our current situation fine. There will be time to get back to normal when your case is over."

"True. However, you're getting a slice of normal back at Jake's as soon as we get there."

I smile, kiss his lips, and rise to stand. "Let's go then!"

"Now you're excited, and you don't even know what your surprise is."

"I'm sure it's wonderful if you took the time to put it together."

He stands, threads his fingers with mine, and hurriedly walks back to Jake's. We slip through the back wrought iron gate and climb the back porch.

I see Deni chatting with Norah through the French doors. "How did you...? You brought her here!" I pepper his lips and face with kisses. "Thank you. Thank you."

"You're welcome. Come on!"

We step inside, and Deni throws her arms around me before Javier releases my hand.

"Yay! Hey, girl!" Deni croons.

We're jumping up and down like fools. Javier and the girls—Norah, Madeleine, and Callie—have huge smiles on their faces.

"*Cariña*," Javier calls to get my attention. A chorus of oohs and aahs echo around us.

I drop my head.

"I'm joining the guys at Connor's." He presses a kiss to my temple and turns to leave.

I draw him closer and whisper, "I will thank you properly later."

"Does thanking me include clothing?" His voice is equally soft.

"Not a single thread."

I feel his face widen with a grin. "I'm looking forward to it. Have fun." He presses a kiss high on my cheek and slips away.

As soon as the door closes, Deni can no longer contain her thoughts. "Are you sure he doesn't have a brother? I'm hot and bothered from the heat of you two fully clothed."

"Deni! I can't with you."

"What does the nickname mean? His level of hot skyrockets when Spanish falls from his lips, and he's one of the hottest men I've ever seen!" Deni asks.

"That one means sweetheart."

Deni asks, "There are more?"

I grin. "Yes, but I'm not sharing any of the others." They aren't dirty but private, and I'll keep them close if I can.

Callie laughs and agrees.

"She isn't wrong. The temperature in here dropped significantly the second the door closed," Norah adds and hands me a glass of my favorite wine.

"Javier and I are…."

"Intense," Callie suggests.

"Hot as hell," Madeleine adds.

The five of us dissolve in laughter. "He's more than I ever thought I could possibly find in one man. All the pieces fit, especially the prickly ones."

"That's how you know he's a good one like Jacob."

"Ewww gross, Norah. Jake is my brother."

Norah laughs. "I said nothing about the bedroom, Jill."

"Please don't!"

Callie and Madeleine sip their waters.

"Nothing to add, ladies?" My question pointed at them.

"Nope, considering you think of our other halves like brothers too," Madeleine confirms.

She isn't wrong. "Point taken."

We each take seats in the living room and laugh and giggle for the next few hours. Our discussion pings from my relationship with Javier, to Callie and Connor's twins, to my soon-to-be nieces or nephews from Norah and Madeleine.

A harsh reminder of my reality comes crashing down on me when my phone lights up with a text from Jesse's grandmother.

Jane Sandstone: I'm sorry it's so late. We wanted to let you know. Jesse passed away about an hour ago.

I clutch my phone until my knuckles turn white. I knew this moment would come.

"Jill? Everything okay?"

"No. Jesse is gone."

Deni looks over from her seat. "Let's take a walk to Cruz. Yeah?"

"Yes."

CHAPTER TWENTY

JAVIER

I'm floating on a cloud simply from her smile. Never before have I ever wanted to make a woman smile as much as I do Jillian. I can only imagine how hard the girls are ribbing her right now. The snow crunches beneath my feet as I walk to Connor's home. Connor built their home on an available lot at the farm, complete with a recording studio for Callie.

I open the door slowly and contain a chuckle when I step inside. Amara is screaming with tears rolling down her cheeks. Myers is squirming in a small chair beside his sister Sutton who is sound asleep.

Connor appears to be warming a bottle. "Connor, how can I help? Where are Jake and C-Top?"

"The guys are out back handling a work issue that sprang up after the accident. Amara needs to eat, and Myers likely needs a fresh diaper. Pick your poison. There are supplies for both tasks in the small dresser to your right."

I search for a burp cloth, unbuckle Amara, and take the bottle from Connor. Before taking a seat, I offer the bottle to her, and the crying instantly ceases. I settle into the armchair and feed Amara. While she eats, Connor changes Myers and sets him back into his seat where he drifts peacefully back to sleep.

"Do you want me to take her?"

"Nah." I set Amara on my shoulder and pat her back until she burps. Then I cradle her in my arm again, and she goes to work on the rest of the bottle.

"How are you holding up, Cruz?"

"Not worried about me." I'll worry about Jillian every day for the rest of my life and every tiny human we create.

"Welcome to the club."

I grin at Connor. "Thanks. It's pretty fantastic, even with the circumstances I brought to her doorstep."

"Not your fault, Cruz. If I've learned anything since Calliope stole my heart, you can't control other people or their actions. You can control your reaction to the happenings in your life. You'll close the case again, for good this time, and move forward with Jill."

Sutton lets out a whimper and then starts to wail.

"I'm on it, Sutton." Connor scurries back to the kitchen.

While he makes a bottle for Sutton, Amara finishes and burps again like a champ. I set her down on the playmat off to the left of the couch.

"You're a natural, Cruz," Connor states as he feeds Sutton.

"You know being a dad is in the top three on my priority list."

"True, but most guys shy away from a screaming infant. Hell, you're surrounded by infants, and you didn't blanch at all."

"I finally found the one to grow old with which will include fatherhood. I need to secure her world first."

"We need some boundaries about sharing since you started dating my sister," Jake announces as the guys come in from the backyard.

"Everything good, Jake?" Connor asks.

"Yeah, there was a small issue with Miss Forrester and customs coming back from Thailand with Callen. It's been handled."

I respond to Jake's statement. "I have no intention of sharing anything that might make you want to strangle me, Jake. Frankly, it's none of your business. Jillian makes me happy, and I do the same for her."

"Works for me." Jake raises his water in acknowledgment, and the line of questioning ceases.

Christoph flicks on a basketball game, and we watch until Myers wakes from his power nap and his cries ramp up.

"He need to be fed too?" I ask Connor.

"Yup."

"Hook Uncle Cruz up." I unbuckle Myers and rock him while Connor fixes his bottle.

Both Christoph and Jake glance in my direction but stay silent.

"Are you sure, Cruz? You already fed Amara," Connor asks.

"Yeah, I'm sure." I take the bottle from his outstretched hand and start to feed Myers. He doesn't take as well to me sitting, so I stand and pace the floor while feeding him. I set the bottle on the island and shift him to my shoulder. As I do, I notice the ladies walking toward the house with flashlights.

"Everything okay with the girls?" I ask without turning around.

"As far as I know, why?" Jake asks.

"They're headed this way."

Connor moves to the front door and opens it as our better halves step onto the front porch. "Only guys allowed here." In direct contrast to his words, he drops a kiss to Callie's lips.

"Consider your guys' night over," Madeleine informs us.

My eyes pin to Jillian's. Her expression is hard to read given she's trying to mask her true feelings considering the company we're in. She steps in front of me and rises on her toes. "You look hot as hell holding him." She skims her lips across mine.

"Jesse?" I whisper.

Her head drops against my chest beside Myers. "Jesse is gone. Can we go home?"

"Anything you need," I murmur.

She looks up at me. I press a kiss to her forehead and hand Myers off to Callie.

"You're quite the baby whisperer, Cruz."

I grin at her and thread my fingers through Jillian's. "Jake, I'll call you in the morning to figure out the details."

"Okay. We'll be right out to get her home."

I escort Jillian out the front door, and we meander toward the cars. "How are you holding up?"

She lifts one shoulder. "I knew it was coming. Doesn't make it any easier though."

"I imagine it wouldn't. I will get you to his services." I surround her with my arms and kiss her softly.

"Thank you."

The guys join us with Deni closely behind. If Jake is uncomfortable with our level of PDA, he doesn't indicate as much.

"I'll talk to you soon." Deni hugs Jillian, who refuses to release my hand.

"Thank you for coming, Deni."

"Of course. Talk soon!" Deni hurries into her car to get warm.

"Let's get you home," Jake states.

I assist Jillian into the Blackthorne SUV. Jake follows in my truck, and Christoph follows in Jillian's car. Cam was called into the firehouse. Within thirty minutes of leaving Jake's, she's stripped down to a lacy camisole and panties and slipped beneath the cozy covers on our bed.

"I'll be right back." I press a kiss to her head and leave her in bed.

"Is she okay?" Jake asks.

"Not really. Wouldn't expect her to be. I'll call you when I have the details of the service."

"We'll get her there, even if I have to cover it with you myself," Jake promises.

"I appreciate it."

"Take care of her, Cruz."

"I will as long as she'll have me."

Jake extends his hand to me. I take it and bro hug him at the same time.

I lock everything up, shuck my clothes, and wrap my body around Jillian.

"Is he going to let me go?" Her tone is uneasy and concerned.

"I'll make certain of it."

Her head moves slightly in acceptance before she nestles deeper into my embrace until morning.

When I wake in the morning, Jillian isn't in our bed anymore. I don't sleep deeply given my military training, especially considering the security concerns currently surrounding us. The mere fact she slipped out of my grasp is unfathomable.

"Breathe, Javier." Her voice settles over me like a warm blanket as she appears at the threshold of the bedroom. "I went to make us coffee." She sets two cups on the nightstand, sets her robe on the foot of the bed, and waits for me to scoot up against the headboard. She joins me, then hands me my cup. We both savor our first cup of the day.

"How did you know I was worried?"

"I know you. You may be able to disguise your feelings from everyone else, but not me. I won't leave and make this situation harder."

"*Muy apreciado, cariña.*"

"You're welcome. I assume you need to meet with Jake today?"

"Yeah, probably by phone though."

She smiles over the rim of her cup. "I'll make sure I'm properly dressed."

I laugh, set my cup on the other night table, place hers beside it, and haul her beneath me. "It would be worth it to see his head explode if I'm paying attention to you and not him."

"True, but this time your call will be beginning not wrapping up. I'll be dressed as frumpy as I can pull off."

"It doesn't matter what you wear. I'm learning every gorgeous dip, curve, and spot to kiss and suck to steal your breath. Your efforts would be futile. Besides, you couldn't be frumpy no matter how hard you try."

"A challenge?"

"No, sweetheart, a statement of fact." I lower my mouth closer to hers.

"I give." She cranes her neck and takes my lips in a sensual kiss. She catches my bottom lip between her teeth before releasing it.

I swallow a groan and travel over her chin to the top of her shoulder. Rocking back onto my heels, I lift her cami over her head and return to my spot. I nip, suck, kiss, and savor the sweet-smelling valley between her breasts and down the midline of her body. I drag my tongue over her hip bone and the flare of her hips. She squirms beneath me. I climb upward to confirm Jillian's sweet spot. When I savor the skin just inside her hip, she attempts to move away.

"No way, gorgeous." I set one hand on her other hip and the other splayed beneath her breasts before resuming my slow, sensual torture of her skin near her pelvis.

Her eyes clamp closed, and her lips purse. I travel to her other side and note her left is more sensitive than the right. Without discontinuing my exquisite tasting of her skin, I draw two fingers along her folds.

"You're soaked."

"Yes." Her reply is breathy and needy. "I need you."

"*Si, corazón. Yo también.*"

Her eyes fly open to meet mine.

I will never tire of her reaction to me speaking Spanish to her, even if she doesn't always understand. It's sexy as hell. I widen her legs and grasp her inner thighs as I push forward into her heated center. Her hands encircle my wrists, and she meets me thrust for thrust. Her inner muscles pulse around me. My name falls from her lips as she crests the edge of bliss. Mere moments later, I follow her over.

I lower onto my forearms and skim my lips over hers.

"That one is a keeper too," she grins.

"Noted." I'm game to try every position fathomable with her.

We share the scalding hot water in her Carrara-tiled shower with waterfall showerhead. She put as much thought into the master bathroom as she did in the kitchen. After a leisurely brunch, Jillian shares the details for Jesse's services with me, and I reach out to Jake.

"Hey, Jake."

"Hey. How is she doing?"

"As well as can be expected, I suppose. The services are set for St. Ignatius Church at ten in the morning on Monday, followed by internment with his parents at Meadowbrook cemetery. The family plans to hold a reception at the school to allow for the students to be present. I realize I'm the new guy and not involved in planning, but I would like to assist for Jillian."

"I would expect nothing less. Plus, if you suggest something instead of me, she'll examine it differently."

"True."

"Staff wise, I have you, me, Christoph, Maia, and Barrett available."

For the next hour, we consider options for the three locations before bringing Jillian into our discussion.

She sidles beside me at the dining room table. "Hi, Jake. Thank you for doing this. I'm sure you're completely against me leaving the house for a public event."

"You treat your students like they're your own children. If I don't figure out a way to make it safer for you, you'll go unprotected, which isn't an acceptable option."

Jake is spot-on there.

"Thank you."

I fill her in on the details we discussed, knowing she won't be fully pleased when I get to the end. "First we'll leave here in two vehicles. You'll have to go with Jake and Maia. I'll go with Barrett." I point to the drawing I created while talking with Jake. "This is the floorplan of the church. You'll enter and exit through the side entrance and take a seat to the side near the door. Barrett and Jake will remain near the door. Maia and I will sit with you."

"With us so far?" Jake asks.

"Yeah. Keep going."

"We'll leave the church through the same door and make our way to the cemetery. You'll stay in the vehicle until the service is about to begin and hurry back as soon as it ends."

"Okay."

I pull the drawing for the school out with Xs clearly marked in almost every ingress and egress point in the building. Jillian is astute enough to know the marks can't bode well for her. I take a deep breath before continuing.

"You need me to forgo the reception." It's a statement not a question.

"Preferably… yes. There are too many unknowns."

Dejected, she leans into me. "I understand. Thank you for figuring out a way for me to honor Jesse."

I press a kiss to her temple.

"I'm sorry we can't do more, Jill," Jake offers.

"I appreciate this more than you know, Jake. I'll take what I can get."

"Cruz, I'll call the church and speak with Barrett and Maia. Please be ready to leave at eight on Monday. Jill, please contact Platt and take a personal day for the services."

"Will do," Jillian and I answer at once.

"Call me if anything changes," Jake requests.

"I will. Thanks, Jake."

"You're welcome."

I end the call and pull her into my arms. "I'm sorry we can't make it all happen, *cariña*."

Her voice is muffled against my chest. "Don't be. Jake was right. I would've gone regardless of the security plan. Most of the services is more than I expected."

I truly don't want to ask her, but it needs to be done. "Before we knew about Jesse, I planned a date for tomorrow. Do you want me to cancel?"

She inhales sharply. "You did?"

"Absolutely. It's our first one."

I can see her beautiful brain is spinning, so I give her time to think it through.

"No, but thank you for asking." Her fingers dip beneath the hem of my tee and she eliminates all the space between us. "Do you have work to do this afternoon?"

"No."

"Will you watch Jesse's favorite movies with me?"

"*Sin duda.*"

"What does that mean?"

"Without question or definitely. Do you have popcorn?"

She cocks an eyebrow at me. "Do you know me at all?"

I'm not sure if I should be offended or laugh. Thankfully, I wait long enough for her to burst into laughter.

"Come with me, my love." She leads me into the kitchen to the tall cabinet beside the refrigerator. After dutifully pulling out an air fryer and a waffle maker, Jillian kneels on the floor before reaching into the recesses of the cabinet and produces a popcorn maker.

I can't suppress the grin on my face. "You're full of surprises, aren't you?"

"Stick around. I'll share all my secrets."

"I plan to, gorgeous." I offer her a hand up and kiss her breathless.

With gourmet ingredients, Jillian pops white cheddar popcorn and buttery classic popcorn. We grab drinks and curl up on the couch for a movie marathon in honor of Jesse.

"What are his favorite movies?"

"In no particular order: *BFG, Cars, and Cars 3*.

"Cool. I've never seen any of those in their entirety. Why not *Cars 2*?"

She giggles softly. "Jesse didn't like the storyline. Also, Doc Hudson, who was voiced by Paul Newman, wasn't part of the storyline. He was very particular about his movie plots. *BFG* first?"

"Sure."

She presses play and curls against me on the couch. As I watch the movie and her, I have so many questions.

As the credits roll, she asks, "What did you think?"

"It's kind of sad at the beginning, then it gets better. Why was it one of his favorites?"

A sad smile appears on her gorgeous face. "He felt like Sophie. His parents left him because of his disability."

"How awful."

"Yeah. He didn't speak for the first few months of school."

"He was lucky to have you, Jillian."

She shrugs. "I think it was the other way around."

We snuggle up again and watch *Cars* and *Cars 3* with only a short break to order pizza. While I clear our dishes, I confirm details for our date tomorrow. When the last movie ends, we collapse into bed until morning.

My gorgeous woman is still in dreamland. I slip out of bed, change, and head downstairs to work out. As I near the end of my long run, her cute, pink toenails descend the stairs. I slow my pace to a light jog. "Morning."

"Morning." She takes a seat on the floor and stretches her legs in front of her.

When I finish, she turns on the television to a yoga session. As she begins, I steal a kiss and leave the basement. While she exercises, I make breakfast and formulate a plan to keep her busy until our date. With our breakfast nearly complete, she crests the top of the staircase.

"Happy Valentine's Day, *cariña*." I hand her a cup of perfectly sugared coffee and a single red rose and plant a soft kiss on her lips.

"Thank you. Same to you." She lifts the flower to her nose before sipping her coffee.

"You're welcome. I need a small favor from you. Actually, it's a large favor."

"Okay." Her voice is laced with concern.

"I need you to stay upstairs from one until four so I can set everything up with my worker bees. Maybe you can take a long bath and read before getting ready for our date. Cocktail attire is required."

She starts to speak but thinks better of it.

I wink at her and continue, "I'll pick you up at four."

"I'll be ready." The sliver of excitement in her response gives me hope. She was steady in her request for me not to cancel.

"Thank you." I plate our breakfast, and we lounge around until the first delivery arrives.

Jillian scurries upstairs as I approach her front door.

"No peeking," I call up after her.

Her sweet laugh echoes down the staircase.

CHAPTER TWENTY-ONE

JILLIAN

Not only with security but Jesse's passing too, Javier planned a date for our first Valentine's Day together. Only briefly did I consider asking him to cancel. After hiding away in a luxurious bath with lavender bath salts, I'm properly buffed and scrubbed. I blow out my hair and apply a small amount of makeup. When I finish everything other than slipping into my dress, I curl up on my cozy chair and read. Just before four, I shimmy into my red dress and step into my sexiest heels.

True to his word, Javier knocks on our bedroom door at precisely four.

I giggle before answering, "Come in." *Hot damn!* My man looks mouthwatering in his tailored suit with crisp white shirt.

"You look hot, *corazón.*" He hands me a bouquet of roses and sets his hand on my hip.

"Thank you. You look hot yourself. When did you sneak your suit out of our room?"

He gifts me with one of his trademark, genuine, heart-stopping smiles. "I've been planning this for a while." He steals a kiss and offers me his arm.

Nothing looks different until I turn at the base of the staircase. Fairy lights hang from the exposed beams on the ceiling and provide romantic lighting. My dining room table is now set in front of the living room fireplace. A red and orange fire is already roaring, and the table is elegantly set for a fancy dinner with china from my mother's collection.

I turn and pin my gaze to his. "How did you do all this?"

"I had some help from Cameron and your parents. The rest though, I did myself while you were upstairs relaxing."

I exhale slowly. "No one has ever done so much for me as you have."

"No one will ever get the opportunity to try again. This doesn't come close to what you deserve."

I cup his face and brush my lips over his. "I don't need all of this. I only need you."

"You have me, but I'll choose to do this and more for you every chance I get." He kisses me breathless before whispering near the shell of my hear, "Get used to it. It won't change."

All I can do is nod slowly.

He leads me to my chair and dutifully pulls it out for me. After I take a seat, he pours our wine and hurries into the kitchen.

"What are we eating?"

A sexy grin graces his face. "I took the liberty of making all of your favorite restaurant foods from appetizer to dessert. The theme is mostly about your favorites rather than a cohesive style of cooking."

I purse my lips and watch him unveil the appetizer.

"No way! How did you pull this off?"

"I did a bunch of research and recreated these while you were teaching and froze them."

"You somehow recreated southwestern eggrolls like the ones at Chili's?"

"Yes, I did. Try them."

I savor the bite. "Mmmm. Oh my… this is amazing!"

A mixture of joy and pride appear on his gorgeous face. "One down, a few more to go."

We sip our wine and devour the plate of eggrolls. Without a doubt, I consumed more than half the plate.

"Ready for dinner?"

I grin at him. "Yes." I attempt to recall what I shared as my favorite dinner all those years ago and come up empty. Now the manicotti from Romano's would be atop the list. However, there's no way for Javier to know. I never shared with him. I remember my favorite dinner dish is from Olive Garden—well, it was back then.

He sets our plates on the table and uncovers mine with flair. My plate has angel hair pasta, cherry tomatoes, asparagus, and shrimp in a light garlic sauce. Shrimp scampi—perfection on a plate.

"You're two for two."

Pride laces his response. "I remember every word, *cariña*, even if it wasn't time for us yet."

I do too. I spin the pasta around my fork. The garlic sauce is perfect, the pasta al dente, and the shrimp expertly cooked. "Delicious, Javier."

He smiles and polishes off his plate while I do the same. Soft music surrounds us after he pushes a few buttons on his phone. "Jillian, may I have this dance?"

"Yes." It takes me a solid minute in his arms to recognize the song. Truthfully, I focused more on the emotions coursing through me. The same feelings were present at the wedding. "This is the first song we danced to at the wedding."

He nods. "Yes. 'Slow Dancing in a Parking Lot' by Jordan Davis. I made a playlist of every song played while your body was pressed against mine before I crashed at my hotel."

"You're a romantic, Javier."

"Only for you."

We sway and twirl around the dining room, lost in each other. Here in this moment, everything in my world is right. I'm safely tucked in Javier's embrace, our breathing and heart beats in sync. I have no concerns other than searing these moments into my brain. It isn't until the playlist restarts that I'm willing to separate from him.

His kiss makes my knees weak before he suggests dessert. This man knows how to sweet-talk a girl—bone-melting, scorching kisses and my favorite restaurant dessert. What more could a girl want for a second date?

He serves me his attempt at red velvet cheesecake from The Cheesecake Factory.

The first bite melts in my mouth. "Javier, yours is one hundred times better than the restaurant!" Almost everyone else in my life expects me to cook, given my aptitude and enjoyment for cooking, except him. Cooking for me is one of the many ways he shows his love.

A proud smile graces his lips. I lean over and kiss him thoroughly. "More dancing or sleep?"

"More dancing, tangled sheets, then sleep," he suggests.

I slip my hand into his and step into his arms. We don't make it past the second song on the playlist before our clothes start descending to the floor. Each step toward the bedroom, more articles of clothing denote our path. A few hours later, after testing a few different positions and chasing bliss at once, Javier leaves our bed and collects our clothes. As soon as he returns, I drift off to sleep.

Near two in the morning, I wake and find Javier starting at the ceiling. "Want to talk about it?"

"No." His response is flat and laced with angst.

"You're worried about tomorrow?"

He shifts onto his side to face me. He only drops his head slightly.

"Are you worried about me or you?"

Javier leans forward and presses a kiss to my forehead. "Mostly you."

Without hesitation, I state, "If you need me to skip it entirely, I will."

"No, absolutely not! I will not allow you to sacrifice anything else for me. It's more than enough for you to teach from home." The anger in his tone is harsher than I've ever heard.

I cup his face with my hand. His jaw tics beneath my touch. "Isn't it my choice?"

He hauls me against him, his hold tight but not overly so. "Yes, but… if anyone isn't going, it's me. I'm in a bad-worse situation, *cariña*. I want to be beside you and support you. However, my presence could increase the danger to you."

"Jake is extremely thorough. If he can't render this outing safe, no one can. He would forbid me from going, like he did the hospital, if he wasn't confident in his ability to protect me at the services tomorrow."

"I understand in my head, but the pesky organ in my chest is another matter."

Oh, Javier. "Only you are more protective of me than my brothers. If Jake feels it's safe, I need to go. However, if for any reason your gut tells you something is off tomorrow at any time, say the word and I'll come straight back here. No questions asked."

The tension in his corded arms decreases, and the muscles of his jaw loosen as well. "Thank you."

"We should try to get *some* sleep," I suggest.

He draws me closer and murmurs, "I'll try."

In my experience, the weather always seems gloomy on days like today. Javier paces the length of our bedroom while I fuss with my outfit and shoes. A few passes ago, I stepped in his path. If anything, I need him to relax. I won't suggest remaining home after his reaction early this morning, but he's wound tight.

When I'm ready to go, I step in his way again. I wrap my arms around him and set my head against his chest. "Javier, talk to me."

"Leaving you here with Ben is one thing. It's even another to take a drive to Jake's. Right now, I'm terrified in equal measure like I was at the cottage."

I add space between us to look up at him. "If you won't compromise and allow me to stay here, all I can do is promise to listen to Jake."

His eyes close, and he drops his head once. "The moment you knocked on my door, everything in my world shifted to revolve around us. It will break me if something happens to you."

"I trust Jake and his team. More importantly, I trust you. We'll be fine." His deep-rooted concern for my safety is chipping away at my resolve. On the other hand, he won't let me choose to stay home. Before I can figure out a better plan, Jake and his team arrive.

Jake, Barrett, Maia, and Christoph make my living room feel tiny. Hell, Barrett could on his own. However, my recollection of the plan only calls for two of them plus Javier.

"Can I have a word with you, Cruz?" Jake asks.

"Sure." Javier takes a step toward the kitchen.

After he considers his question, Jake adds, "Jill, could you join us too?"

Javier reaches back for my hand and leads me into the kitchen. "Given the availability of the team members, we made some changes to the plan." Jake looks Javier straight on. "Cruz, you are not working today. You will be escorting Jill only as her other half." The slight stutter in my brother's voice is endearing and sappy. "Connor provided some valuable insight into your mindset given his experience with Callie and her performance at the 9/11 museum. Coupled with my difficult choice to separate from Norah for her FBI meeting, we realized you need to be there today only for Jill."

Javier's fingers tighten around mine, but his body relaxes a fraction more each moment Jake's words sink in.

Jake finishes explaining the changes. "Any questions?"

"No. Thanks, Jake," I reply.

"You're welcome."

The ride to the church is silent and uneventful. With Barrett and Maia in front of us, we step through the side door and take the closest pew. Carol, Kate's mom, and Stevie's parents acknowledge me as I take a seat. It pains me not to rush over to Kate and Stevie, but Jake's rules are what they are. I won't push my luck.

The sheer pain on Jane and Marty's faces is unbearable. If not for them, Jesse would have been a ward of the state. Given his disabilities, it likely wouldn't have been as beneficial for Jesse. The pastor begins the service. Every so often, a muffled wail or sniffle echoes around the church. Near the end of the service, the pastor opens the floor to anyone who would like to speak.

Without a second thought, Kate and Stevie walk to the front of the church. Stevie speaks first. "I had two... no, three friends at school: Miss

Jill, Kate, and Jesse. There aren't a lot of kids like us. I'll miss him forever."

Javier leans closer and whispers near the shell of my ear, "I'll get you back to school as soon as I can."

I nod once and refocus on Kate.

With her computerized voice, she addresses the mourners for Jesse. "Stevie is right. Our special world is a bit smaller and a bit dimmer without Jesse. He was our friend, and I'll miss him too."

Stevie hugs Kate, and they move back to their seats and accept hugs from their parents. As the pastor wraps up the service, Barrett taps Javier on the shoulder, and we move to the side door of the church. As I'm about to step outside, I notice a couple huddled together near the rear of the church.

"Look left," I murmur to Javier.

He turns his gaze and observes the couple. "Do you know who they are?"

"I have a thought, but let's get to the car. Then I can verify." As the answer leaves my lips, the couple advances down the aisle.

"Let's move a bit faster," Javier recommends forcefully.

Sandwiched between Barrett and Maia, we walk briskly to our car. Jake is dutifully behind the wheel while Christoph stands ready to open the door.

Once we settle inside, I pull out my phone and hope my instinct is right. As I pull up the images on my phone, I hear a commotion outside the car. Instantly, Javier tenses beside me.

I lean into him and whispers, "Breathe, Javier. They're Jesse's parents."

He relaxes but not enough for my liking.

"We just want to talk to her. To thank her." Their words are forced out between sobs.

I turn and look through the rear window. It's tinted so they can't see in. It's the same couple.

"I'll let her know what you said," Christoph states before sliding into the front seat beside Jake. "Go."

Jake pulls away and drives toward the cemetery.

"Do you know who they were?" Christoph asks after a few blocks.

I turn my phone so he can see the images from Jesse's student file. "They are Jesse's parents. They took off when they couldn't handle his disability any longer. Jane and Marty have been his caretakers since he was diagnosed near six months old."

The remainder of the day is smooth. Maia escorts me—Javier glued to my side—to share my condolences with Jane and Marty. I drift toward the back of the crowd and stand surrounded by Jake's team. I'm even able to talk to Kate and Stevie briefly as they leave the cemetery. Walking away from them is harder than I anticipated. It's one thing to know they're safe in the classroom while I'm at home. Here I feel as if

I'm risking them a bit. However, I needed to pay my respects to Jesse and his family.

The next few days are a blur. The realization that Jesse isn't coming back and the impact on Kate and Stevie is markedly obvious. During my lunch break, I arrange for a visit from the district's therapy dog whose handler just happens to be a counselor for special needs students.

During their visit at the end of the week, I simply observe and listen as Gina gently walks them through their feelings about Jesse while Rosie gratefully accepts all the belly rubs she can handle.

CHAPTER TWENTY-TWO

JAVIER

I don't recall how well, or perhaps how poorly, I handled my grief when my father passed. I was young and solely focused on my role as man of the family at fifteen. As far as I can tell, Jillian is trudging through for Kate and Stevie. She booked a therapy dog visit with a counselor for her students this afternoon.

After lunch, I reach out for updates about the case, starting with Sam.

"Hi, Cruz."

"Hey, Sam. How are things there?"

He pauses as if searching for the correct words. A sweet wail carries through the phone.

"Congratulations!"

"Thanks. Savannah and Bennett are doing well. Emme is doting on both as best a two-year-old can, such as delivering water to Savannah and a pacifier to her little brother."

"Great name! I can call back at a more convenient time."

"Thanks. I appreciate the offer, but no need. Right now, life is a fuzzy movie on repeat with not enough sleep, feedings, and playtime with Emme until the little guy gets onto a schedule."

Sounds perfect to me. I can't wait to be a bleary-eyed new dad.

Sam continues, "I retained Samara Livingston to locate and retrieve the painting about a week ago. She provides weekly updates. At this point, it was all I could do. Bishop indicated he was near the end of his legal retrieval options. I read between the lines. Samara has pulled off the impossible more than once for me. Ideally, she can again."

"You only employ the best. She'll get it done this time too."

"I certainly hope so. I need this case to go away for good this time, as I'm sure you do as well."

"Yes. Jillian's safety is atop my list of priorities."

"How is Jake handling your relationship with his younger and only sister?"

"Better than I expected." I hear a sweet, muffled voice, probably Emme. "I'll let you go. Please extend my well wishes to Savannah. Let me know when you have an update."

"Thanks, Cruz. I will."

Jillian and I will get there with little people underfoot. Before I talk myself out of it, I call Bishop. Sam gave me a small update, but Bishop may know more.

"Hi, Cruz."

"Bishop. I just finished talking with Sam. Any other updates, outside of tracking the painting, you can share?"

"You were my next call. Caitryn Spillane has been lying low. Procedurally, there isn't anything left for her to do. It leads me to believe she knows where the painting may be. However, I have no grounds to pull her in for questioning. Not one shred of evidence connects her to the armored car theft."

"Understood. Until she makes a move, there isn't anything else to do. Has Babylon resurfaced?"

"I wish. No one has seen him since Tyson almost three weeks ago. Were you able to identify the women who visited Babylon?"

"Most of them. Blaine provided me video from the security camera across the street. I was able to positively identify three of the four women. I had Blaine run a search on them, and they appear to have worked for a high-end escort service run by Olga Petrovski. The disconnected number can be traced back to a private event planning corporation. Blaine was able to pull the business records. Olga is listed as the president, and the business has been in the red since it was formed."

"The events company is a front for Ms. Petrovski's escort service," Bishop shares.

"Almost certainly. Like Caitryn, there isn't anything I can do with the information at this point. As far as the fourth woman, there wasn't a clear enough image even for Blaine."

"Unfortunate. It means we have only two avenues of investigation right now: Babylon and recovering the painting."

"Pretty much," I reply. "Babylon has disappeared completely. I would think he has spy craft training if I didn't know better."

Bishop laughs. "No kidding. The only people I know who can disappear as well as he has are spooks." There must be a different way to track him. I push the thought aside.

"Anything from Davidson?"

"Nothing since your last official day of work under his command."

"Okay."

"How often does your gut turn out to be wrong, Cruz?"

"Rarely."

"Same. We keep Davidson on the board until we can figure out why both of us are on edge about him."

"Understood. I'll let you know if I learn anything of value."

"Same here. Later, Cruz."

As I end the call and lean back away from the island, the doorbell rings. I notice Jillian hasn't left her office yet. The counselling must be running over.

I open the front door but leave the locked screen door between myself and the delivery guys.

"I have a delivery from Gemma Watson," the young man states.

"You can leave it on the porch."

"No problem. There's a lot." He makes upward of six trips to and from his van with bags loaded with groceries. Are we having a party I'm not aware of?

After he makes the final trip, he waves and pulls out of the driveway. I pull the bags into the foyer and relock the front door. Then I move the bags into the kitchen.

On my final trip, Jillian steps out of her office. "Oh good, the food is here."

"Are we having a party?"

She pulls her lower lip between her teeth.

My woman slays me with that move, and she knows it. "Stop that!"

"Uh-uh."

I round the island and haul her against me. She releases her lip with a squeak.

"I may have volunteered to host a family dinner tomorrow."

"Does Jake know about this?"

She huffs in my arms and laughs. "Yes, dear. My big, bad, protective—though not as protective as you—brother signed off on this party. It was already scheduled for everyone to meet the twins. He approved moving it here instead of me going to the farm again."

"Okay."

"We met the twins."

"I know, but my parents and Cam haven't."

"Are you working out?"

"No, not today."

"How are Kate and Stevie?"

She shrugs. "Anytime they get to spend with Rosie is fun. I'm sure talking to Gina will help going forward."

"What about you?"

"Jesse isn't the first student I've lost, but it's still hard. I knew going in I would likely outlive most of my students. They're all special to me." Her arms tighten around me.

Truly, there are no words to comfort her. She needs time. Of all people, I understand. I'll get to Arlington as soon as I can. I owe it to Adams, Jones, and Carter to fulfill my promise.

I press a kiss to her head. "Let's put the perishables away, make dinner, and curl up in front of a blazing fire."

"Sounds perfect."

While she starts dinner, I put away the perishables and set the remaining food on the dining room table. "How many people are you cooking for tomorrow?"

"Just my family."

I do a quick count in my head and come up with about thirteen people. "What are we cooking?"

"You're going to help?"

"Of course. I love cooking with you."

She leans over the island and plants a kiss on my lips. "I plan on chicken parmesan, eggplant parmesan, ziti, garlic bread, and antipasto boards as appetizers. For dessert, I have ingredients for a make-your-own cannoli bar."

"I'm officially salivating now."

She laughs softly. "You're going to have to wait for those dishes until tomorrow, but dinner for tonight is almost done."

"Already?"

"Yes. I set up everything for our dinner during lunch while you were working."

She plates burgers with gorgonzola cheese, bacon, caramelized onions, a red jam, and sweet potato fries. We chat about the updates from Sam and Bishop while we eat.

"Interesting. Now you just wait until Samara finds the painting or Babylon makes a mistake?"

"Pretty much," I reply.

As planned, we clean the kitchen and snuggle up in front of a blazing fire until sleep calls us both.

CHAPTER TWENTY-THREE

JILLIAN

A family dinner prepared by me is about as close to a normal Saturday as can be. True, I can't leave my house, but everyone will be here later.

"Rise and shine, babe. We have tons of work to do."

Javier groans and turns toward me in our bed. "How did you slip away again?"

"Perhaps you sleep more soundly with me than without."

His lips curl up into a small smile. "Maybe." He peeks at the clock. "*Cariña*, it's barely after six in the morning on a weekend."

I laugh softly. "I know, but we need to get started on cooking for my family."

"Fine, I'm coming." He rises, steals a kiss, and moves into the bathroom.

"I'll make you a cup of coffee." I return to the kitchen and prepare a second cup for me and one for Javier.

When he joins me, I take a moment to enjoy the view over the rim of my mug. My man is always gorgeous, even post-workout. However, fresh out of bed with mussed hair and his dark-rimmed glasses is my favorite version. We drink in silence. When he reaches the bottom of his cup, he notices the kitchen has turned into a pasta factory.

"How long have you been up exactly?" He surveys the island and food prep I already completed.

I shrug. "Not too long. Since five-ish."

"I'm partially caffeinated. How can I help?"

I start Javier cooking the noodles for the ziti and then direct him to the antipasto boards while I work on the main dishes. We work for about two hours, then take a break to eat a small breakfast. With our bellies full, we move on to seasoning the garlic bread and preparing the filling for the cannoli. Then we add more tables and chairs in the living room.

Near noon, I set the food into the oven with a timer to start in an hour and hurry upstairs to shower. As I'm about to step out, Javier blocks my exit.

"We don't have enough time for friskiness in the shower," I remind him.

"There's always time."

I make the mistake of setting my hand on his chest. The heat of him beneath my fingers liquifies my resolve, and it flows down the drain with the water bouncing off our bodies. With one large step, he pins me against the cool tile and drags a finger down my belly. I widen my legs inviting him to touch me. Without hesitation, he spears me with his fingers.

"How are you this soaked for me if we don't have enough time?"

I exhale and reply, "I never said I wasn't turned on or unwilling. Dripping with need is a given when you're nearby. It is when you're not too. I only reminded you of the time constraints."

"Want me to stop?"

"Hell no."

He lowers his lips to mine. "There's my feisty woman." After teasing me to the brink of orgasm, he withdraws his fingers, strokes himself twice, and sheaths himself to the root. He anchors one hand at my hip while the other wraps around my waist.

I dig my fingernails into his shoulder blades to assist in balancing on my toes of one foot. *Holy hell!* "Feels… damn."

We find our rhythm and chase our release faster than ever before. I shudder around him as he tenses and explodes inside me. After recapturing our breath, I rinse expeditiously and hurry out of the steamy enclosure.

"What's the rush?" He catches my arm as I step out.

"If I stay with you, I'll want a repeat performance."

"I'll happily oblige."

I kiss him and respond, "I know. We truly don't have any more time now though."

He frowns and kisses my hand before releasing me.

I scurry around the bedroom and throw on some clothes. As I hit the bottom step, Callie knocks on the door.

"Hey. Kudos for being first with three infants," I say after opening the door.

Connor sets the twins on the floor of the foyer, then lifts Amara's carrier.

Callie scoffs. "It's a piece of cake when you've been up for hours on end. Thank you for hosting."

Javier hustles down the stairs, bro hugs Connor, and takes a crying Amara into the living room.

"Want to borrow her for a bit, Cruz?"

"Only for some snuggles, then I need to move on to Sutton and Myers. I need to be fair to all three." Within moments of Javier lifting her from her carrier, Amara is quiet.

Callie's eyes dart to mine. "I thought it was hot after girls' night. He's truly a baby whisperer."

I can't wait until the baby is ours. "Yeah, he is."

Soon after they get settled, I move into the kitchen and set out the appetizers. Javier greets a steady flow of guests, usually with one of the babies cradled in the crook of his muscled arms. I've known about his desire to have a large family since we met. Seeing it with our nieces and nephew is something else. *So damn hot!*

"Earth to Jill," Norah breaks into my thoughts.

"Hey, Norah. Do you need something?"

She shakes her head. "You need to stop looking at Cruz like he's your last meal or your brothers are going to lose their minds. Sweet mercy! You're going to start a fire in your own kitchen."

I feel my cheeks heat up. "You know how you and Jake can't seem to keep your hands and lips to yourselves, even when people are around?"

"Yeah."

"Well, Javier is equally, if not more, affectionate than Jake."

"Oh."

I nod curtly. "Yeah. I'm completely on board, except the guys will freak out. Hence why I'm swooning over him with the babies from a distance. This morning's shenanigans barely took the edge off."

"I guess you weren't kidding."

"Not even a little." Exploring new positions with Javier is fast becoming my favorite pastime.

Jake steps into the kitchen, slides his arm around Norah, and kisses her possessively. After pulling away, he says, "Thanks for hosting, Jill."

"Thanks for allowing me to, Jake."

I excuse myself and check on the food.

Javier corners me in the dining room with Sutton sleeping on his shoulder. "Hi, *cariña*. Are you trying to avoid me?"

"Not exactly." I motion for him to step into my office and close the door behind him. "Norah already called me out for gawking at you with the babies. I'm trying and failing to hide the effect it has on me apparently."

"I'll hand them back to their parents."

I rise on my toes and skim my lips across his. "No. Get in as many snuggles as you want. I'll keep my hands in my pockets and attempt to school my face."

He laughs. "Good luck with that!"

"Ha ha ha."

I slip out of my office and greet my parents with a huge hug. "Hi. Thank you for coming."

"I'm glad Jake let you host. It seemed easier than moving you," Dad offers.

"I agree."

"How are you holding up?" Mom throws her arm around my shoulders.

"It's a lot with the remote teaching and losing Jesse. I would prefer to be present for Kate and Stevie, but I understand why I can't. The guys will get me back there as soon as they can."

"They will. How is it having Cruz here suddenly?" Mom asks.

"Being with him or living with him?"

"Both, I guess," she replies.

I assumed Dad would share with her. "It isn't as sudden as it seems." I loop my arm around hers, and we take a seat in my office while Dad heads into the kitchen to talk with the guys. I share the same information with her as I did with my dad with a little extra gushy love stuff. She can handle it.

"Oh, Jillian. Is he the guy you mentioned a few years ago? The one where the time wasn't right for either of you?"

"Yes, he is."

"What a beautiful beginning."

I smile at her. "Thanks. He's incredible and—"

Javier interrupts, "Don't let me stop you from sharing my finest attributes with your mom."

I beam at him. "Everything okay out there?"

"Yes, except the warmer timer is about to expire. Time to eat, right?"

I laugh. "Are you ever not hungry?"

"Nope."

Mom adds, "Spoken like a true guy."

We laugh, and I get to work in the kitchen serving dinner with Javier by my side. After dinner is a feeding frenzy for the babies. I handle Myers, Javier takes Sutton, and Mom feeds Amara to give Callie and Connor a break.

"It's been a long time since I fed an infant. Norah and Madeleine, how are you feeling?" Mom asks them.

"I'm ready to be done," Madeleine offers.

"Same," Norah agrees, "but we both have at least a month to go. Can I help set up the dessert bar, Jill?"

"I'll take him," Javier offers, even though he's still holding Sutton who is sound asleep.

I raise an eyebrow at him. "I'll set him on the blanket."

I hurry into the kitchen and set up the cannoli bar on the island.

Mom soon follows to assist. "Does Javier have any nieces or nephews?"

"Just these three so far. Why?"

"He'll be an amazing father someday."

I smile inwardly because, to me, it isn't a new revelation. "Yes, he will."

There isn't one person who isn't raving about the dessert. Aside from seeing my students progress, my family stuffed with food I prepared is all the thanks I need.

Slowly, our guests leave. I tidy up and move the extra chairs back to the garage. I catch Jake before he and Norah leave.

"Can we talk about an outing for Javier?"

"Where?" Jakes asks.

"To visit Adams, Jones, and Carter."

Understanding crosses Jake's face. "He shared the entire story with you, huh?"

I drop my head. "Yes. He needs to visit though. He gave them his word."

"I assume you want to be beside him?"

Sin duda runs through my mind. "Without question."

Jake nods. "I'll create a plan, but perhaps you can go when the case is closed instead, no security necessary."

"Thanks, Jake."

"You're welcome."

After I return inside, we collapse onto the couch with a glass of wine.

"Thanks for your help today."

"I was going to apologize for not helping enough."

"Why would you think an apology is necessary?"

He grins at me. "I spent most of the day with the guys and the babies."

"One isn't necessary. I'm grateful you have a good relationship with them personally too." Doesn't every girl want her man to get along with her family and their significant others?

"Me too." When we finish the bottle, we climb into bed hand in hand.

CHAPTER TWENTY-FOUR

JAVIER

The next few weeks have been smooth sailing. Sam's risk on hiring Samara paid off—sort of. She located the painting yesterday. However, where she found it proves difficult.

"Are you serious?"

Sam scrubs his hand down his face on the screen. Bennett is sound asleep beside him in a swing. "I wish I was kidding. Samara traced the painting to a luxury condo on the Upper East Side. The owner of the condo is Moniker Inc, the parent company of Olga Petrovski's event planning business."

"How is Olga connected to Caitryn, if at all?"

"I don't see one aside from Babylon using her escort service unless Caitryn used her event planning services."

"So Moniker has a legal and illegal side of the business."

"Yes, it seems that way."

"We can't retrieve the painting because Samara located it by less-than-legal means," I guess.

"Yes."

"Now what?" I ask even though Sam won't have a satisfactory answer.

"We wait until someone slips up or we find another connection."

"Has Bishop found any connection between Caitryn and the armored car company?"

"Not as of my last call with him. He's on my list for today though."

Sam nods. "Please let me know if he has additional information."

"I will. Any security issues since Maia left?"

"No. I have no interest in the case other than the fact Morgan Insurance is the actual owner of the painting. For a painting I want nothing to do with, it's taking up a significant amount of my energy."

"I understand. I need the case over too. Hopefully, someone will make a mistake soon."

"Thanks, Cruz."

"Welcome. I'll update you when I know more." I end the call and lean back against the couch.

"Not a good update?" Jillian asks as she steps into the living room.

"Is it lunch already?"

She leans forward and kisses me lightly. "Not quite. Kate and Stevie are attending a schoolwide assembly in the gym. I have a short break."

"Sam's retrieval specialist found the painting."

"But?"

"It's in a condo owned by Moniker, Inc. The president is Olga Petrovski, and we can't use any of her intel to reobtain the painting."

"Is that Caitryn?" She points to the file on the tufted ottoman.

"Yes." Caitryn is a tall, thin woman with fiery red hair and distinctive green eyes.

"She's pretty. Intriguing given she might be running one of the largest mob families on the east coast. Babylon?" Jillian points to the man in the file to the left.

"Yeah."

"I wonder if the awkward nerd look is for show."

"Could be."

"At least you've made progress, right?"

I shrug. "I guess."

She draws my attention back to her face. "Javier, I have faith in you. With the guys, Bishop, and Sam, you'll close the case."

"Thanks, *cariña*. Get back to class."

She steals another kiss and walks back to her office.

I sort through the information from Sam and call Bishop. "Morning, Bishop."

"Cruz. What can I do for you?"

"Nothing. I have an update." I share the information I learned from Sam.

"Well, at least we located the stolen masterpiece, even if we can't touch it," Bishop observes. "Hold on, Cruz."

I move to the refrigerator and rummage for fixings for lunch. With the phone on speaker, I prepare lunch for the two of us. Jillian joins me right before Bishop rejoins the call. I raise my finger to my lips.

She nods.

"Cruz?"

"I'm here."

"There has been a development. I stepped away to take a call from Tyson. It appears Stephen Babylon returned home late last night. He collected his mail and asked not to be disturbed."

"What can we do with this information?"

"I've put a tail on him and will monitor the helipad too. It's the only conceivable way he left the building the last time. I also have units on Caitryn, as well as Jimmy merely because he's her brother. It was a tad tricky to get her tail without revealing I know where the painting is. I'm going to work my contacts to see if I can find an avenue to bring Caitryn in for a discussion. She's savvy, so I don't know if she'll come without Attorney Jameson. If I can arrange it, I would prefer you to be present."

"Understood."

Jillian freezes with her sandwich in midair at his request, worry plastered on her beautiful face. I would have to go into the city and sit in a room with Caitryn Spillane, who likely levied the current threat against me, my fellow officers, and their families. If it will close this case, I'll sit in a conference room with her despite the fact her brother attempted to abduct me at the cottage.

"I'll reach out when I have more." Bishop ends the call.

I set the phone down and surround her in my arms. "Knowing Babylon's whereabouts and the location of the painting is progress. I'll go sit in a room with Caitryn and her lawyer if it will close this case." I need to for her, for us, regardless of the risk I would be taking.

"I need to get back to class. Can we talk more about this later?"

"Of course." I press a kiss to her temple and let my hands slide down her form until she's out of reach.

I exhale sharply. My next call may be rough.

"Hey, Cruz," Jake answers on the first ring.

"There have been some developments." I share all the latest information with him and wait for him to formulate his thoughts and opinions.

"You want my opinion whether Jill can go back to teaching in person safely given all the parties have been located and are under Bishop's surveillance?"

"I would appreciate some insight, feedback, and perhaps the start of a plan to get Jillian back to school, whether I go or someone else."

"Maia, Alex, and Barrett are local right now. Let me see what the schedule will look like if you need to go to the city."

"Thanks, Jake. I hate her being stuck here because of me."

"She doesn't feel stuck, Cruz."

"I know, but it still doesn't sit right with me." Even though I promised to stay out of her office, I move to the door and call her name.

She turns the camera to the side as I walk around so her students can't see me in the office. "Everything okay?"

"Yeah, but I need to sit here if you don't mind."

"I don't mind." She kisses me and resets the camera. Jillian continues teaching for the next two hours while I stare in admiration. I'm sure watching her teach in front of her students is even more awe-inspiring.

She signs off and curls up in my lap. "Want to talk about whatever is bothering you?"

"It's nothing you don't already know. It hit me hard today when I agreed to meet with Caitryn in New York. We don't have any proof she sent the threat, but it still doesn't make me feel better about the whole thing, and I'm sure it makes you want to hurl."

"Your description is disturbingly accurate."

"I know it needs to be done, but I'm stuck between the reality where I have no choice and the consequence is the case doesn't get closed."

Jill cups my face with her small hands. "To get where we want to be, you need to go to New York, and I need to control my reaction to you putting yourself in danger for us."

"I don't want you to hide it from me."

"Not what I meant. I need to control it for me too. In my head, I know you'll take every precaution you can. My concern isn't for something you don't do to protect yourself, but something unexpected someone else does you didn't think of. I know it's grasping at straws. Your job has inherent risks. It's hard…."

"I know. You also planned on sharing your life with private security personnel where the risk is drastically less. Yet I'm still working with

Bishop at the same level of danger as with the NYPD. I need you to know, the only place I want to be is safely with you."

She nods and snuggles deeper into my arms.

"Jake is working to see if we can get you back to school in person soon. There's no reason for you to stay here when every key player in the city is under FBI surveillance round the clock."

She lifts her eyes to mine. "Really?"

"*Si, cariña.*"

She pulls her lower lip between her teeth and rolls over it. As she releases it, I suck it into my mouth. Without another word, she leads me into our bedroom where we stay twisted around one another and our sheets until Jake calls near seven.

I shift against the headboard with Jillian's naked curves plastered against me. "Yeah, Jake," I answer to be sure she knows who is calling.

"I'm going to send you a tentative schedule. I need to confirm with Platt. She requested to meet whoever will be with Jill before agreeing."

If Platt wants to meet the team, it means we won't be relegated to the parking lot.

"Whatever will make her comfortable, I'll do it."

"I thought you might. We'll likely meet with her tomorrow late morning. Dad will spend the day with Jill."

"She won't leave, Jake."

"I know she won't, but it'll make me feel better knowing she isn't alone."

"Same. I'll confirm more details in the morning."

I end the call with Jake, set an alarm for the morning in case we sleep all night, and wiggle back down into bed.

The alarm blares at five.

"Snooze, press snooze!" Jillian whines.

"Just one," I reply. I press a kiss to her head and silence my alarm for ten more minutes. I failed miserably at just one. Nearly thirty minutes later, we're scrambling to get ready before class starts for Jillian.

"I would apologize for stealing your workout time, but I'm not truly sorry."

I grin at her. "These abs take work, sweetheart. Can't skip workouts, especially with your spectacular cooking."

"I would love you without them."

"How sweet. Hustle up, Kate and Stevie will be waiting." I steal a kiss and gently shove her toward her office. "I'll bring you coffee."

"You're the best."

"Only for you. Now go!"

After brewing coffee and making a small breakfast, I sneak into the office and back out.

Ben and Jake arrive near nine. "Morning, Cruz."

"Morning, Ben. She's in her office."

Ben nods and moves into the kitchen.

"Hey, Jake. Where is the rest of the team?"

"Morning, Cruz. Waiting in the car. We weren't sure where she was set up to teach. Didn't want to interrupt."

"Okay. I'll be right back." I leave Jake, grab a fresh cup for Jillian, and poke my head into the office.

"Leaving?" she whispers and takes the cup.

I nod. "Love you."

"Love you."

I slip out and come face-to-face with Jake. "You done?"

"Seriously, Jake?"

He cracks a smile. "I'm still getting used to you dating my only sister."

"Okay."

"In all seriousness, I'm happy the two of you found one another."

"Thanks. Let's get my woman back to school."

"Cruz!"

I raise my hands in question. "What? Too far?"

Jake laughs. "Too far. Too soon."

I laugh and follow Jake out the door. If I'm not mistaken, Ben is laughing at the granite island too. Barrett, Maia, and Alex greet me when I take the open seat in the vehicle. I reply in kind.

When we arrive at the school, Janice ushers us into a conference room beside the main office. "Principal Platt will be right with you."

"Thank you, Janice," I respond for the group.

"You're welcome," her voice is shaky given her diminutive stature and the sheer amount of space we consume in a room.

Almost immediately, Principal Platt joins us. "Good morning. Thank you for coming in."

"Morning. Nice to see you again," Jake greets her.

"Likewise. In an effort to keep things calm around here, I felt Jill's students should meet your team before they are fixtures in her classroom."

"Understood. Mainly, Cruz will accompany Jill to and from work. However, it's probable one of the other team members will be here, so I brought them all."

"Thank you."

Jake introduces each team member to Platt, ending with me.

Platt speaks next, "What do you need from me?"

"We need to walk to her classroom, and we'll be on our way for today. One team member will be here with Jill until the security issue is closed, which should be sooner rather than later. We'll scale down when the case wraps. However, Jill feels her students will be better served with her in the building rather than remotely, although she greatly appreciates your accommodation."

Platt nods. "Janice will escort you to Miss Blackthorne's classroom. Suzie is present with Kate and Stevie. Of course, Jill is remote teaching as well."

We follow Janice down the hall to Jill's room. After a light knock, we enter the room.

"Suzie, the team wanted to see Jill's room."

"Hello," Suzie replies.

Collectively, the team acknowledges her.

"Smile Guy!" Kate perks up, her words coming through the computer beside her.

"Hi, Kate. Nice to meet you in person." I extend my hand to her.

"Did you know he was coming, Miss Jill?"

I look over my shoulder, and my gorgeous woman is blushing. Maia and Alex are grinning, and Barrett is completely ignoring Kate's name for me.

"I did, but they arrived sooner than I expected. I planned to prepare you first. Kate and Stevie, these people work for my brother Jake. He's the one with the blue shirt on."

Jake waves to them.

Jill introduces everyone by name. "One of them will be with me at school for a while."

"Are you sick?" Stevie asks.

"No, stuff outside of school is complicated, so I'll have an escort to school."

"Cool. You're really tall," Kate looks up at Barrett.

He crouches down beside her. "Hi, Kate. Yes, I am. It just means the rain hits me first."

Kate chuckles.

"When are you coming back?" Stevie asks.

Jake replies, "Tomorrow."

Kate and Stevie cheer while Jillian beams. Even though she's on the screen, her joy is abundantly clear. She misses her classroom.

We chat with the students a bit more and exit the classroom.

"What is the status of the ingress and egress during the school day?" Maia asks.

Jake shares the details of the building and the timing while we ride back to Jill's, as well as the schedule of staff who will accompany her to school.

"Thanks, Jake. Later, guys." I offer.

Each mumbles a reply of some kind except Jake. "I have a call with Blaine later. I'll let you know if I learn anything pertinent."

I nod, hop out of the SUV, and hurry up the front steps. As I step inside, Ben is approaching the door, ready to take down whoever is intruding.

"Cruz, you had me worried there for a minute."

"Sorry, Ben. I'll knock or call next time."

"Hopefully, there won't be a next time. Jake indicated you were close to wrapping up your case."

"True, at least I believe we're close. All the players are under FBI surveillance, which allows Jillian to physically go back to work."

"I'm sure she's thrilled."

"She is. Thank you for spending your morning here."

Ben sets his hand on my shoulder. "I'll do anything for my children, their significant others, and my future grandchildren."

"Thank you." In this moment, I'm sure when this case is complete, I'll just be me. Javier Cruz, a man head over heels for Jillian Blackthorne. Her family will welcome me without hesitation for any danger I may bring with me. It's also nice to have a quasi-father figure in my life again. I miss my father every day. Having the Blackthornes in my corner is appreciated.

CHAPTER TWENTY-FIVE

JILLIAN

I'm nervous for today. There's no reason for me to be nervous.

"Ready, *cariña*?"

"Yes. Do we need to go over the ground rules again?" I follow him to the garage and climb into the passenger seat of his truck.

He purposefully pouts at me. "No. I don't like your ground rules, but I understand why we need them."

"Javier, we need to be cognizant of my students and where we are. No touching and no kissing while we're in the building."

"I'll do my best. I crave the taste of you on my lips and the softness of your curves in my arms."

I turn away from him and push out a breath. "The things you say."

"It's how I feel, Jillian."

"I know, and I feel the same. However, we need to act like adults, not two people madly in love while we're in the building."

"I promise to try to be on my best behavior."

The ride is uneventful, and we make it with plenty of time. About ten feet from her classroom, Deni loops her arm around mine and joins us.

"I can't believe you're here with arm candy too!"

I can feel my face heat up. "Stop, Deni! It's too early."

"As if you haven't done the deed already at least once today."

I glance over at Javier. It was more than once. Given my nervousness of returning, we've been awake since before five. The multiple, all-consuming orgasms took the edge off my nervousness until I got into his truck.

"Ohmigod! I was kidding around. I need details! Then, you need to clone him for me. I could use some wake-up sexy times myself."

I would apologize for her, but it won't matter. Deni is Deni. I giggle, hug her, and shoo her back to her own classroom. Javier settles into a chair off the side, and I wait for my students.

"Good morning, Kate," I greet her when she arrives. The parents were given advance notice and bio information for the team members who may be with me.

She indicates she wants a hug, and I happily oblige. "You too, Smile Guy!"

Javier ambles over to her and allows her to hug him.

Kate whispers something to Javier, but I can't make it out. They hook their pinkies together.

He smiles. "I will, pinkie promise."

I raise a curious eyebrow. Javier doesn't even attempt to explain his alliance with Kate. I'm quickly distracted by Stevie entering the room.

"Yay! You're back!"

We go through our practiced handshake. Stevie nods to Javier and takes his seat. The first morning back moves smoothly. Thanks to Suzie, Kate and Stevie are still entrenched in their school routines.

Suzie joins us and escorts Kate and Stevie to the cafeteria for lunch. I lock my door, draw Javier into the only private spot, and kiss him breathless.

Kiss.

"For the record—" he attempts.

Kiss.

"I'm not the one—"

Kiss.

"Who caved first."

I laugh against his mouth and kiss him again until I feel less caged. "Noted."

I unlock the door, lead him to my desk, and we share lunch. The afternoon ends quickly, and we escort the students to the dismissal area.

"Can I make a request?" Javier murmurs near my ear after taking the driver's seat.

"Yes." My voice sounds uncertain.

"When you don't need an escort to work, will you create a reason for me to join you at least once a month?"

My heart tightens in my chest. He wants to visit my students even when I don't need a bodyguard. I swallow the lump in my throat. "I'll see what I can do."

When we arrive home, we both change to work out since he exchanged his morning gym time for sheet time—morning sexy time I'll willingly repeat daily. After my workout, I cool down while ogling him on the treadmill. There's something about the way his abs move as he runs—

"Stop staring at me like I'm a piece of meat!" he bellows.

"Nope, not a chance. You can stare whenever you want, so can I."

"I'll keep it in mind for future reference." He slows down to a jog and then to a fast walk before ending his workout. "How are you feeling about today?"

"I think it went well. However, you aren't allowed to keep secrets with my students."

A wide smile grows on his sweaty face. "Kate said she liked you before we met, but this version of you is happier. She made me pinkie promise not to leave, at least until she isn't your student anymore."

My eyes widen. "I only get two more months! Damn, too bad. I was beginning to love having you around."

"No, *corazón*, you can have every second you desire."

"Javier, I'm kidding. I'll work on my sarcasm tone. Two months will never be enough, neither will two years, or two—"

Before I can finish, he covers me with his body and kisses me senseless. After stripping out of our clothes and chasing bliss for the third time today in the basement, we crest the stairs to shower. How many rooms are left to christen? I wonder.

"Where did your mind go?" he asks as we make our way to the shower.

I wrinkle my nose instead of answering.

"Still adorable. Now spill, gorgeous."

"I was mentally checking off a list of rooms in the house where we've been together."

"Oh, I see. Well, I need a list so we can check off each room."

"I'll happily oblige after dinner."

We make dinner, discuss locations for our list, and Javier fields a call from Bishop.

Over the next week, our days and nights are similar. Not exactly the same, but we make a dent in the list of rooms to be crossed off the naked list. Our domestic bliss comes to a screeching halt when Bishop schedules a meeting with Miss Spillane, her attorney, and Stephen Babylon for tomorrow afternoon.

Panic overcomes me in the span of the minute it takes Javier to fill me in. My pulse is racing, and my heart is pounding in my chest. Thankfully, I'm able to calm myself some before he notices. I take a seat on the couch.

He lowers to the ottoman, straddles my legs with his, and links our hands. "Jillian, I'm going to the FBI office in the city. Bishop will escort me from the airport. I'll take every precaution possible."

"You must realize by now, I trust you. It's everyone else I don't trust. I'll be fine. Who is staying with me at the house?"

"No one."

Intriguing. "Barrett will escort you to class tomorrow. Then Maia will be your shadow for a few days afterward. The number will depend on the outcome of my meeting with the interested parties. Please only go to school and then come home."

"I will."

We sit in silence for a few minutes. "I should pack," Javier states.

"Takeout?"

"Sure." His tone indicates the last thing he cares about right now is dinner.

Nearly an hour later, the only sound is our silverware in our food. I'm to the point where I can't handle the quiet. I'm concerned what may be going through his mind.

I cover his hand with mine and force him to lift his eyes to mine. "Talk to me, Javier."

"I don't know what else to say. Before us, I never had anyone looking out for me at home. It was just me, no one pacing the floor worrying about my safe return. My choices and decisions at work only impacted me."

"What are you saying?"

He pushes out a harsh breath. "I'm saying my gut is telling me not to leave your side."

"Okay. Do you have a choice?"

"Not sure. I'm certainly going to try to get one though." He leaves the table only to grab his phone from the island.

He calls Bishop and sets the phone between us on speaker.

"Cruz. How could you possibly know?"

"Know what, Bishop?"

"Caitryn slipped her tail."

My breath catches in my throat. His gut was right.

"When?" Javier asks.

"Within the last two hours. What were you calling about?"

"My gut told me something was off. A call felt warranted."

"We make quite a pair," Bishop acknowledges.

"Yeah. What's the plan?"

"Stay put for now. Clearly, Caitryn won't show for our meeting if she isn't in the city anymore."

"Will do. Call me when you know more."

"I will. Later, Cruz."

He ends the call and dials Jake. When he doesn't answer immediately, he dials Connor.

"Hey, Cruz."

"Everything okay? Jake didn't answer."

A laugh flows through the speaker. "Everything is fine considering Norah's water broke and Jake is freaking out."

Aww, I'm ecstatic for them. We hear mumbling in the background.

Connor speaks again, "I take that back, both Jake and Christoph are losing their minds. Madeleine appears to be in labor too. What can I help you with?"

Javier updates Connor with pertinent details about the planned meeting, Caitryn, and the plans for me.

"Okay. Give me twenty, and I'll review the plans for Jill and call you back."

While we wait, we clear the table and dishes. He escorts me to the couch but refuses to sit down in the meantime.

"Babe, everything is fine right now. We're safe here."

He stops midstep and turns toward me. "True, but I just got you back into the school building. I won't take it away, not even for a few days."

"Since I know you'll refuse the suggestion, I won't offer to stay here. What can we do to make you feel more comfortable?"

He moves again on a quest to wear a path into my area rug. "What other safety measures does Jake have in place that he thinks you don't know about?"

I smile. "Aside from the extra features on the alarm, there's a tracker on my car and my phone. Neither of which will help since I won't be driving and I don't have my phone on me during class. The Blackthorne vehicles have tracking too."

"Could you keep your phone on you until this is resolved?" Javier pleads.

"Yes, I can carry my phone."

"Thank—" His phone rings. "Yeah, Connor."

"For now, Barrett will still accompany Jill to school tomorrow, and you can go too. Barrett can monitor the outside while you're inside. If you need to leave, Barrett can move inside."

"Okay."

"Cruz, I've been where you are. You gut is screaming not only to protect Jill but to close the case. Determining which facet will win is the most difficult choice you'll have to make. We've got both of you covered, whatever needs to be done."

"Thanks, Connor."

"Keep me in the loop if anything changes."

"Will do." He ends the calls and takes the spot beside me.

"We should try to get some sleep," I suggest.

"I'll join you, but I doubt sleep will come for me anyway."

"Worth a try."

I hustle upstairs, strip down to lacy panties with a fitted tank, and dive into bed. It's chillier than I anticipated.

His eyes widen as he enters the room. He hurries out of his sweats and tee to join me. As he hauls me close, I twine my legs with his and tuck my head under this chin.

"Better?" I whisper.

"Everything is with you snuggled against me."

"It'll be only us sooner than you think," I murmur against his warm skin.

"I hope so."

"No need to hope. You're the most resolute man I know, even more than my brothers—all of them."

"When it comes to protecting you, absolutely."

I press an open-mouth kiss to his chest. "Try to sleep, Javier. It'll help. I love you."

He kisses the top of my head. "Good night, *cariña. Te amo.*"

Hours later I stir and find him sound asleep. I cuddle closer and let sleep reclaim me.

CHAPTER TWENTY-SIX

JAVIER

Near five in the morning, my phone rings. I attempt to silence it but fail.

"Sorry," I whisper to Jillian before answering. "Hello."

"Morning, Cruz."

"Bishop." My voice is low and scratchy.

"At least one of us got some sleep."

"Not much. You have an update?"

"According to Attorney Jameson, Miss Spillane has been in her condo all night."

"We both know she's wrong or lying."

"True, but the attorney doesn't know about the tail."

"Any word on how she slipped away?"

"Not yet. My team is still questioning the agents on duty and the concierge at her building."

"What do you want me to do?"

"Can you be prepared to log in to a video conference call at two, even though it's unlikely Caitryn will show?"

"Yeah, I can. Send me the details, and I'll get things set up here."

After ending the call, I locate my glasses and pad to the kitchen for caffeine. I brew a cup of coffee and attempt to settle the frustration and fear in my head.

"Go back to bed for a little longer," I urge Jillian when she shuffles into the kitchen.

"I won't sleep knowing you're out here planning, worrying, and walking through each aspect of my day."

It's uncanny how much she's like Jake. I suppose thinking like private security is a learned behavior rather than ingrained—at least it is for the Blackthornes.

"I'll call Connor in a little bit, but I'm debating whether to join you at school in the morning and come back for the conference call with Bishop."

"Either will be fine. I'm sure your concern has skyrocketed with Caitryn's location unknown."

"Yes." I brew a second cup for myself after she makes her first.

"Whatever you decide, I'll get coverage for recess and stay in the building all day," Jillian offers to assuage my rising trepidation of allowing her to go to work.

"Thank you." Then I realize my increasing fear matches my growing love for her. Guilt is consuming me for failing—potentially failing—Jillian like I did Adams, Jones, and Carter. Arguably, I didn't fail my unit mates. I wasn't there to stop it either though. Failing Jillian is not an option. I'm confident her brothers agree.

"I'll do whatever I can to make our situation more palatable. You've already nixed my suggestion for me to stay home. Short of you changing your mind, outdoor recess is all I have left to give."

I set my cup down and draw her close. "I'm torn. I want you to teach in person. You're talented. Kate and Stevie need you present, not via video. I refuse to take it away again."

"Your need to protect me is precisely why I'm willing to switch back again. Both actions exemplify our deep-rooted feelings for one another."

Damn! "How do you do that?"

She lifts her sky-blue eyes to mine. "Do what?"

"Take every single thought in my head and feeling in my heart and boil it down to a succinct explanation."

She smiles. "It's a gift."

I kiss her deeply and send her to get ready for school while I call Connor.

"Morning, Cruz."

"Hey, Connor. Sorry it's so early."

He chuckles. "I have three children under the age of one. I assure you, you didn't wake me."

I share the update from overnight with Connor. "I'm going to join Jillian at school for the morning along with Barrett. Will you be able to pick me up around one and bring me back home?"

"Sure."

"Any update from Jake and Christoph?"

"As of eight last night, both Norah and Madeleine were both in labor. Nothing new yet."

"I'll see you later. Thanks, Connor."

"Welcome."

Within an hour, we're headed to school with Barrett. The ride is uneventful, precisely how I like them.

"Morning, Jillian. Cruz," Deni says as we approach.

"Morning, Deni."

Deni hands Jillian a bag and a tray with two coffees.

"You're the best, Deni!"

"Only because you love me the mostest!"

"Right back at you."

When we enter her classroom, I wrap my arms around her and bring my lips close to Jillian's ear. "I thought you loved me the most."

"How I love you is exponentially more and different than anyone else on the planet. It always has been, even when you weren't mine yet."

"I'm glad we agree."

Carol and Kate squeal with joy when they step into the classroom.

"Sorry, *cariña*." I'm truly only sorry we were caught. I'm sure Jillian isn't happy about sharing more of her personal life with her students. Although, if our family is correct, we don't hide our emotions well at all.

"Morning, Kate. Hello, Carol. How was your evening?"

"No need to stop canoodling on our account," Carol states.

I shake my head and move to my designated spot in the corner—fitting considering the scolding I deserve for breaking the rules in her classroom.

"Thank you, Carol."

"Kate had a good night."

Kate agrees by pushing her cheering button on her computer. Soon thereafter, Stevie arrives and his dad leaves. Once they're entranced with morning announcements, Jillian moves closer to me.

"How mad are you?"

Her smile always lightens my load. "I'm not mad. However, I'm glad it wasn't Platt or one of the office staff."

"Happy to not be in the doghouse for something else," I mumble.

"I didn't put you there. You put yourself there. When the case is closed, balance will be restored. For now, we make the best choices given the information we have."

"Okay."

She turns back to the class and inspires their young minds until lunch. To miss the throng of students in the hallway, Suzie escorts the students to the cafeteria ten minutes before the bell rings. According to Jillian's schedule, Kate and Stevie are also the last to leave the cafeteria.

"I'll see you at home tonight." My words are meant to make leaving the building easier for her. Mostly, they're for me.

She murmurs, "I'll be fine," against my lips as I force myself to leave the room.

With another kiss to tide me over, I reluctantly step into the hallway. As I reach the front of the building, I cross paths with Barrett.

"All quiet out front," he advises me.

"Same inside."

"I'll bring her home immediately."

"Much appreciated." I walk through the door and slip into the passenger seat of the waiting Blackthorne SUV.

"Hey, Connor."

"Hey."

"Any updates?"

"Elizabeth Harper and Sam Benjamin were born within fifteen minutes of one another late last night. Both Norah and Madeleine are doing well," Connor shares.

"Awesome. Jillian will be crazy excited to have another niece and nephew to dote on."

"Jillian? You mean you."

I laugh. "True."

"Otherwise, all quiet." Connor pulls into our driveway about twenty minutes later.

"Thanks. I'll keep you updated."

Connor pulls away as I enter the house. I shuck my jacket and boot up my laptop in the office facing the bare wall. The last thing I need is for Babylon or Caitryn to see something they shouldn't. I login and find Bishop and Babylon already present in the room.

"Afternoon, Cruz," Bishop greets me. "We also have Stephen Babylon present. We're waiting on Miss Spillane and her counsel, Shannon Jameson."

"Afternoon, Special Agent Bishop and Mr. Babylon. Thank you." I glance at the clock and note both women have about five minutes to arrive on time.

Soon after two, Caitryn's attorney arrives. We dispense with introductions quickly, and Bishop starts right away with questions.

"Attorney Jameson, thank you for coming. Where is your client?"

"She was aware of this meeting and her requested attendance. I last spoke with Miss Spillane last evening near nine," Shannon answers while shifting in her seat.

"Did Miss Spillane indicate her intention to attend this meeting?"

Perhaps Caitryn was lying to her lawyer. The bigger question is why. Being at this meeting would give her insight on how to reclaim the painting or at least strike a deal with Morgan Insurance to pay for it.

"My client stated she intended to be present to move this along."

Clearly there was no mistake or misunderstanding. Caitryn was aware her presence was expected.

Bishop turns his attention to Babylon. "Mr. Babylon, what is your position regarding the painting?"

"Thank you for hosting this meeting. I have no interest in reimbursing Morgan Insurance for the painting. The company can dispose of it as they wish." Stephen Babylon's reply feels terse and forced.

Who is pulling his strings? Nothing in his file nor the information we gathered while investigating indicates he's anything more than a rich, nerdy bachelor who has a penchant to pay his multiple sexual partners.

If Bishop is thrown by Babylon's answer, he doesn't show it. "Why didn't you come forward and share your disinterest in owing the actual painting with our earlier requests?"

"I hadn't made up my mind yet. Also, given the increased value from the appraisal, I don't have adequate liquid assets to reimburse the insurance company."

Only three people know what the new appraised value is: me, Bishop, and Sam. I fire off a text to Sam and Bishop.

Me: How does Babylon know the new appraised value?

I'm not expecting an answer, so I refocus on the call. Bishop asks Attorney Jameson to reach out to her client and determine if she plans on arriving late.

Then my phone indicates an incoming text. The words make my blood run cold.

Jillian: Rule 69. I love you, Javier.

CHAPTER TWENTY-SEVEN

JILLIAN

I point to the restroom two doors away from my classroom as Barrett approaches. Thankfully, he doesn't stand guard outside the door. Knowing Jake, the entire team memorized every door, corridor, room, and odd space in this building before he agreed to let me teach in person again. I'm perfectly safe in the ladies' room. At least I thought I was.

The fire alarm blares as I finish washing my hands. I exit the restroom as Barrett steps into the hall.

"They're in the cafeteria," I relay and take off running toward my students.

Despite his considerable height and bulk, Barrett gets swallowed up by the students moving to the exits. When I reach the cafeteria, I locate my students. Suzie and I escort them outside and around the building to the far corner of the parking lot according to safety protocol.

Once Kate and Stevie are in line, I scan the crowd for Barrett. I'm merely worried because we were separated. Instead of locating him, I locate a woman with fiery red hair who doesn't belong anywhere near here. I recognize her from the photos—Caitryn Spillane. Immediately, I pull out my phone and text Javier.

Me: Rule 69. I love you, Javier.

He's well versed in Gibbs' rules. Rule #69 is never trust a woman who doesn't trust her man. The only reason Caitryn Spillane is within arm's distance of me is she and Babylon are a couple or at least in cahoots regarding the painting. Otherwise, she would be in New York at Javier's meeting where the topic of discussion is the painting she believes rightfully belongs to her family. I'm not sure how Babylon failed Caitryn, but she doesn't trust him to play his part anymore. How I'm mixed up in it, I'm not sure yet.

I don't see Barrett as the redhead sidles beside me.

"Do you know who I am?" She's taller than me by a considerable amount and dressed in black dress pants, sneakers, and a parka.

I push down the bile rising in my throat and attempt to untwist the knot forming in my belly. "Yes."

"You need to come with me," her demand quiet but resolute.

"If I don't?"

"You will never see Javier Cruz again."

Shivers cascade through me "If you assure me you won't hurt my students, I'll come with you willingly."

Caitryn nods once.

At least her devious plans don't include harming innocent children.

Deni's class finishes lining up beside Kate and Stevie. "All good, Jill?" Deni asks.

"Yes, I'm going to take another pass around the building to check on stragglers. Can you make sure they get back to New York?"

Deni's eyes widen, her fear for me evident as she nods furiously. Caitryn takes two steps back, and I follow. She leads me to a dark-colored sedan and puts me in the back seat.

As she rounds the car to drive, I text Javier again and then call him but lower the volume completely on my phone.

Me: Black sedan VA BAX-9531.

"What is your plan here?" I ask Caitryn as she pulls into traffic.

"My plan is to get what's mine."

Which is? "The painting?"

"That's part of it. I plan to avenge my brother too." She continues away from Crescent Bay.

Damn! "What else are you after?"

"None of your concern."

"Abducting me is only the beginning of your problems. Crossing state lines will only make it worse."

The guys will find me before it's too late.

"Washington, D.C. isn't a state. I thought you were a teacher. Shouldn't you be smarter?"

I'm smarter than you, Miss Alleged Irish Mob Mastermind. You didn't even think to check for my phone or a weapon. "Cute. What's the deal with the painting anyway?"

"It belonged to my family, and I want it back."

"Can you prove ownership? I mean, it would certainly go a long way to persuade the authorities."

"I have evidence it was hanging in my great-grandfather's office long before I was born. Then the Noonans messed everything up."

"Have you shown this alleged evidence to the authorities?"

She shakes her head and turns toward the old post office. "What's with the questions?"

"I'm merely trying to help you support your theory regarding the painting. Oh, can we drive by the Ellipse?"

"This isn't a guided tour," Caitryn snaps back.

"Sorry, I haven't been into the capital in a while. Back to the painting, did you share the evidence with your lawyers?"

"Of course. My lawyer decided to request the appraisal. Then the painting was stolen again."

"Oh, I didn't know." A complete lie, but Caitryn doesn't know the extent of my knowledge of the case. "Has it been located yet?"

"Not that I'm aware of." There's no waver in her gaze. I can see her eyes in the rearview mirror. Perhaps she doesn't know where it's located. Seems odd given it's her endgame.

I play along, even though I know where the painting allegedly hangs. "Maybe it'll turn up. What is the next step in proving it's yours? Who owns it now?"

Caitryn pulls up to the valet at a fancy hotel. Before she gets out, she turns to me, "Follow my lead, and I won't hurt you."

I nod. When she closes her door, I slide my phone into my pocket and hope I don't disconnect it.

"Have a lovely afternoon, ladies," the valet croons and takes her keys.

"Thank you," I reply and follow Caitryn inside.

"This hotel is fancy. J.W.—"

"Pipe down. Let's not draw attention to ourselves."

I dutifully follow Caitryn to the bank of elevators in the center of the lobby. We ride to the tenth floor, change elevators, and then head to the top. "The penthouse, nice." I'm taking a risk reiterating all these details, but I know the guys will figure it out.

The penthouse is stunning and opulent. There's a sitting room and two separate suites as well as a dining area complete with a table for eight. The view of the city is unparalleled.

The sole reason my mind isn't racing along with my heart is the probability of Javier hearing everything I'm saying. I'm sure Deni will come through whether she talks to Barrett, Javier, or both. "You didn't answer my question. Who owns the painting now?"

"Some renowned insurance company. The problem is... the appraisal my lawyer requested increased the value substantially. It was valued at five million more than I expected."

"Oh, that's unfortunate."

Caitryn is pacing the length of the Berber carpet. "You really aren't bright, are you?"

"Excuse me?"

"You think this is going to be easy and tidy. I let you call your boyfriend, and he swoops in to rescue you. You might as well make yourself comfortable. We're not going anywhere until the painting is turned over to my family.

I consider challenging her about Jimmy, but I don't. Not yet. "How do you plan on going about it unless you know where the painting is?"

"I already told you I don't."

"Let's say I don't believe you. If you knew where the painting was, then what?"

She isn't stupid enough to walk me through her plan, is she? "If, and I emphasize *if*, I knew where the painting was located, I would share the information with my lawyer… you know, privilege and all. Then, I would instruct her to strike a deal with the insurance company to get the painting back."

"You said you didn't have enough money though."

"Not as dumb as you look, huh?" Caitryn turns to face me.

The longer I keep her talking, the better. She won't realize I'm still relatively unharmed. Freaking out on the inside, absolutely, but physically, I'm fine. "Just a good listener, I guess."

"I can get the money from my boy… a friend. A friend can lend me the money to make up the difference."

"Why haven't you made the call yet?"

She stops pacing and stares directly at me. "I wanted as much leverage as I could get." Her stare darkens in my direction.

"Me? I'm nobody. I have nothing to do with the painting or the insurance company."

"You're full of yourself. You shot my brother!"

"I shot your brother because he put a gun to the temple of the man I love. I did nothing wrong. I protected myself and Javier. I wouldn't hesitate to do it again."

"Awww, don't care. This is all your fault!"

"Is it?"

"Of course it is! You shot him!"

"No, it's yours." Now I'm pacing the floor parallel to her to stay out of her path. "You sent him to find Lieutenant Cruz." I pause.

She stops walking but says nothing.

"Why?"

"I wanted to use Lieutenant Cruz for leverage, just like I am with you now."

"I'm not worth anything." When Javier hears my last statement, I'm confident Spanish expletives flow from his lips.

"You're the best I can get right now. Lieutenant Cruz will come for you. You may not have realized it, but we've had eyes on the two of you since you left the city, and my family has been tracking Lieutenant Cruz during his tenure with the NYPD. So unfortunate he didn't get the promotion."

We have a traitor among us. Who? What does she mean 'unfortunate'? "You're right. He will come for me. Still doesn't explain what you believe he can do for you."

I'm wracking my brain to determine the traitor. I can eliminate my brothers and their significant others. Certainly, it's not Javier. Who was involved in this case? Who knows about the painting? I recall Javier mentioning the circle was tight.

"He has an in with the insurance company, the NYPD, and the FBI."

She isn't completely off base there. "Why the cat-and-mouse game? Why do you need leverage at all?"

"I'll use anything I can to get what I want. First on the agenda is the painting." She stops pacing and checks her phone.

"How do you propose to do that?"

"Why would I share with you?" Her tone is incredulous. She has no idea what she has shared already in her haze to abduct me from school.

"You don't have to. I could call Javier and tell him where we are."

She laughs heartily. "No need. He'll get here soon enough."

"How?"

"My man will lead yours right here."

Interesting. She clearly isn't aware I have the phone line open. Who is her inside man then? There are only two options: Finn and Barrett. The rest of the staff haven't had anything to do with my security. Could she have one at the NYPD too or even the FBI? I'm not sure if I should be proud as a woman at her gumption and ability to command her alleged mob family or disgusted these men are following her every whim, no questions asked. At this point, all I can do is wait for the cavalry unless Caitryn does something to give me an opportunity to escape. I won't hold my breath.

CHAPTER TWENTY-EIGHT

JAVIER

Panic is coursing through my veins. Despite all our planning and attempts to protect Jillian, Caitryn abducted her. At least, I'm fairly confident that's part of what her text means.

I pull up his number and dial. "Barrett, talk to me."

"Cruz, there was a fire drill during lunch. She was in the restroom. When the alarm sounded, Jillian ran to the cafeteria. Then I lost her as the students filled into the hallway and out of the building."

"Did you locate her at all? Hold on, Barrett."

My phone indicates an incoming text. I read it and make note of the vehicle information Jillian sent. Then there's an incoming call from Jillian.

I disconnect Barrett and answer, "Hello?"

She doesn't respond, but I hear her talking to someone, presumably Caitryn. "What is your plan here?"

Instead of risking losing Jillian, I hurry to the land line and call Barrett again.

"Sorry, got disconnected from you."

"No problem. Denise is here. She said Jillian told her to reach out to you."

"Thanks, Barrett. Please tell Denise I'm working on finding Jillian now."

I hear mumbling and furiously tap an email to Connor, include the vehicle information, and send it. Almost impossibly fast, he responds that he's on his way with Maia and Nolan. Plus, he sent Blaine the details about the car and reached out to Bishop.

"What's next, Cruz?" Barrett is back on the line after talking to Denise at the school.

"Can you inform Principal Platt? We need Suzie or someone else to cover Kate and Stevie."

"On it and then?"

"Hold tight. I'm working with Connor."

"Will do," Barrett responds.

As I wait for Connor and Maia, I listen to Jillian's conversation with Caitryn. She says something about Washington D.C. A while later, she mentions the Ellipse.

My woman is calm, collected, and a goddamn genius! At least she sounds calm and collected. The genius part is unquestionably true. Not only is she drawing information out of Caitryn but dropping hints about her location.

I slip on my vest, grab my weapons, and prepare to leave the house and jot notes from Jillian's open call.

By the time Connor, Maia, and Nolan arrive, I know where Jillian is located. I pile into the SUV. "Maia, please call Barrett. I had him hold tight at the school." Once he answers, I share the details I know. "It appears Caitryn Spillane abducted Jillian from the school." I divulge the other details that I've learned from the open phone call, including the fact she's in D.C. at the J.W. Marriott hotel, more specifically, in the penthouse. I pushed one wireless earbud into my ear to continue to listen as we move toward Jillian.

"Where do you want me to meet you?" Barrett asks.

Connor replies, "Have the local police arrived?"

"No, they aren't aware Miss Blackthorne has been taken yet."

Ice pulses through my veins. Blackthorne protocol would dictate Barrett contact local authorities as soon as he learned Jillian was taken, not only because it's Jillian but because a crime has been committed. We have no actual law enforcement authority. The unmistakable look on Connor's face bolsters my opinion.

"Please reach out to the local police and wait for their arrival. Give them a statement, and we'll contact you with more information when we have it," I instruct him.

"Roger, Cruz."

Maia ends the call and exchanges a look with Nolan.

"What the fuck! He's a former cop; he knows the first hour is critical. He also knows our protocol. How did our extensive background check miss the connection between the Spillane family and Barrett?" Connor bellows.

I shush the team to listen to Jillian. "My man will lead yours right here," filters through the earbud. She's still holding it together well given the circumstances she finds herself in.

Completely my fault.

Not the time, Javier!

Connor's phone rings while I chastise myself for not seeing Barrett for the traitor he appears to be. He answers on speaker, "Yeah, Bishop."

"Stephen Babylon is spilling details about his agreement with Miss Spillane and the heist to steal the painting. I can't leave here. I've reached out to the D.C. field office. Special Agent Audrey Davenport will be at your disposal. I've texted you her contact information. She's expecting your call. Before you ask, I trust her with my life; you can trust her with Jillian's."

"Thanks, Bishop," Connor states and ends the call.

"What do we do about Barrett?" My question directed at Connor.

"Nothing. We need to see what he does."

I glance at Connor to confirm I heard him correctly.

His stare indicates we don't have another choice. Connor pulls our vehicle along the curb around the corner from the hotel where Jillian is being held. He swipes a few times on his phone. "Maia, I just sent you the map of the hotel. Review it with Nolan and look for the safest way to enter."

"On it, Connor," Nolan replies.

"What other personnel is available?" I ask.

"Aside from us, Lane. However, given the failure with Barrett's background check, just us four for now."

"Understood."

I overhear Jillian request to use the restroom. Caitryn indicates which direction. I hear a door close and lock. Then I hear running water. Within seconds, a text comes through.

Jillian: Barrett is a traitor. Babylon might be her bf.

Me: We're nearby waiting for local backup. Be careful, cariña.

Jillian: I will. You too.

Me: Always.

I hear the water stop and the door reopen. I return my attention to Connor.

"Here." Connor hands me his phone. "Call Agent Davenport and see how long until she arrives," he requests.

I dial and wait for the call to connect. "Davenport."

"Good afternoon. Cruz from Blackthorne Security."

"Pleasure. Bishop indicated you needed local assistance."

I share the current situation and information we know at this point. If Bishop trusts her, I have no reason to question her.

"How many agents do you need?"

"We have four bodies, a few more couldn't hurt."

"I'll be there in fifteen with some additional support."

I end the call with Davenport and attempt to focus on Maia and Nolan's plan. Bile rises in my throat when I realize the call with Jillian is no longer active. *Deep breath. Jillian will be fine. She can handle herself. Hell, she saved me at the cottage.* I pull myself out of my spiraling thoughts and focus on Maia and Nolan's plan to rescue Jillian.

"The penthouse is only accessible by one elevator. You take one from the lobby and then a private one from the tenth floor. There's direct access to the roof, which will need to be secured. Do we know if Caitryn is armed?"

"We don't, but Jill wouldn't blanch if she were," Connor shares.

"True." Maia shares the layout of the penthouse. There's only one entrance and two exits, which is good and bad tactically. As Maia finishes her explanation, Agent Davenport arrives and closes off a portion of the street.

"Javier Cruz, Connor Michelson?" she addresses us as we step out of the SUV. We extend our hands to her. She takes them in turn. Audrey Davenport is stunning—dark, sable hair tied in a loose ponytail at the base of her neck, piercing blue eyes, just enough curves, and extensive firearms and investigative training. "Pleasure. Audrey Davenport.

We explain our plan for entry as well as the need for a team to land on the roof to prevent her from egress like Babylon did in New York. We also share about Barrett and his status as an alleged traitor.

"I'll get a team to the roof. Do you have a photo of Barrett Beaumont I can share?"

I swipe through my gallery and turn my phone toward her. "I sent it to you."

Davenport pulls out her phone and starts barking orders.

The last few hours have taken years off my life. Jillian is being held captive due to one of my old cases. I take some comfort in the fact she can protect herself better than most people. Pacing the sidewalk beside the SUV, I consider barging into the hotel and rushing headlong to rescue her. My head knows it would endanger Jillian more, my heart doesn't give a damn.

Connor stops me in my tracks. "Cruz, whatever you're thinking, forget it. Bottle it up."

"Easy for you to say. You went into danger, not Callie."

"True, but thanks to Ben and Jake, Jillian can handle herself, which she proved already."

"Fine, but I can't be comfortable with my woman in danger because of me."

Connor shakes his head. "Cruz, stuff the guilt, worry, and fear away. We need to remove our client from this harrowing situation."

I push out a harsh breath. He's right. *Focus, Javier!* "Let's do this."

Agent Davenport leads us into the building to the elevator bank, along with two of her agents. Nolan and Maia take the roof. When we reach the tenth floor, we encounter Barrett waiting for the penthouse elevator.

"Set your weapon on the ground, Barrett! Now!" I demand.

He lowers his weapon to the floor, then withdraws a knife from his ankle holster. "She has my daughter." Barrett's response is shaky.

"Thanks to you, she has my better half." I'm fuming, and preventing myself from putting my fist through his face is taking substantial amount of restraint.

"I know, and I'm sorry. Kendall is all I have left."

Fuck! My gut tells me Barrett is telling the truth. I only know a bit about his story, given how twisted my life has been since I started at Blackthorne. Clearly, his past hasn't been rosy.

Davenport tells her team to hold.

"What are you supposed to do for her?" Connor asks in a calmer tone than Barrett deserves.

"Caitryn said she would release Kendall if I tracked Jillian's whereabouts and reported back to her, which I did. I'm profusely sorry. I'll give my life for Kendall. Letting Caitryn take Jillian was supposed to be the end. Caitryn said my daughter would be released after she boards the chopper. Now, I'm supposed to escort her to the chopper she has waiting on the roof."

"When is the last time you saw your daughter?" My tone is steady.

He exhales sharply. "Two days ago, she was taken from school. I didn't—"

Connor interrupts, "We'll deal with your misdeeds later. Do you have any idea where your daughter is?"

"No."

Connor changes the plan on the fly. "You're going to go to the penthouse and attempt to get Caitryn to the roof."

Barrett nods.

"We'll follow closely behind. You'll be arrested on the roof with Caitryn by the agents stationed there. Work for you, Davenport?"

"Yes."

"What about Kendall?" For a large, hulk-like man, his voice is small in this heart-wrenching moment.

Damn him for not reaching out sooner. We would have found Kendall first.

"We'll find Kendall and then worry about the rest," Connor assures him.

"Thank you."

"You may not have realized it before, but joining Blackthorne makes you family. We've got your back, despite your misdeeds."

I fist his shirt in my hands. "Barrett, I will kill you if Jillian is harmed."

Agent Davenport clears her throat.

Barrett mutters, "I'll deserve it, but Kendall is all I have left worth living for."

We revamp the timing of our plan and put it into action.

CHAPTER TWENTY-NINE

JILLIAN

Caitryn keeps looking out the window and checking her watch. Evidently, she has a detailed plan for how today will go. The question is when Blackthorne will destroy it.

A phone call pulls her attention away from the time. "Jimmy?" I can only hear one side of the conversation. "I don't have time for details." After a short pause. "It was you. Didn't think you had it in you." Another pause. "You have it in your possession?" She waits for a response, then ends the call. After a few moments to recalculate, Caitryn addresses me. "Time to move, princess!" Caitryn grabs my arm and urges me into the suite on the right.

I hate being called princess! Her brother called me the same thing. "Where are you going?"

"I'm leaving. You're staying. I can't be caught with you. Then I'll most certainly spend the rest of my life in prison, and I'll have failed to protect my family's legacy."

"That's happening either way!"

Caitryn rears back and slaps me across the face. "Shut up! Being bold now won't help you. I'm going to get what's mine and restore my family name."

That's laughable. Don't see how she's going to do that leaving me here, but I won't correct her. She has no idea how bold I am.

She ushers me into the bathroom, has me sit on the vanity bench, and binds my hands and feet.

"My revenge will come when you least expect it, Miss Blackthorne."

"For what?"

She doesn't respond. Instead, Caitryn ambles to the door and looks back once more before locking me in. It's apparent Caitryn doesn't resort to violence frequently. If she did, she wouldn't have made the rookie mistake of binding my hands in front of me. I lift my wrists to my mouth and work on the knot. Once I free my hands, I pull my phone out of my pocket and realize the call disconnected sometime after I left the bathroom earlier.

While I wrestle with texting Javier, Caitryn is talking to someone in the sitting room.

"You're late."

"Where is my daughter?"

The voice is familiar.

"She's in there."

"I need to see she's okay before."

Caitryn bellows, "Fine, make it quick. I've already been here too long."

After hearing there's another captive, I take a risk and text Javier.

Me: Caitryn grabbed someone else too. She's in the left suite.

Javier: Hold tight. We're coming in soon.

Heeding his words, I cower beneath the vanity and unbind my feet.

I strain to hear Caitryn's conversation.

"Let's go! The chopper is waiting," Caitryn shouts.

"Fine!" the deep, husky voice basically growls in response.

Ohmigod! That's Barrett! I consider throwing open the door but talk myself out of it. My judgment is winning over my anger right now!

I hear a door slam closed and then chaos as measured voices echo around me as they clear the penthouse. The door to the bathroom opens and Javier steps inside and clears the room.

"*Cariña*, are you hurt?" He holsters his weapon and runs his hands down my sides before tightening his hold on me.

"No, I'm fine. There's another person here."

"Connor is checking it out."

Instead of backing away, he draws me even closer. If I could burrow into him, I would, but not because I'm scared. A wave of relief washed over me when I heard them clearing the penthouse.

Our moment of peace is interrupted by Caitryn's loud voice. "You can't do this! I didn't do anything wrong. This is a setup!"

A beautiful FBI agent is reading Caitryn her rights. "You have the right to remain silent. Anything you say can and will…."

I tune her out and notice a teenager sitting on the couch. She looks tired but otherwise uninjured. The FBI agent hands Caitryn off and takes a seat beside the young girl. She's tall and thin with platinum blonde hair.

"What's your name?"

"Kendall Beaumont."

Barrett has a daughter?

"Hi, Kendall. I'm Special Agent Davenport. Can I get you some water?"

"No, I'm fine. Where's my dad?"

"He's being held in another room for now. Can you walk me through how you got here?"

Kendall exhales and shares her story with Agent Davenport.

Connor joins Javier and me to await further instruction from Agent Davenport. Soon thereafter, Maia and Nolan come over. Maia offers me a water.

"Thanks," I mumble while twisting the cap. As I take a sip, I start to feel a bit dizzy and latch on to Javier's muscled forearm.

Swiftly, he opens the door to the bedroom and guides me to the dressing bench at the foot of the bed. "Adrenaline wearing off?"

I nod.

Javier props me against his body and asks, "When did you eat last?"

"I ate some of my lunch."

Agent Davenport moves to the threshold of the suite. "Miss Blackthorne, I understand your quick thinking led to this successful outcome. Well done."

"Thank you. Truthfully, I didn't know Kendall was here until Barrett arrived asking about her."

She nods to acknowledge my statement. "Connor. Cruz, a word?"

Javier presses a kiss to my temple, and Maia sits beside me.

"How are you really?" Maia asks.

"Overall, I'm fine. Pissed at Barrett and Caitryn and worried about Kate and Stevie. I can only imagine the impact my disappearance had on them."

"I understand. Perhaps we can call them later," Maia suggests.

"Thanks, Maia."

About fifteen minutes pass before Javier returns. "We're going to reconvene at the Blackthorne office," he informs me.

"Okay." I take his outstretched hand and thread our fingers together.

Connor, Maia, Nolan, and Agent Davenport surround me and Javier until we exit the building and I slide into the back of a Blackthorne SUV. I'm sandwiched between Maia and Javier in the back seat with Nolan and Connor up front. Javier's arm is over my shoulders and his other hand is threaded with mine on his thigh.

The ride takes about thirty minutes. Connor pulls into the lot behind the building, and we enter the conference room.

Gemma rushes over and throws her arms around me. "I'm so glad you're okay!"

"Thanks, Gemma."

"I took the liberty of ordering enough food to feed a lot of people. Let me know if you need more or need something else," Gemma shares.

Connor thanks her, and we dig into the food. Agent Davenport joins us soon thereafter.

"Please help yourself," Javier offers.

"Thank you. Bishop will be ready to update you in about ten minutes via video conference. I assume you have a secure link."

"Yes." Connor pushes a few buttons and logs in to his laptop in the conference room. We chat amongst ourselves until Bishop appears on the screen.

"Good evening, everyone. Miss Blackthorne, glad to see you're relatively unharmed."

"Thank you, Agent Bishop."

"I'll get right to the update, as I'm sure all of you need some rest. While Caitryn was running loose in D.C., her boyfriend, Stephen Babylon, was spilling details of her plan to avoid jail. Caitryn Spillane ordered Jimmy to abduct Cruz. When he failed, she cast him aside and worked the appraisal and Davidson angle. According to Babylon, the unidentifiable woman with purple hair on the security feed is Caitryn. She has been in his stable of rotating women for the last eight months or so. She led Babylon to believe, if he disappeared, she would be able to secure the painting and he would be able to keep the money from Morgan Insurance."

I'm riveted by Bishop's words.

He continues, "Fast forward a bit when Babylon learned the painting was stolen during transport, he returned home believing Caitryn failed to follow through on their deal. Babylon indicated he spoke with Caitryn, and learned she couldn't afford the increased value from the recent appraisal by Ms. Caffey."

"I'm sorry to interrupt, but that isn't the story Caitryn told me."

"Go ahead, Jill," Bishop yields.

"Caitryn indicated her boyfriend, I assume she meant Babylon, would give her the additional funds to make up the difference."

Bishop interjects, "She wasn't lying. She meant a different boyfriend." I motion for Bishop to continue. "Sam's retrieval expert located the painting in Olga's condo but couldn't reclaim it given her gray-area methods. Phone records show Caitryn reached out to Captain Davidson and requested he prepare to move the money."

Davidson is on the wrong side of this too.

Javier stiffens beside me. "We were right about Davidson?" he asks Bishop.

"Yes. Not once in my career has my gut steered me wrong. I'm glad we left him on the board."

"Me too. Please continue," Javier states.

"Davidson sent two of his officers to relieve my agents who were tailing Caitryn."

"Why didn't they reach out to you for confirmation?" Agent Davenport interjects.

"They believe they did. A call was placed from Agent Diamond's phone to my desk. The person who answered approved their request to leave Caitryn's detail."

"Who approved it?" Davenport asks.

"A low-level secretary in the New York field office is apparently Davidson's niece—a significant detail that was missed on her background check and conveniently left off her application."

"How does Barrett fit in?" Connor asks.

"Caitryn only reached out to Barrett as insurance in January. She threatened to abduct Kendall. To thwart the abduction, Barrett agreed to feed her information about Jill's whereabouts."

"Caitryn said she had eyes on me since I left the city."

Bishop nods. "She likely meant Davidson and Barrett. When Babylon returned, he met with Caitryn but she didn't know about Jimmy's agreement with Davidson."

"Davidson was working both siblings?" Cruz adds.

Bishop nods. "It appears so."

"That's where I come in?" My words come out unintentionally loud.

Javier's grasp tightens even more.

"Yes. When Jimmy failed, Caitryn set out to use you as bait to get Cruz to show his face. Caitryn believed it was the only way to get the painting back because she believed Babylon double crossed her."

"She isn't the brightest woman I've ever met. Do we know what her plan was had she escaped the hotel?"

The room erupts in laughter as Bishop wraps up. "Not fully. The helicopter was set to bring her back to New York."

"I may know some more details." I share with Bishop and the others Caitryn's hypothetical plan if she knew where the painting was, including how it was unfortunate Javier didn't get the promotion.

"That part actually does make sense," Bishop offers.

"It does?" Javier asks.

"Yeah, Caitryn and Jimmy were going to frame you for the theft after the heist as if you had been in on it since the beginning when you investigated with Sam."

"Caitryn is cunning," I add aloud.

"Yes, she is. With all this information and Babylon's cooperation, Caitryn Spillane is looking at many years behind bars."

"That all makes sense except for one missing piece," Cruz adds.

"Which is?" Bishop asks.

"How does Olga fit into all of this other than housing stolen property?"

Bishop nods. "We did forget about her, didn't we? Olga is Jimmy's girlfriend and has been for the last eight months."

"They were never seen together," Cruz states.

"True. No one looked at Jimmy or tracked his comings and goings until he came after you," Bishop replies.

"What happens to the painting?" Javier asks.

As soon as the question leaves his lips, Jake and Christoph barge into the conference room.

"Sorry, Bishop. I had to check with my own two eyes," Jake admits as he yanks me into a hug. He passes me to Christoph.

"Same, Bishop."

"I'm fine. Don't you both have newborns to tend to?"

"Yes. Norah and the baby are resting. I have about thirty minutes before I need to get back."

Christoph laughs. "Betty kicked me out of the house. Said she needed girl time with her future granddaughter and great-granddaughter."

"Congrats, guys!"

"Thanks, Bishop. Please continue," Jake urges.

"The painting belongs to Morgan Insurance. Sam can dispose of it as he likes. Neither Caitryn nor Jimmy will be able to afford to reimburse the company for the value of the painting."

"Sam could probably fetch a hefty penny if he were to sell it now given the storied history it has," Connor offers.

"He probably could. However, I bet Sam locks the painting in a vault and leaves it there for years before making that decision."

We laugh. Bishop thanks Davenport for her assistance and signs off, indicating we'll talk more in the coming days.

"Thank you for your support, Agent Davenport," I extend my hand to her.

"If you're looking to change careers, Jill, give me a call."

I laugh. "I appreciate the offer, but I'm fine with my students."

"I understand." Agent Davenport makes the rounds and leaves the conference room.

Gemma rejoins us, cleans up the remnants of our late dinner, and slips away silently.

Jake speaks next. "Truly, Jill, how are you?"

"I'm fine, Jake, just exhausted like I imagine you are."

"I'm bleary-eyed, but I love it. It reminds me of the sleep deprivation of basic training."

"Christoph, what about you?"

"Jake's description is accurate."

"We should talk about Barrett, at least briefly, before you hustle out of here," Connor recommends.

"I need more information first," I tell them.

The four of people left in the room turn and gawk at me.

"What?" I pause and then offer what I want to know first. "His motivation was protecting his daughter. First, did we even know he had a daughter? Second, she's the first teenager in the Blackthorne family. If she inadvertently mentioned the name of her dad's new employer at school or on social media, what are the chances she's the one who started the entire chain of events? I'm absolutely not suggesting there shouldn't be consequences for leaking intel. However, it shines a bright light on a missing aspect in the vetting process of the employee and their family."

"Her points are salient and valid. However, consequences are required in my opinion," Jake adds.

"I agree more details are necessary regarding the entire timeline. That said, I should get back. I have further to drive than Jake," Christoph adds.

I rise and hug them. "Thank you both for coming so soon after your children were born."

"Never considered it an option not to. Take care of her, Cruz," Jake orders.

"I will. Please give our well-wishes to Norah and Madeleine. We'll visit soon."

"Sounds good," Christoph replies as he rushes out as fast as he came in.

"Ready to go home?" Javier asks.

"Yes. Um, how are we going to do that?"

Connor laughs and tosses a set of keys toward Javier. "Take one of the SUVs. We'll work out picking it up in a few days."

Javier snatches the keys from the air.

"Nicely done! We'll talk on Monday." Connor's words follow us out the door.

I wave backward and melt into Javier's side. After he escorts me to the passenger side of the truck, he hurries around the front, making faces as he goes.

"You're silly."

"Your smile was all I was after. If I need to be silly to get one, I will." He lifts my hand to his lips.

After he lowers it between us, I lean over and kiss him softly. He pulls onto the road toward home—a home where I can come and go as I please again. Even though I'll stay put more often than not, I miss my trips to browse the shelves at the Nook.

"Want to talk now that it's only me?" he asks.

"Only you? You're everything."

"*Tú también eres todo para mí, cariña.*"

His words make me giddy. His words in Spanish make my heart pound faster, even if I don't know what he's saying some of the time.

"She didn't hurt me. Mentally, I'm exhausted, not only from today but overall. Part of me is relieved too. We don't have to be on edge anymore. I can go out if I wish, even though I don't wish. We can focus completely on us."

He's silent for a few minutes, his emotions playing out on his face and through his fingers still threaded with mine. "There aren't enough words for me to appropriately thank you for standing beside me. If I knew she would take you, I wouldn't have—"

"No. We agreed now is the time for us. I don't care if there are five more cases like this one. We'll be together through it all."

"I won't ask that of you."

"Are there?"

He pulls into our driveway and shoves the truck into park before turning to lock his gaze to mine. "Are there what?"

"Are there five more cases? Ten?"

"No, none." His words are resolute and unwavering. He's sure there are no more loose ends at the police department.

"Even if there were, I'm here with you. I love you, Javier."

"*Te amo, cariña.*"

Feeling like a weight has been lifted off my shoulders, we walk with our fingers linked into our home.

CHAPTER THIRTY

JAVIER

It has been a few weeks since Caitryn abducted Jillian. She has resumed her normal life before I disrupted it, and I'm taking regular assignments with Blackthorne. I'm currently on assignment with Lynn Smith at the opening of her new movie directed by Ellis Barnett. This event is the red-carpet premiere in New York City.

It's the first time I've returned since Jillian's visit. The second she knocked on my door, my entire world shifted. When I return from this assignment, I'm going to ask her to be mine during this long holiday weekend. I realize it may seem soon to some people, but my feelings for Jillian will only grow stronger.

"Ellis, congrats on your film."

"Thank you, Cruz. Please meet my wife, Kelly. She designed the costumes for the film."

"Nice to meet you."

"You as well."

"Cruz, nice to see you again," Cash Morgan states as he enters the green room before the premiere.

I extend my hand to him, and he draws me into a bro hug. "Cash, good to see you. You must be Noelle." I extend my hand to the tall, gorgeous, red-haired beauty standing beside Cash.

"Pleasure to meet you in person, Cruz. Cash and Nicholas have mentioned you on numerous occasions." Nicholas is Ellis Barnett's given first name.

"All good things, I hope."

Noelle laughs. "Only good things."

The lights dim, and we move into the theater to watch the premiere of the movie. I dutifully escort Mrs. Smith back to her hotel suite and immediately leave for the airport.

Me: I'm on my way home to you.

Jillian: I'm here waiting. Let me know when you land. I'll cook.

Me: I will.

A bumpy flight and landing later, I deplane and let Jillian know I'm almost there. She replies with a wink and smile emoji. Who even knows what that means? Jillian isn't an emoji-type person. It can only mean one thing—she's up to no good.

I groan and hurry home. While Jillian owned the house before we became a couple, I don't feel out of place.

"*Cariña*, I'm home."

Jillian meets me with a toe-curling kiss as I latch the front door. "I missed you."

"I missed you too."

"What deliciousness do I smell?"

She lifts one shoulder and leads me into the kitchen. "No helping, please. I'm going to pull off your favorite traditional dinner on my own."

"Okay. First, how do you know my favorite traditional dinner?"

"I called your mom."

I raise an eyebrow in interest.

"Well, technically, I called Marisa and then your mom. This is going to take another fifteen minutes if you want to change or unpack first."

"I'll be back." I kiss her thoroughly and leave the kitchen.

When I return, she's plating dinner. She has clearly been slaving all day, or at least she did the day she made the *pastelles*.

"You did all this work for me?"

"I would have preferred you teach me, but this works too. I had some time on my hands. I experimented with your favorites. According to Marisa, you don't eat all of this in one meal, but I had time and tried all the recipes. The three for tonight are after two failed attempts."

She sets a plate with two *pastelles* in front of me and hands me a fork. "Oh, I almost forgot." A trip to the refrigerator later, she sets a bottle of hot sauce nearby.

"My mom was thorough, huh?"

Sheer joy is plastered on my woman's face. "She was and patient too."

"What do you mean?"

"I failed at the *pastelles*. The masa wasn't the right consistency. She walked me through it yesterday on a video chat."

I lift the first bite to my lips and groan. "These are perfect, sweetheart."

"Thanks. I was serious when I said I wanted to learn."

"I know. Things were a bit hectic until recently."

She leans over and kisses me. "It's over now though."

"Yes, it is. What else did you make?"

A twinkle takes root in her ocean-colored irises. *"Pernil y arroz con gondules* for dinner. Did I say that correctly?"

"Yeah, you did. How many times did you practice?"

"More than I'm willing to admit."

"Gracias, cariña."

"You're welcome."

Jillian sets the plates at the dining table and sits in the chair I pulled out. Despite all her skills with other dishes, she's nervous.

"Stop worrying, *corazón.*"

A small smile graces her face. "I will once you taste it."

I lift the *pernil,* which is seasoned, slow-cooked pork, and pause before slipping the fork between my lips.

"Javier." Her tone is exasperated.

"Do you have any idea how sexy it is when you say my name, especially when you're irritated with me?"

"Quit stalling."

I savor the first bite and then try the rice. *"Es perfecto!"*

"Really?"

"Si, cariña." My phone rings on the island, but I let it go to voice mail.

We chat about my assignment and the last few days with her students. Then we discuss our weekend plans.

"Did you pack for a weekend away yet?"

She lifts her eyebrows at me. "No, I was kind of busy in the kitchen. It won't take long. I can do it after dessert."

"You made my favorite dessert too?"

"Of course I did!"

Aside from agreeing on major aspects of a marriage, Jillian is also willing to risk failing to make me happy like I will for her.

"Pack first, then dessert?"

"Voice mail, pack, then dessert in bed," she suggests.

"Hell yes!"

"No peeking though."

"I already know what you made. What difference does it make if I see *arroz con dulce* sooner?"

She purses her lips. "I give."

"Am I right?" I surround her with my arms and press a kiss to the sweet-smelling slope of her neck.

She giggles. "You know you are."

With the dinner dishes done, I check my voice mail. I know from the prefix of the telephone number, I may not like the message.

"Good evening, Lieutenant Cruz. Chief Roberson of the NYPD. Please give me a call back at your earliest convenience."

My eyes close almost involuntarily. There's only one reason for the chief to call me personally. My chest tightens, and I steal a glance at Jillian. I don't want the job anymore. I want a life with her and at least a few tiny humans with her eyes and her breathtaking smile.

How Jillian feels I need her close before I can ask is something I'll never understand. Our silent communication is remarkable. She reads me as well as I read her.

She slides her arms around me and sets her head on my chest. "Who called?"

"Chief Roberson."

"Did he say what he wanted?"

"No, but there's only one reason for him to call me personally."

"How do you feel about it?"

"Even if the department realized they made a mistake with Davidson, I didn't earn it from the start. I want us. I want to build a life with you."

"If you want to hear him out, I understand. I support you either way."

"You would leave your students?"

"For us, I would."

"I applied for the job, and I didn't earn it. I chose Blackthorne instead of opting for another opportunity to be captain. I chose us. I'm not changing my mind now when the department realized they chose wrong."

"I'll be beside you whatever you choose."

"Nothing to decide."

"Are you returning his call now?"

"No, I'll do it on Monday." I press a kiss to her forehead and lead her upstairs and pack for our weekend getaway. She only knows a few details, which is a switch for her. I appreciate her not pushing me to know everything even though it's her nature.

"Do I need anything fancy?" she asks, standing at the threshold of our closet.

"No, not fancy."

Sooner thereafter, we curl up in our sleeping clothes with dessert. Even though I'm dying to try it, I offer her the first bite.

"It's delicious, but honestly I've never had it before so it could be terrible."

I laugh. "Highly doubtful." I scoop a spoonful, and the flavors explode on my tongue—cinnamon and coconut. "*Delicioso*! Almost as delicious as you."

Her cheeks burn red. I take her dish and mine and set them on the floor and spend a few hours before we leave the house nipping and tasting every inch of skin on Jillian's body. Throughout the night, we worshiped each other two more times between bouts of sleep.

"Rise and shine, gorgeous." I hand her a steamy cup of coffee and rejoin her in our bed.

"Thanks. Are you going to clue me in on our itinerary?"

"Today, we're going to Arlington. I would prefer to keep tomorrow's itinerary a surprise now."

"I'm proud of you for following through on your promise."

"Me too."

The ride to Arlington isn't exceedingly long. I pull into one of the visitor's spots and step through the gate with Jillian tucked against me. We walk the grounds and view all the points of interest, including the Tomb of the Unknown Soldier and the Kennedy Family burial site.

"Did you find out where to go?"

I kiss her temple and reply, "Yes. Jake handed me the plan he created for you."

"Oh. I asked him to create a plan if it took a significant amount of time to close the Spillane case. I wanted to be beside you for this. You may not have mentioned your promise to them specifically. However, I knew you weren't telling me the whole story when we first met."

"I'm not mad you asked him to create the plan. I know you didn't break my confidence." I stop our slow walking and turn her to face me. "Thank you for not pushing me before I was ready."

"I know baring your soul to me about Adams, Jones, and Carter was difficult enough. Pushing you to fulfill your promise wouldn't help. I simply wanted to be prepared to join you."

I take a deep breath and turn down one of the well-manicured aisles marked with uniform, white gravestones. Given they died in one attack, my unit mates are buried within ten yards of one another. I set a single white rose on top of each marker. With Jillian beside me, our fingers interwoven, I let my guilt seep into the soggy grass beneath my feet.

In my head, I set myself free. *I'm sorry for taking so long to get here. I wasn't ready or willing to accept my lack of control over my life on that day and many that followed. It took a wise woman, who all of you would've loved, to make me realize I can only control so much in my life. The mission where we lost all three of you wasn't one of them. Controlling my reaction to it is. I'm here, albeit quite late. Rest in peace, guys.* I tighten my grip on her hand and gaze down at her.

Her eyes are pinned to mine. "All set?"

I nod and lead her back to the car. We grab a late lunch at a local grill and bar before driving to our hotel for the evening.

About halfway to our accommodations, Jillian asks, "Still not going to share where we're going, huh?"

"Nope. Please let me surprise you, sweetheart."

She raises her hands in surrender. The hotel I chose won't give anything away. We're about twenty minutes away from our date location. I have the entire day planned for both of us.

When I wake, Jillian isn't in bed anymore. I don't panic anymore, but I preferred when she wasn't able to slip out of my arms so stealthily.

"Morning," she murmurs and hands me a cup of coffee.

"I would rather serve you coffee in bed."

"Awww, you're incredibly sweet. You're salty because I slipped away without waking you."

"So what if I am?"

"The Spillane case is closed. No one is looking for either of us. Besides, I have no intention of straying too far from your side. It's quite unrealistic for me to be glued to you whenever we're together though."

"I volunteer us to give it an actual, honest attempt to be stuck to one another whenever we aren't required to be apart, like for pesky things like work."

She laughs. "You would."

"We have about an hour before our first appointment of the day."

Her confused look tells me I singlehandedly pulled off our surprise getaway. "What are you talking about? We're going to visit your family in New York, aren't we?"

"Not exactly. I may have pushed them off until next weekend and they're visiting us."

"All of them?"

"*Si, cariña.*"

"Don't start with the Spanish, Javier. It won't make me forget you bamboozled me. Now I need all the details."

"I won't divulge all the details for the rest of our getaway just yet. However, our first appointment is an early breakfast, but the one immediately following requires us to be comfortably dressed."

"I told you I'm not a fan of surprises, right?"

"*Si, mi amor.*" The more Spanish I speak, the closer I am to forgiveness for surprising her for the rest of the weekend. "Am I forgiven yet?"

"Not yet."

Our breakfast arrives precisely at eight. I may have over ordered, but when you stay at a fancy hotel, you have room service breakfast and indulge a bit. As expected, Jillian selects the Belgian waffle with fresh strawberries and a heaping helping of crisp bacon. Whereas I start with the western omelet, hash, and toast. We finish our food, and I escort her downstairs to the spa.

"We're going to a spa?"

I grin at her. "We have two appointments here today before our date this afternoon."

"Miss Blackthorne. Mr. Cruz, right this way." Our hostess, a tiny, older woman, ushers us inside.

The spa has a modern theme with clean lines and muted colors. There is a distinct fresh scent in the air. It's soothing. The only thing overly feminine is the list of treatments available, some of which I've never heard of even though my sister owns a spa.

Our hostess leads us into a private room for pedicures. "Your treatment specialist will be right with you."

I assist Jillian into her chair and sit beside her.

"Have you ever had a pedicure before?" she asks.

"Nope."

She smiles. "Today is going to be interesting."

Our specialists fill the basins with water and set our feet in to soak. We chat about everything and nothing while they work. My feet are insanely ticklish. Chatting with Jillian is helping me ignore the sensations on my feet from the buffer and the callous remover. It isn't until it's time for the foot massage that it takes a turn. I end it right after the top of my foot almost crushes the spa worker's nose.

"I'm so sorry."

"No problem, sir. I'll continue on then," she informs me.

I nod, and she sets my feet down and pats them dry. When she finishes my toes, I notice Jillian's are freshly painted and drying. Next, we move on to manicures, which is a more pleasant experience for everyone.

"How did I not know your feet are so ticklish?"

I shrug. "Not sure, but now you do."

A twinkle flashes in her eyes. "You are moving toward forgiveness, Javier."

"Well, let's see if you can completely forgive me by the time our couples massage is complete."

She peppers my lips with kisses as we settle onto the massage tables. One hour later, I feel like jelly and completely relaxed. I'm not nervous about her answer. I'm more nervous about choosing the right words.

"Ready to get dressed for our date?"

"Yes. Are you going to share where we're going?"

"No. I'll share we're going to a late lunch though."

After dressing, I sneak out of the bedroom and accept a delivery as discreetly as I can.

Jillian exits the bedroom wearing a simple wrap dress in navy blue, which makes her eyes shine even brighter.

I kiss her lightly and offer her a bouquet of red roses. "You look gorgeous."

"Thank you. You look pretty good yourself."

I offer her my arm and lead her to the car. The ride is only twenty minutes, but I'm working through my words in my mind. I'm so wrapped up in my head, I almost miss the entrance. I swipe my hands down my pants to dry them before I open her door.

"What is this place?"

"Remember when we were asking questions of each other, and one was what would you do if you didn't need to earn money for a job?"

"Sure. I would open a pay-what-you-can-afford restaurant."

"A well-known rock star happens to have two, and this is one of them."

"Seriously?"

"You didn't know?"

Her eyes widen at the prospect of having a meal in her dream type of restaurant. "No, not at all. I mean, the concept isn't farfetched. I didn't realize there was one so close to home. You researched this for me?"

"*Cariña,* as much as you don't like the idea of it, I will sacrifice myself for you and every tiny human we create. I knew from the moment we met you were going to change my life for the better. Now a few years later, I know we were meant to meet." Now is as good a time as any. "I planned to do this later, but...." I drop to one knee before her in the parking lot. "Jillian, *te amo hasta lo más profundo de mi alma. Sería un honor para mí si fueras mi esposa.*"

She may not have understood the words exactly, but the single tear falling over her cheek leads me to believe she got the gist.

"Jillian. I love you to the depths of my soul. It would be my honor if you would become my wife."

"The honor would be mine."

As I slide my ring on her finger, applause erupts around us. A small crowd gathered behind us. Despite them, I kiss my fiancée breathless. Congratulations and other well-wishes surround us as the crowd enters the restaurant.

I wipe the happy tears from her cheeks and kiss her deeply. "I have one more question to ask before our reservation. What does your dream wedding look like?"

"Small and elegant, why?"

"Do you mind if our engagement is short?"

She wrinkles her nose. "How short do you have in mind?"

"I'm thinking July 16th is a spectacular day to change your name to Mrs. Jillian Cruz."

"Yes, absolutely, yes!"

Thank you so much for reading *Protecting Us*!

I hope you love Jillian and Cruz. Find out what happens with his Blackthorne teammate Alejandra. Will she find happiness after a rough first attempt?

Pre-order Alejandra's book on my website or your favorite retailer now so you don't miss it!

Check out Lina and Gugliotti's HEA in *Worth the Chase* coming soon!

COMING SOON

New stories are coming soon!

A York Beach Novel
The Cappellis
Worth the Chase

The List
Smithson & Scarlett

Blackthorne Security
Alejandra & Jordan

MY BOOKS

YORK BEACH SERIES:
A New Beginning with You
Taking A Chance on Me
Just One More
Kiss You Like You're Mine
Only with Him
My Once in a Lifetime

THE CAPPELLIS
Chasing Forever
Chasing My Sunshine

MORGAN BROTHERS SERIES:
One Unforgettable Favor
Until I Kissed You
Always Have, Always Will

BLACKTHORNE SECURITY
Protecting My Forever
Protecting Our Future

For a complete list of Nicole's books, visit:
https://www.nicolevidal.com/books

Did you love *Protecting Us*

Thank you for taking the time to read it. I hope you loved it!
If you liked this book or another one of my books, please consider
posting a review. A short line or two will be perfect!
I appreciate your support and feedback.

www.ingramcontent.com/pod-product-compliance
Lightning Source LLC
Chambersburg PA
CBHW072342020726
47506CB00004B/968